"You will not walk away from me or my offer," he called out after her.

"Oh, but I will," she said over her shoulder, marching her way toward the door. "Observe."

The duke quickly came in from behind and grabbed her arm, forcing her to not only stop but to also turn and face his dense, muscular body.

Maybelle froze as the scent of sandalwood, one she remembered all too well, surrounded her. Every bit of her body now blazed beneath his powerful stare and for one crazed moment, she actually wondered what it would be like to be at his command again. With his hands on her body. His length deep within her, making her feel wanted, needed.

He slowly released her but inched closer, bringing in more of that sandalwood, which was sensually tinted with the heat of his body. "Your grandmother's school is going to complicate your life in a way you aren't even prepared for. Admit it. My offer is a good one."

Finally grabbing hold of her wits, Maybelle stepped back and crossed her arms. "Oh, is it? You might say I'm a bit concerned about being deprived. On every possible level."

He stared at her for a long moment, his dark eyes slowly turning into a smoldering invitation. "I would never deprive my wife of *anything . . .*"

MISTRESS OF PLEASURE

DELILAH MARVELLE

ZEBRA BOOKS
Kensington Publishing Corp.
http://www.kensingtonbooks.com

To my amazing husband, Marc,
who has held my hand every step of the way
for so many years
and has shown me time and time again
an unwavering love
that goes beyond any romance I could ever write.
Thank you for all the weekends you gave up for my writing.
Thank you for all the weekdays you gave up for my writing.
But most of all, thank you for having always believed
in my writing.
I love you, baby.
Always.

Acknowledgments

So many, many people go into writing a book. Perhaps not literally, but mentally and spiritually, and as such, I wish to acknowledge each and every one of them.

Maire Creegan, my critique partner. I don't know how fate threw us into each other's path, but I do know that my writing would have never flourished without your watchful eye. Thank you for being an inspirational critique partner and a wonderful, wonderful friend. London, baby!

Victoria Dahl, for putting your name on the line and getting this book into the hands of John. Thank you, thank you, thank you.

My editor, John Scognamiglio, for all the unseen hard work and countless hours you put in day in and day out. Thank you.

My agent, Pam Hopkins, for stepping in when I needed it most.

Nadia Cornier, for keeping me in the game and being a personal cheerleader for my writing even when I felt there was nothing to cheer about.

Rose City Romance Writers, for all of its amazing members who have given me endless support throughout the years and friendships I will forever cherish.

The Wild Cards, my fellow 2005 Golden Heart

Finalists, for being wild at heart and sound of mind. Or at least most of the time!

And last, but most certainly not least, RWA, for being an amazing organization that allows organized writing chaos and creativity to thrive.

Lesson One

What defines a woman?
Why, she does, of course.
                    —The School of Gallantry

London, England—May 1830

When Maybelle first discovered at the tender age of twelve that her beautiful, silver-haired grandmother was in fact a French courtesan, it had been most . . . *awkward*. Yet equally fascinating, to say the least.

Being left in the care of such a sexually liberated woman certainly made for an unusual upbringing. For instance, French was taught, not out of cultural or educational necessity, but because her grandmother believed that the rolling off of French from one's tongue was erotic. As such, French words always had to be sprinkled here and there like powdered sugar over the not-so-orgasmic English language. At fourteen, Maybelle refused to adhere to the woman's ridiculous French/English rule. Mostly because she felt like a want-wit who couldn't decide between two languages.

At fifteen, Maybelle was further astonished to discover that naughty little books were not only permitted. They were required. So unlike other girls who took to sneaking pornographic books and keeping them under their bedroom pillows, Maybelle was forced to sneak volumes of Voltaire. For there was only so much copulation a girl could ingest day in and day out.

Needless to say, after spending nine years under the perpetual rule of her grandmother, there really wasn't much in this world that could actually astound her.

Or at least that is what she'd thought.

Maybelle eyed the full glass of cognac, which had been set onto the gleaming surface of the walnut table before her, and heaved out an exasperated sigh as she eased into one of the parlor chairs. She had expected the last morning spent with her grandmother to be difficult. But cognac? Honestly.

She met her grandmother's attentive gaze from across the French crimson parlor and drawled, "I take it there is no tea in the cupboards?"

"Och. Tea. The English are overly obsessed with it." Her grandmother rose from the settee, rustling not only her full verdant skirts but also all three sets of stringed pearls dangling over her more-than-generous bosom. "We have every right to toast to all of our upcoming adventures. After all, you will finally get to visit your beloved Egypt, while I, I will finally have my School of Gallantry."

Maybelle paused. Then blinked. "Your School of Gallantry?"

"Ah." Her grandmother bustled over toward the small writing bureau set in the corner of the parlor and snatched up a piece of parchment from atop a pile of correspondences. Turning, she bustled back again and halted before Maybelle. Smiling ever so charmingly, she held out the sizable cream-colored parchment by the tips of her manicured fingers.

Maybelle stared at the parchment dangling before her.

MADAME THÉRÈSE'S SCHOOL OF GALLANTRY
ALL GENTLEMEN WELCOME.
LEARN FROM THE MOST CELEBRATED
DEMIMONDAINE OF FRANCE
EVERYTHING THERE IS TO KNOW
ABOUT LOVE AND SEDUCTION.
ONLY A LIMITED AMOUNT OF
APPLICATIONS ARE BEING ACCEPTED
AT 11 BERWICK STREET.
DISCRETION IS GUARANTEED AND ADVISED.

Well. That certainly explained why her grandmother had kept to herself these past few months. She'd been busy creating a school. For men.

Heaven help her. This was going to follow her straight to the pyramids. At least the woman had used a nom de plume. Although it was only a matter of time before the gossip papers found out who was really behind it.

"Well?" her grandmother prodded, still holding out the advertisement. "What do you think?"

Ever since her father's death left her in the care of his mother, she often felt as if *she* were the guardian. And enough was damn well enough.

Maybelle rose from her parlor chair and snatched hold of the parchment. "Our reputation is already limp. Why on earth do you feel the need to flog it to death? You promised Papa that you'd never return to being a demimondaine. You promised."

Her grandmother arched a silver brow. "This is not a return. I am merely selling techniques."

"Techniques?" Maybelle smacked the parchment with the back of her hand. "It's ludicrous. What man would ever admit to needing lessons in seduction? You of all people should know that it comes natural to men."

"Does it? How odd. I suppose the thirty men who have already enlisted are merely looking for entertainment." With that, her grandmother snatched the advertisement back and smoothed the edges of it carefully between her manicured fingers.

Maybelle's heart jumped. Thirty men had already enlisted?! Who on earth were all these naughty blighters? And what did they think they were going to learn?

Calm. She needed to remain calm. There had to be a perfectly good reason for all this. There were always reasons. No matter how far-fetched. "Are we having trouble with our finances?" she prodded, stepping toward her. "Is that it?"

Her grandmother frowned. "Non. Our finances are exceptionally good. Although I did have some assistance from the lovely widow Lady Chartwell. The woman fondly shares my vision of educating men."

Maybelle's eyes widened. England's widows were actually donating to this plight? Although Maybelle wanted to outright demand why her grandmother would stoop to such a crude level of disrespect toward herself, her lips were simply too numb to form a single intelligible word.

"You are not pleased, I see." Her grandmother sighed heavily and wandered back toward the bureau, carefully setting the advertisement onto it. She tilted her head to one side, causing her thick, silver chignon to shift, and centered the parchment before her as if she were straightening a painting. "London has always been so boring compared to Paris. I am used to more excitement. More passion. As you know, I have long sworn off my occupation and sadly, have no great grandchildren to occupy my time. What is worse, you and I have completely different interests. A pile of old rocks set upon endless hot sand is nothing short of torture. I am too delicate for such things."

Oh dear God. There it was again. The pity-me routine. "No one forced you to stay in London. You chose to stay here. Furthermore, I won't have you calling the pyramids a pile of old rocks. They are amazing historic monuments worthy of genuine fascination. I've

already postponed my trip four times because of you
and every time I was forced to pay my designated trav-
eling companion ten pounds despite the fact that I
never traveled anywhere."

Maybelle crossed her arms over her chest. "So
what is it that you want this time? Aside from great
grandchildren."

Her grandmother turned and feigned shock as
her slender hand flew to her bosom. "*Want?* What
would make you think that I want anything?"

Maybelle narrowed her gaze knowing a seasoned
actress had stepped onstage. "You know exactly
how I feel about these things, which is why you are
trying to leverage this against me. Otherwise, you
would have never told me. You would have waited
until I left England and *then* opened the school."

Those soft blue eyes, which were a mere shade
darker than her own, remained fixed on Maybelle.
"I am not trying to leverage anything. The adver-
tisements have long been sent and the townhouse
rented. It is done, chère. Classes begin next week.
And in the end, I confess that the most difficult
aspect was having to choose only four out of the
thirty who had originally enlisted."

Maybelle hesitated then drawled, "You are rent-
ing out an entire townhouse to host only four
men?"

"Oui, but it is only temporary. Until I regulate the
schedule and coordinate the lesson plans. As time
goes on, I will add more men. Which of course will
mean more work. It will require more teachers.

More hosts. More toys." Her grandmother paused and eyed her. "You would not consider staying and becoming a hostess for a few months, would you? Though we should qualify you more by dispensing of your virginity."

Maybelle choked on a horrified gasp, then quickly cleared her throat. Twice. "I believe you are the only grandmother in the history of England to ever say such a thing to her granddaughter. That aside, do you even realize what you'll be promoting by opening such a school? Do you?"

A mischievous smile appeared on those full pink lips. "I will proudly be promoting the pleasure of all my fellow women who are fortunate enough to come across my étudiants."

Maybelle lowered her chin slightly but did not break their gaze. "No. You will proudly be promoting the idea that women are poodles and should be petted at will."

Her grandmother tsked, puckering her lips. "Chère. If a man knows nothing about seduction, the courtship becomes merely poom-poom. Animal copulation. And it is the woman who suffers, for a man can always find pleasure. But a woman? Not so. We cannot keep men from the conquests they seek, but we can educate the lust-ridden fools and in turn bencfit, oui?"

So. It had come to this. Cheap bargaining. "All right. Name your price."

"Price?" Her grandmother blinked. "You mean

for the school? I agreed on one hundred pounds per week."

A gasp escaped Maybelle, despite the fact that her grandmother had completely misunderstood. "*One hundred pounds per week?*" she squeaked. "For mere advice? Are they mad?"

"It is a very respectable price. Understand that an experienced demimondaine such as myself could actually demand much more."

"Grand-mère, please. I will gladly bargain with you, if need be, but for heaven's sake, you must close the school before you become an even bigger celebrity of the wrong sort."

"I will not bargain for the school *but*—" Her grandmother paused, then turned abruptly toward her. "I will bargain for the money you wish to travel with. Since I still hold all the purse strings."

Maybelle blew out an exhausted breath. She knew that trying to leave London was going to be an adventure in and of itself.

Her grandmother's sharp features softened and her blue eyes took on a form of pleading. "Once, chère. It is all I ask."

Maybelle lifted both brows. "Once what?"

Her grandmother slowly made her way toward her, her eyes never leaving hers. "I have taught you everything I know, and yet here you are at one and twenty, and have only kissed one man. Why?"

"I did *not* kiss that man," Maybelle sternly corrected, holding up a rigid finger and shaking it. "He kissed me." And the mere thought of that pock-ridden bastard stating his never-ending noble intentions, only to then grab her and shove his sour tongue down her throat made her queasy. Sadly, it summed up her relationship with every man thus far. For they all seemed to think that just because she was the granddaughter of a courtesan, any approach would do.

Her grandmother sighed. "I do not understand. You have no intentions on ever marrying, and yet you hold onto your virginity as if it were worth a dowry. A woman's innocence is only valued by men. The moment you dispense of it, you take your first step toward freedom. Your first step toward ensuring you do not belong to anyone but yourself."

"Yes. I am well aware of that."

"Then what is the problem?" A concerned look crossed her face. "Do you prefer women? Hm?"

Maybelle could actually feel her cheeks growing hot. Unbearably hot. "I want it to be memorable, is all. I want to look upon a man and say to myself, *oh, yes, I'll bed that one please.* Besides. You know the *ton.* They keep all the titled, good-looking men to themselves and give us their horrid remnants no one else wants."

Her grandmother paused before her and shook her head. Almost pitifully. "You think the *ton* is keeping the good men away? Pffff. The *ton* has no power over us. We arc our own government which no man rules. *We* define ourselves. And that is why I am asking *you* to define yourself. Without the *ton*'s ridiculous restrictions. I say, storm the Season. Claim the man of your choosing and enjoy life. Perhaps then you would not be so horribly tense."

Maybelle glared at her grandmother. "Horribly tense? Need I remind you, we cannot even attend social gatherings unless they're being hosted at a brothel."

"You, Maybelle, are my granddaughter." Her grandmother smiled and swept on open hand toward their surroundings. "As such, you have the ability to place every man at your feet. Make a name for yourself and the sort of men you want will come by the dozen."

"Grand-mère, I am not interested in becoming a demimondaine. Life is difficult enough with you being one."

"But you have the makings of greatness."

"Greatness indeed. I learned from Papa long ago never to overextend myself to anyone as it leads to very bad things. Surely, you remember how obsessed he was with Mama. And she'd been dead for twelve years."

"Henri was born a romantic. What can I say." Her grandmother sighed, reached out, and took hold of Maybelle's hands, squeezing them tightly. "Have I returned to being a demimondaine after becoming your gardienne? Non. Yet why is it men continue to roll at my feet, begging to be patted at any cost? Because I cannot escape the name I have created. Nor do I want to. I enjoy sex."

Sex, sex, sex. It was all the woman ever talked about. Maybelle released her grandmother's hands, shook her head, and stepped back. "I will not watch you destroy whatever integrity London has left by teaching all the men how to take advantage of women. It is not right."

Her grandmother grew unusually serious, the laugh lines around her eyes clearly fading. She lowered her voice. "I will tell you what is not right, Maybelle. Because of who I wish to be, because of who I have always been, I have not only sent my son to an early grave, but am now forcing his child to flee from me in the same manner he did. I know what will happen once you leave today. You will not return. You will disappear from my life. As Henri had."

Maybelle swallowed and closed her eyes, inwardly fighting with the reality of her situation. For although, yes, life in London was unbearable, and had been for many years because of her grandmother's reputation, she had no desire to flee. As her father had.

At sixteen, the man had altogether left France assuming he could escape his infamous mother, and upon arriving in England, set out to marry a respectable woman. That woman being Maybelle's own mother, who died giving birth to her.

In the end, her father's stubborn pride kept them from changing their name, thus making it difficult to escape all the back turning that came along with being associated with a renowned courtesan. When he eventually grew ill and lay dying, he realized there was no one to hand his twelve-year-old daughter to.

No one but the mother he'd been running from all his life.

Maybelle opened her eyes. Stepping forward, she took hold of her grandmother's slim shoulders and squeezed them gently, assuredly. "I would never abandon you. Ever. Seeing the pyramids is a dream of mine. You know that. And the way that Ferlini man is going about destroying them, there may very well be nothing left for me to see. You've read the papers. He is damn well smashing tops off pyramids and plundering tombs wherever he goes."

Her grandmother pinched her lips together, her blue eyes now glistening with tears. Tears Maybelle hadn't seen since the woman had arrived from France and threw herself at Papa's bedside while he lay dying.

Her grandmother must have realized her faux pas, for she quickly blinked back those tears, pulled away, and sniffed. Waving a hand, she muttered, "Go. Follow your heart, your love. I will pay for everything and manage the school on my own. You will see."

Maybelle slowly exhaled, feeling guilty and exhausted. For in the end, her love, not to mention her very heart, belonged to her grandmother. Would always belong to her grandmother. And considering the outrageous endeavor the woman was about to embark upon, she needed support. For she knew there would be little of it from anyone else. "I will stay for two months," Maybelle finally announced. "But only two months."

Her grandmother turned back toward her, those blue eyes lit with beautiful mischief once again. She clapped, rattling her emerald bracelets. "Two months will be magnifique! You will join me at the school on opening day, oui? Aside from all the men you will meet, I have countless rooms filled with all sorts of treasures and adventures."

Treasures? Adventures? It sounded like a pirate ship. One she wanted no part of.

Maybelle pointed at her grandmother and kept herself from altogether poking the woman in the shoulder. "Let us not get carried away. I am not interested in schoolboys learning how to please a woman. I know more than the basics thanks to you. Understand, Grand-mère, that the trouble with most men, even the experienced ones, is that they are forever seeking out attachments and are for the most part quite possessive. Albeit in different forms, but it all ends the same. If it isn't a wife they require, it is a mistress, and if it isn't a mistress, it is some other form of convention that they ultimately define in their own terms. Which is why I see absolutely no point in pursuing a single one of them."

Maybelle took in a deep, calming breath and let it out. "Now. I propose that over the next two months we point all of our efforts in the direction of your school and then in the direction of my travels. Then we will both be happy. And that is what we want, yes? To be happy?"

"Ah!" Her grandmother held up a finger in the

air, causing all of her bracelets to fall down the length of her wrist. "I have an idea."

Oh, no. Not an idea. Maybelle stepped back.

"Lord Hughes owes me a favor. A considerable one, I admit." She winked with great exaggeration. "I shall therefore see to it that he invites us to several of his soirées. He does not care what the *ton* thinks." Her grandmother smiled and smugly folded her hands before her. "I promise to find you a man incapable of demanding any attachments."

Maybelle's eyebrows rose. Why, that sounded horrid. Not in the least bit promising.

"And when we find him," her grandmother went on, gesturing toward her ever so graciously, "it will then be entirely up to you to make the best of it."

Which is exactly what she was afraid of. For there was a rather big difference between knowing everything about men and actually dealing with them. Maybelle sighed ever so softly. A pile of old rocks set upon endless hot sand sounded rather perfect as of now.

If only she wasn't so bloody softhearted.

Lesson Two

Not everyone is capable of seduction.
Yet everyone is perfectly capable of being seduced.
                    —The School of Gallantry

London, three weeks later at the house of
Lord Hughes, evening

Elegantly dressed men and women whisked in and out of sight, adorned in perfectly tailored and expensive satiny hues of onyx, periwinkle, and alabaster. Beautiful is what they were. All beautiful.

On the outside, at least.

And although, yes, the orchestra played loud enough for the deaf to hear, and the candles from the crystal chandeliers had dripped more wax on her than the wood floor throughout the evening, it was still mildly entertaining. Mildly, only because she'd spent most of the night tucked between the oak-paneled wall and her grandmother.

A grandmother, who by the by, had received more amorous stares and conversations from men during the past few hours than she had in her entire life. And unlike the snobby women around them who refused to acknowledge their existence, the men were proving to be exceptionally friendly. Exceptionally.

And one might only imagine why. After the school's grand opening, her grandmother had become a celebrity of sorts. For only the men, of course.

A mustached gentleman grinned and nodded his pleasantries toward her grandmother as he passed by. Her grandmother returned his nod and set her chin once again.

Whoever thought one could be so popular in society and yet so equally despised? It made no sense whatsoever. But then that was the *ton* for you.

Maybelle sighed and leaned back against the wall. After attending a total of seven soirées in three weeks, she had hoped her grandmother would come to terms with the fact that she had standards. Thank goodness.

Maybelle peered past the double bouffant sleeves of her grandmother's low-cut, plum evening gown, but could barely see the dance floor. She pushed away from the wall and was about to tap her grandmother on the shoulder so that the woman might step aside and give her a better view when a tall, muscular dark-haired gentleman strode past.

Maybelle's heart skipped as her eyes unwittingly followed him. Now *there* was a chariot worth riding into hell on.

The man was clad in black, thigh-hugging trousers that tapered narrowly down the length of his long, muscular legs and was finished off by a pair of black lacquered shoes. If not for the evening jacket, which brushed past his upper thighs, she had no doubt his bum would have been a heavenly sight to behold.

Of course, there was still plenty to admire. His perfectly tailored black jacket paraded the width of his chest and the muscles in his arms. A high, crisp white collar surrounded his strong jaw and neck, which was even further accentuated by a perfectly pressed pure white cravat. His thick black hair, which had been combed back with tonic, was a bit on the long side, going entirely against fashion, but the way it brushed over the back of his high collar was in and of itself fascinating.

Although he was almost out of sight, the man paused from his steady stride, and turned, as if sensing someone was watching him. His lean, shaven face; sharp nose; black eyes; and straight brows came into view.

Maybelle inhaled sharply. *Oh, yes, I'll bed that one please.*

The man scanned those around him, and although she inwardly pleaded that he might meet her gaze at least once, his dark eyes swept past her.

Drat. Perhaps her grandmother was in the way. Maybelle gathered her cream satin skirts and quickly scooted out from behind her grandmother to place herself on better display.

To her disappointment, the man had already

turned and made his way back through the crowd. Maybelle released her satin skirts and let them drop to the floor right along with her heart. She watched as he rounded the dance floor and disappeared through the French doors leading out onto the darkened terrace.

It was for the better. A man of such appearances was most likely married. And if not married, then engaged. And if not engaged, then looking to be. And as one woman never sufficed the thirst of any man, there was no doubt a mistress involved. Several of them, if she had to guess. One for every single of his vicious, lusty whims. Yes. He certainly looked the sort.

"You have very good taste," her grandmother drawled, still staring out onto the dance floor. "That, chère, is none other than the Duke of Rutherford. Better known to London as the man tragically ruined by his father's lust."

Maybelle's eyes widened. Certainly not the sort she had imagined. She leaned toward her grandmother. "Ruined by his father's lust? You don't mean his father actually—"

"Och, mais non! Where is your mind tonight?" Her grandmother glanced around, snapped open her ostrich fan, and leaned toward her, gossip overtaking her blue eyes. She hid the bottom half of their faces behind the confines of her fan and lowered her voice. "You see, a little over six years ago, his father died in the arms of a courtesan. Laudanum overdose. Dreadful, dreadful scandal. But then the réel rumors commenced. That the woman was not a courtesan at all, but a lady of high, respectable society."

Her grandmother clucked. "Well. That made it even more difficile for the *ton* to accept and ever since, the duke's poor mama has desperately tried to marry him off to whoever will have him. Despite his dire circumstances, the man refuses to compromise his lineage and will not marry below him. And so there you have it. Ruined by his own father's lust."

How sad. And yet . . . how utterly perfect if she were to ever seriously consider being debauched good and well by any man. She wouldn't have to worry about the duke wanting the daughter of a courtesan for a wife. And his father's death certainly should have altered if not entirely affected the man's perception of wanting a mistress. Which was rather promising. A bit too promising.

Maybelle eyed her grandmother and blurted, "What if I wanted him? For a night, that is. What would you suggest?"

Her grandmother leaned away and snapped her fan closed, letting it dangle by its velvet string attached to her gloved wrist. If the woman was in any way pleased, she hid it rather well. She shrugged. "Seeing you want only one night, I suggest you keep it simple."

"How simple?" Maybelle prodded.

Her grandmother lifted her other hand, pulled out a small, tin box from the wrist of her glove, opened it, and held it out for her. "Here. Have a mint. I will make an introduction for you before the end of the hour."

An introduction indeed. The man wasn't even likely to notice her from behind her grandmother's overpuffed sleeves and large breasts.

Maybelle lowered her voice a touch more. "Why an introduction? Is it because of his rank?"

Her grandmother laughed. "Of course not. It is because of *my* rank. You want him, oui?" She shook the box at her, rattling the candies within. "Do take one, chère. Men adore the smell of mint. It seduces their senses."

Maybelle wrinkled her nose at the thought. But if there was anyone who would know what men adored, it most certainly was her grandmother. Maybelle plucked up the mint and tucked it into her glove. For later use.

Maybelle impatiently watched the doors leading to the balcony, hoping that the duke would return soon. "So how does one even go about seducing a man of such status? Surely it complicates matters."

"A title is but a barrier, not a complication." Her grandmother plucked up a mint, placed it onto the tip of her pink tongue, and slid the tin back into the unbuttoned space at the wrist of her glove. "Perhaps you should consider visiting the school and sitting in on a few lessons. We discuss social barriers all the time."

Maybelle refrained from snorting. "No. No, thank you. I shall manage. Without stepping onto your pirate ship."

Maybelle eyed the balcony once again. Though a part of her contemplated seducing the duke to keep her grandmother from ever nagging her again, a much larger part wanted to finally discover the truth behind all of the excitement. And who better than with a man who sent her pulse thundering with but a glance that had not even been directed at her?

Etiquette and delicacy be damned. She was wasting time. "I wish to approach him out in the garden. Might I?"

Her grandmother sighed dramatically as if she were dealing with a petulant child. "I will not argue." She paused. "But. Before you go. Be certain that I do not notice you are abandoning me or I shall come across as a very bad chaperone."

Ha. A demimondaine shouldn't even *be* a chaperone. But yes, yes. She understood. Discreet. She could do that. Maybelle paused for a moment, then took to busily arranging her skirts. As she did so, she snuck one dainty step to the left. Toward the direction of the balcony. Then another. And another.

Her grandmother lifted her chin and continued to stare out before her, appearing genuinely occupied with listening to the orchestra and watching all of the couples whirl and dance.

Ever the brilliant actress.

Edging farther and farther away, one step at a time, Maybelle scanned the festivities around her. Fortunately, no one seemed to notice her change in direction. All of the earlier female gossips who might have actually noted what she was up to had long taken leave for supper. A blessing indeed.

When she eventually retreated far enough from her grandmother to warrant a complete escape, she turned and sashayed toward the French doors leading outside.

Exude confidence. Yes. Confidence.

The cool, night air made her pause on the large, round stone terrace. She took in a deep, satisfying breath and let it out. Free. Free to finally step outside the endless, stifling rules of the *ton*.

Eyeing her dim surroundings, Maybelle stepped farther out. Quiet couples leaned against the limestone banister. A banister that wrapped around the entire terrace, and only allowed for an opening on the left, which led out into the darkness of the garden.

He must have gone out into the garden. She slowly ventured down the wide terrace stairs, her gown rustling in the silence as it dragged behind her. As she wandered farther and farther down the garden path, outlined with neatly trimmed tall hedges, it grew very quiet, save for her own movements. And dark. Without a single bit of moonlight to guide her.

Her pulse quickened as she swallowed against the dryness in her throat. *This is idiotic. Even if you do find him, what do you intend on doing with the man? Regardless of his reputation, he is still a duke.*

Maybelle paused and bit her lip. Hard. She

should return. Immediately. Before she made a want-wit of herself.

She turned and hurried down the darkened path, toward the lights of the ballroom that glowed in the far-off distance. Between her unsettled nerves and the pasty dryness in her mouth, it was almost difficult to swallow. Let alone breathe.

Still keeping a steady pace, she glanced down toward her hands and blindly searched in the darkness for the mint tucked inside her left glove. Just as she placed the candy onto the tip of her tongue, she collided straight into what could have only been a stone pillar.

The mint popped out of her lips like a lead ball from a cannon and she snatched at whatever was before her to keep from falling back. To her surprise, the pillar had a waistcoat.

A male voice exclaimed, "What in—"

The waistcoat she clung to ripped, and they both tumbled to the ground, landing between the hedges beside the garden path.

The man's hard body held her pinned to the ground, knocking the breath out of her. The night sky whitened as pain seared through her. She gasped, unable to breathe or move.

The man immediately pushed himself up, removing his entire weight off to the side. His broad, muscled body, however, continued to linger above her in the shadows. "Are you all right?"

His deep voice, sensual and low, sent a ripple of awareness through her. The sky above darkened and returned to normal. The ache in her body dissipated as her chest finally expanded. She gulped in a much-needed, almost pleasurable breath. Rich, spicy sandalwood tinged with the sweet fragrance of a cigar unexpectedly filled her nostrils.

It was him.

Her head pounded and the blood in her veins heated. "My corset is still in one piece," she managed.

A deep rumbling laugh escaped him as he completely rolled off, giving her room to breathe again. He rose, looming like one of the obscure surrounding hedges. Two shadowy hands came closer. "Give me your hand."

She gulped in another breath and took his hands with hers. Two large palms pressed against hers, and she was whisked effortlessly onto her feet.

They momentarily stood in silence and though there was no further need for him to be holding her hands, he lingered, transferring the heat of his gloved palms into hers. Maybelle lifted her chin to get a better look at him, but was only able to make out that he was taller than her. Much taller. And broad shouldered.

He released her hands, stepped away, and cleared his throat. "Forgive me. I didn't realize anyone was on this path."

Which meant they were alone. Completely and utterly alone. At long last. This was her opportunity to not only stamp freedom upon herself, but to do it in an untraditional manner with a man who could actually make it memorable. After all, did one truly need a bed?

The question was, however, how was she to do this? Grab him, do what she will, then run? No. She should be polite.

Knowing now was not the time to falter, Maybelle stepped forward and closed the distance between them. "Actually, Your Grace, I was on this path searching specifically for you. I was hoping for a moment of your time."

He paused, his large shadowy frame shifting toward her. "Time for what exactly?" he drawled in a tone that clearly indicated he knew what it was she was referring to but wasn't quite certain as to whether he should be intrigued or not.

Oh for heaven's sake. Any other man would have grabbed her by now. "I find you rather attractive."

The duke was quiet. It didn't even sound like he was breathing.

Maybelle inwardly cringed, knowing she was probably going about this all wrong. Perhaps she should have enlisted the help of her grandmother after all.

The man cleared his throat. Then stepped back. "Amusing. Really. Who put you up to this? Wharton? I should bloody hang the bastard by his trousers." His clothing rustled, as if he were dusting himself off. "So who are you? And what the devil did you spit at my forehead? I believe it left a mark."

Maybelle could have glowed in the darkness from the heat her cheeks produced. It wasn't as if the situation could get any more embarrassing. Perhaps she needed to show him she was quite serious. At the very worst, he would disregard her advances and that would be that.

Stepping toward him, Maybelle grabbed for his muscled arms and pulled herself close to the heat of his body. The muscles beneath his clothing tensed, even though he did nothing to fight her.

Taking in a shaky breath, Maybelle raised herself on her slippered toes, leaned forward, and pressed her mouth against the fuzzy outline of his lips. His lips proved to be much softer and warmer than she had anticipated. Certainly nothing like the last fribble who had tried to kiss her.

Maybelle gently parted the duke's lips and slipped her tongue into his wet mouth. The unexpected taste of brandy flavored her lips as his hot tongue slowly submitted and began circling hers. His hands drifted toward her waist and the pressure of his fingertips dug savagely into her corset. As if he was trying to find all the skin hidden beneath and bury himself in it.

Overwhelmed by his unexpected intensity, and that he was willingly returning her kiss, the garden spun. His tongue traced the inside of her mouth, pushing against her own tongue. Her pulse thundered as she tried to meet his demand.

What now? Though she knew everything there was to know about kissing, sex, and arousal from a hypothetical level, her true inexperience could very well bring an end to all this.

Maybelle pulled her wet mouth away from his and

clung to his muscled arms, trying to calm her heavy breathing. Although she wanted to ask him to altogether take over this matter, she couldn't find the strength to force the words out of her mouth.

"Not as bold anymore?" he whispered huskily down at her.

She swallowed and forced her words out between breaths. "I was hoping you could demonstrate how bold you can be."

A low growl escaped him. He reached around her, grabbed her bum tightly with both hands, and forced the front of her body against the length of his muscled frame.

She gasped, feeling his rigid cock pushing against her belly. He slowly found her mouth in the darkness. His hot, brandy-flavored tongue pushed open her lips and traced the inside of her mouth again.

Ooooh. *This* is what she'd been denying herself? She could actually feel herself growing wet. From a kiss!

The duke suddenly tore his mouth away from hers. "This is madness." His breath escaped in heavy takes. "I don't even know who you are or what you look like. I can barely make out the whiteness of your gown."

His husky voice washed over her entire body and tingled her ears. "My name is Maybelle," she whispered back up at him, wishing she could see more of his shadowed face. "And as for my appearance . . ."

She slipped her hands beneath the warmth of his jacket and slid her hands toward his muscled back, hidden beneath his vest and shirt, savoring the hardness of his body. "Perhaps it is best you allow your hands to be your guide."

He sucked in a breath, grabbed at her gloved hands, and spun her around. Completely. Yanking her against his hard body, he held her backside tightly against him, causing every part of her, including her exposed neck and shoulders to explode with heat.

He bent his head toward her ear, his warm breath teasing her senses, and demanded, "What sort of game is this? Do I know you?"

Her pulse thundered in her ears. "No. Of course not. Tonight is the first I've ever seen of you."

"And based upon what you saw, you flippantly decided to sacrifice both your reputation and all common sense." He tightened his hold on her waist, digging the tips of his fingers into her corset. "I am not a fool, Madam. What is it that you really want of me?"

Maybelle swallowed. Hard. It was as if he was staring straight into her soul, demanding that she contemplate not only her intentions but her state of mind. The trouble was, at that moment, she realized that she actually wanted this. Wanted him. And it went beyond any vow she'd ever made to herself to render herself useless to men.

"If it isn't obvious by now what I want, Your Grace," she murmured up over her shoulder, "then I am at a complete loss of words and utterly disappointed by your inaction. Sadly, I expected more from a man surrounded by so much gossip."

The duke's lips continued to hover beside her ear and his breathing grew heavier with each passing moment. He eventually whispered, "I've never been much of a gentleman and clearly, you are not looking for one." He slowly crossed his arms around her front side and held up both hands before her. "So. Do you want my gloves on or off?"

She bit her lip, her heart pounding. "Off."

"Off it is." He bent his head forward, the side of his face and chin brushing against her hair, then used his teeth to pry off each glove. She froze as his muscled arms flexed with each smooth movement.

He tossed the first glove and then the second into the fuzzy darkness, making them disappear somewhere at their feet. "Now." He lowered his bare hands and encircled her waist. He gripped her hard. "Hold out your hands."

Maybelle held them out, not daring to question his intentions. Only wanting them. Anticipating them.

Knowing full well she couldn't bend at the waist, he slowly guided her face down toward the grass just off the path and set her gently on her hands and knees.

She swallowed as he slowly dragged up her skirts and pushed away the folds from the lower half of her body, exposing her entire backside to him. Half of her dreaded what was about to happen, the other half wanted it knowing it was him.

He leaned over her, his heat and erection pressing against her and although she expected him to enter her there and now, instead, his large hand reached around her and brushed the side of her face.

Gently. Tenderly.

Her cheek tingled against the feathery feel of his warm touch. She pressed it against his hand, wanting to melt into his palm completely.

"You feel beautiful," he murmured from behind.

She closed her eyes and inwardly shivered. He certainly made her feel beautiful.

His hand trailed down from her face down to her neck. His fingers drifted lower. To her breasts. Breasts she didn't know were worth having until now.

Oh, one could learn to love being ruined.

The duke yanked at the front of her gown and nudged her breasts up and out of her corset, freeing them completely. He flicked his thumb across one of her nipples, hardening them against the cool air.

She closed her eyes and gave in to the endless sensations.

His large hand cupped her breast hard for a moment, as if he were savoring each touch as much as she was, before finally releasing it. He then slid his hand all the way up her bare throat to her chin until he forced his finger into her mouth.

She willingly sucked the salty taste of his finger, pulling it deep into her mouth. Wanting to savor the very flavor and warmth of his skin.

"Wet it more," he hoarsely said from behind. "Then push it out." He rubbed against her backside with his erection, forcing its heat to come through the smooth fabric of his trousers.

Maybelle pushed back against him as she slathered his finger with saliva. Slowly, she pushed it out with her tongue.

He brought his hand away and moved back, leaving her to only feel the cool night air caressing her naked thighs. His wet finger suddenly slid from the top ridge of her backside down to the already wet folds between her thighs. She sucked in a harsh breath at the unexpected coolness as he paused on her nub and rubbed that spot in small even circles.

More. She wanted so much more. Which is why she found herself pushing against his finger. Yet it wasn't enough. She wanted to know what *all* of him would feel like. With him inside of her. She tried to look back at him, seeing only that his shadowed frame knelt behind her. "Please. Now."

"Shhh." He continued to rub her with his finger faster and faster. As if he wanted her to lose control there and then.

She bit back a scream as her gloved fingertips gripped the grass, tearing straight into the earth. She felt as if something within her was about to explode. She gasped for air against the tightness of her corset, but felt too lightheaded to properly breathe.

"Hold back," he whispered, his finger never once stopping. "Hold back."

"I . . . cannot," she panted. "I cannot."

"Yes, you can." He stopped and the rustling of his trousers made her realize he was springing himself free. Grabbing hold of her waist with one hand, he brought her back toward him. In that same moment, she felt the warm rounded tip of his shaft slowly work its way through her wet folds.

But instead of entering, he simply rubbed it up and down, up and down against her nub. Teasing her.

She gasped as more wondrous sensations gripped her entire body. She pushed back against him more forcefully, wishing he would simply enter. "Please."

"Is this what you want?" he hoarsely asked from behind her.

"Yes," she choked out.

"Then it is what I want." He continued to rub against her with his cock more feverishly, making her core tighten with each stroke, then rammed the solid head inside of her, shocking her. His entire length slipped in deep. Much deeper than she'd expected. A sharp pain from within made her stiffen and cry out in surprised agony.

The duke froze. As if something was wrong. "Have you ever done this before?" he demanded, his voice rough, almost ragged.

Relieved that the pain had subsided and that it now felt rather perfect, she whispered, "No. Not really."

"Bloody hell." He quickly pulled out, slid her satin skirts back into place, and fell back and away.

It was suddenly quiet. Except for their heavy breaths, which filled the air.

Lovely. Deflowered and yet . . . not.

As the feeling of climax ebbed and completely

dissipated, Maybelle bit back her frustration and shifted into a different position. "I should have probably told you."

He rose, still breathing heavily, but remained silent.

Maybelle momentarily closed her eyes, trying to push away the reality of what she had done. An imbecile is what she was. A complete imbecile.

Of course, she had accomplished what it is she had wanted. And that was all that mattered. She had officially been rendered useless to men.

She opened her eyes. It was time to go. Scrambling to her feet, she arranged her skirts into place and then pushed her breasts back where they belonged. Obviously, the man had nothing more to say. Which suited her. For there was nothing left to discuss.

Drawing in a calm breath that was anything but calming, she abruptly turned and hurried away. It was best she return to her grandmother and finally admit to the woman that she not only needed a few classes on the art of seduction but also quite a few more on men.

"Maybelle," the duke called after her, "wait."

Although she was quite surprised that he even remembered her name, she ignored him and hurried toward the dim lights of the festivities. Whatever had passed between them was best left in the garden. Forever.

When she reached the lightest part of the garden, she quickly slowed her steps, to appear casual to those on the balcony. There was a skidding of feet behind her, and to her surprise, someone caught and hooked her elbow, forcing her to turn.

Thick, broad shoulders clad in a formal jacket blocked her view, forcing her to peer up into fathomless, black eyes. She stiffened as the heat of his intent stare brought fire climbing up her stockinged legs. Her palms perspired beneath her gloves.

The duke, damn him, was even more astounding up close and in the light. His lean smooth-shaven face and full lips complemented his sharp features. The small cool breeze that floated around them lifted his black hair and scattered a few silken strands across his forehead. In the most perfect way.

Maybelle slipped away from his tight grip and stepped back, trying to set a safe distance between them. As she continued to wordlessly return his stare, her cheeks grew unbearably hot wondering what it was he was thinking.

His dark eyes urgently searched her face. "Why? Why did you want me to do it?"

As if he would ever understand the complications of being caught between two worlds. Maybelle lowered her eyes and noted that his white cravat had tumbled out from beneath his dark embroidered waistcoat. Her eyes widened. All the buttons on his waistcoat were missing, exposing the delicate folds of his white shirt beneath. Even his evening jacket couldn't hide the mess.

She stuck out a hand, apologetically touching the mangled fabric. "I certainly didn't mean to—"

The duke stepped back and away from her touch

as if it had burned him. "I wouldn't worry all that much about my appearance. We should, however, tend to yours, Madam. Immediately."

Maybelle swiped at the front of her skirts, glancing down in the process. "Oh, surely it cannot be all that—" She froze, her gloved hands stilling against the cream satin of her gown. Dirt marks and grass stains spattered the entire front of her bosom as well as the length of her knees. She groaned aloud. She might as well have published the details of her debauchery in the *London Gazette*.

"Chère?" a familiar voice asked from behind them.

Maybelle cringed, realizing it was her grandmother. She turned and met the woman's gaze.

Her grandmother smiled warmly and assuredly as she held out a gloved hand. "It is best we leave. People are beginning to gather."

Maybelle eyed the lighted balcony, noticing people *were* gathering. At least a dozen people had wandered out from the ballroom onto the balcony just to look at them. Yes. This could very well make the papers.

The duke stepped toward them from behind. He lowered his voice. "I am to blame for this. Entirely. Allow me to settle this matter in private."

Maybelle turned to him, startled that the man felt in any way responsible. After all, she was the one to initiate all this.

"No need, Your Grace. Bonne nuit." Her grandmother took her arm, slowly turned her away from the duke, and led them back toward the stairs leading to the balcony.

Toward all the people.

"There is no other way to depart except through the ballroom," her grandmother whispered into her ear. "Walk slowly, with dignity, and pretend all is well."

Pretend all is well? After an encounter like that? Impossible! Her heart still pounded and her flesh still tingled long after it had ended. She finally understood why sex was so forbidden. It drove one to lose all sensibility.

Although Maybelle desperately wanted to peer back at the duke, knowing full well it would be their last encounter, she knew it was best to simply let it be. Their moment, whatever she would define it as, was over.

She and her grandmother walked up the remaining stairs of the balcony. Maybelle drew strength from the sudden squeeze her grandmother gave her. She set her chin and did her best to remain calm.

The men on that balcony, both young and old alike, openly gawked at her with unwavering fascination as they passed, while several women leaned in toward each other, whispering behind their elaborate, hand-painted fans.

Maybelle's pulse thundered. A strange fluttering seized her stomach as she walked on. Being the center of so much attention, albeit scandalous attention, felt strangely wild and invigorating. As if she'd finally stepped out from a black and white painting she'd been trapped in all these years and into a canvas-free world exploding with color. This is what it was like to feed one's pleasure and not that of society's. To be one's ruler. It was surprisingly provocative and amazing.

Although thick strands of hair had escaped from her chignon, Maybelle didn't bother pushing them away from her face. Instead, she proudly marched on in a slow procession, past all the endless faces of the *ton*, and bit back the smile that threatened to break free. She could only imagine how proud her grandmother was.

The orchestra's minuet soon faded and she and her grandmother eventually left the ballroom. At long last.

Their steady steps on the marble floor echoed all around them as they headed toward the front door. A part of Maybelle was still in shock as to what had happened, although another part of her was thrilled to be shocked.

"So," her grandmother whispered excitedly, tightening her hold on her arm. "Was he worth the parade?"

Although the man hadn't actually finished, she could well say that it had been worth every damn moment. "I promise to tell you everything later," she whispered back.

"Later, later. You will have me wait that long? Absolutely not. I—" Her grandmother paused, her grasp suddenly slipping from hers.

Maybelle also paused and turned toward her. "Grand-mère?"

A confused look overtook her grandmother's pale, oval face as she took in a deep, ragged breath. Her grandmother shakily placed her gloved hand to her heaving bosom as if she were unable to breathe.

"*Grand-mère?*" Maybelle heard the panic in her own voice echo all around them. She stepped toward her. "What is it?"

"I feel . . ." She staggered back, trying to reach out for her with gloved hands, then collapsed, her slim figure crumpling to the floor with a solid thud.

Maybelle screamed and threw herself to the floor beside her. No! Not now. Not like this. Blinded by an onslaught of tears, she frantically lifted her grandmother's head to determine whether she was breathing. She pressed her cheek against her grandmother's mouth and let out a sob of relief at the heated breath escaping.

She refused to lose the only person who had ever truly understood her. The only person to give her the sort of freedom she had always sought. The sort of freedom her father never could have understood. It never mattered to her what the world really thought of them. All that had ever mattered was that they had each other. But now . . .

Lesson Three

When one is uncontrollably smitten
by an unexpected conquest,
one might think it best to simply
outrun one's attraction and
in turn avoid complications.
Such thinking is pointless and unwise.
For even running shall induce heavy breathing.
—The School of Gallantry

Edmund Worthington, the sixth Duke of Rutherford, continued to stare after the two women who had very calmly, very regally departed past the gathering crowd and into the ballroom. Without hysterics. Without a single pointing of the finger. As if absolutely nothing had occurred.

Which led him to ask, what the hell *did* just occur?

One moment he'd gone out for a cigar and a bit of time away from the noise, and the next he'd been tackled and pounced on by a virgin. Mind you, a very well-rounded and ambitious virgin who knew exactly how to frig a man out of his wits.

Though a part of him wanted to let the whole matter be, another part of him simply couldn't. And he didn't know if it was his moral sense of responsibility or his lower half speaking for him. A lower half that still ached and demanded to finish what had been started.

Edmund roughly adjusted his jacket and gritted his teeth. This was his fault. His fault for letting the situation get out of hand in a very public place. Which is why it was up to him to do the right thing. Whatever that was.

Pushing his way through the small crowd, which continued to linger, Edmund made his way into the ballroom and headed toward the front of the large hall. Pausing for a moment, he searched for the beautiful blonde and her silver-haired French chaperone. Only they were nowhere to be found. Then again, as crowded as it was, he couldn't very well spot an elephant. He grimaced.

"A physician!" A man hurried from person to person. "Is there a physician?"

Edmund spun toward the man rushing by and grabbed at his arm to halt him altogether. "What is it?"

The man turned toward him, his round face flushed. "A lady, Your Grace. She . . . she collapsed. In the entryway. No one is tending to her save one other lady."

There was the *ton* for you. "I'll see to it immediately." Edmund released him. "Keep searching for a doctor."

"Yes, Your Grace!"

Never a dull moment in the life of a Rutherford. Edmund hurried out into the corridor, skidding across the freshly waxed floor. He glanced right, then left, trying to find the woman in need and froze as his gaze snapped toward the front entrance of the house. A slim, silver-haired woman lay motionless on the marble floor, her abundant mauve evening gown crumpled all around her.

The world around him ceased to exist in that single moment when he realized who it was.

He sucked in a harsh breath.

His beautiful mistress from the garden wept silently beside her unconscious chaperone, her dirtied cream satin skirts gathering up and around her corseted waist. Long blond curls, which had escaped from her chignon, glistened in the light of the candles, as her dirt-streaked gloved hands fingered her chaperone's colorless face.

"Grand-mère," she whispered pleadingly, smoothing gray hair away from the woman's forehead. "Wake up. Please. Please."

His pulse quickened as he moved toward her. This woman was actually her grandmother? He kneeled beside her. "What happened?"

Wondrous wet blue eyes snapped up to look at him, suddenly inhibiting his ability to move. He never realized how beautiful a woman's eyes could be. Even in the throws of sorrow.

"I don't know," she whispered, her lips trembling. "I don't know."

"A doctor should be arriving shortly. In the meantime, we shouldn't leave her here." He looked up, noting that the footmen still weren't coming to assist. Where were they? There were always servants loitering the corridors at these functions.

Edmund shook his head, knowing he'd have to do it. He leaned in toward the elderly woman's sizable breasts displayed by her low-cut gown and carefully listened, making sure not to touch her. Shallow breaths escaped her. Thank God. "Fortunately, she is still breathing."

"So why isn't she awake?"

"Let us hope we find out soon enough." Edmund threw off his evening jacket to free his arms and jerked up his sleeves. "The footmen seem to be on holiday. Stand aside."

Slipping his hands beneath the slim frame of the elderly woman, Edmund rolled the limp body toward him, resting her against his chest. He quickly rose, surprised as to how light the woman was considering the mass of her gown alone.

Lord Hughes rushed toward them, his large belly swinging to and fro, and his eyes wide with horror. "This way! At once! To the drawing room!"

Edmund followed Lord Hughes down the corridor and into what appeared to be a small receiving room. When he reached the rose-colored sofa he'd been directed to, Edmund stooped and gently laid out the unconscious woman.

Maybelle, who had been trailing behind him, hurried toward her grandmother. She leaned over the woman, her small gloved hands smoothing the woman's silver hair.

Edmund cleared his throat, trying not to think about how those same hands had earlier grabbed for him. Had earlier begged for his body.

And though yes, he was an inconsiderate ass for thinking about it at a time when her grandmother was desperately in need, how could he *not* think about it?

It was best he leave. For her sake. She didn't need to be further tied to his reputation and there was nothing more he could do to help her grandmother. Edmund strode toward Lord Hughes, who silently and worriedly stood holding his gloved hand to the back of his gray, thinning hair. As if it was his own mother.

Just as Edmund was about to walk past the man and out of the room, he paused, unable to control the searing images of Maybelle that continued to flash through his thoughts. Her moist lips. Her burning warmth. Her smooth thighs. The weight of her full breasts in his hands. All . . . *perfect*.

Bloody hell, he was going to regret it, but he had to at least know her full name. Edmund turned and leaned toward Lord Hughes. "Should anyone inquire, My Lord, who is the lady I assisted?"

Lord Hughes dropped his hand back to his side and blinked at him with large brown eyes, appearing even more astounded than before. "Why, Your

Grace. That is Madame de Maitenon." He leaned in closer and whispered, "She is the most exquisite courtesan known to France and for the sake of all men, I hope to God the woman survives."

Startled, Edmund turned to glance toward the blonde who continued to affectionately touch her grandmother's pale cheeks. Bugger. The granddaughter of a French courtesan had handed him . . . *him* . . . her virginity. And there was no doubt in his mind that this Maybelle de Maitenon was well on her way to becoming a siren in her own right.

Edmund cleared his throat and issued Lord Hughes a curt nod. "Thank you, My Lord." He then strode out of the drawing room, trying to remain as calm as possible.

Shit. *Shit!* He only hoped to God his mother wouldn't get wind of this. The poor woman had been through far too much and this . . . hell, this could very well kill her.

Once outside the room, Edmund folded the doors shut behind him and heavily leaned into them, blowing out an exhausted breath. Why? Why did trouble always come in the form of a woman?

"Edmund? Edmund! What in heaven's name is going on?"

Speaking of trouble. Edmund pushed himself away from the doors and turned toward his mother, the Duchess of Rutherford, as she marched toward him.

Her salt and pepper black hair, which had been set in a mass of heavy curls on each side of her flushed round face, quivered with each determined step she took. She came to a quick halt before him, her drab, bombazine gown swishing into place around her petite and curvy frame. She narrowed her black eyes, yet still said nothing.

She didn't need to.

Edmund cleared his throat. "Allow me to fetch my jacket." He pointed down the empty corridor. "I left it on the floor."

She glanced around, then hissed, "Did you lure some girl out into the garden?"

He grabbed her arm and hastily led her away before anyone could eavesdrop. "Do we need to discuss this here? Now?"

"Do you think it matters where we discuss this? Everyone in the ballroom is already gossiping all about *your* theatrics. Now it is best you tell me what happened. Did you arrange a meeting in the garden? Is that it?"

He released her and swooped down to pick up his jacket. Jerking it on, he glared at her, angry that she would think the worst, as always. "She and I had a running in, of sorts. I swear it was nothing planned."

"An unlikely story." Her eyes traced his overall appearance in a frown of disapproval. She flicked open the fan that dangled from her wrist and fanned herself. "Edmund, you are thirty years old. A man your age does not crawl about the garden with an unchaperoned girl doing—"

She reddened and seemed to fight against wincing. "*You know what.* Do you realize how many people witnessed the two of you emerging from that garden? Half of London, I'd say. And the things being whispered would certainly make an entire ship of sailors blush. Have you heard what is being said?"

Edmund crossed his arms, noting her flushed features. "No. I was occupied. Her grandmother lost consciousness and needed to be tended to."

"Lost consciousness?" She released her fan, letting it dangle once again from her wrist. "Goodness, is she all right?"

"She's breathing, if that is what you mean."

She shook her head, the gold combs in her hair glinting at him. "The poor woman no doubt suffered a stroke after what you did to her granddaughter."

Judging from the older woman's calm demeanor with regards to his apologies, he somehow doubted that. And in some odd, inexplicable way, he sensed that the woman was rather proud of her granddaughter's garden liaison.

His mother glanced about, then drew close. "Come. What happened? You can tell your mother."

"Nothing happened," he growled out. As if he was going to further smear the young woman's name.

What was worse, for the life of him he could not deny what he'd felt when their bodies had been pressed together in the darkness and how damn good it was to have her tight, soft warmth surrounding him. No matter how short lived. He could still smell the intoxicating sweetness of mint that had filled the air with each breath he took. He had imagined her to be pretty and was stunned to discover that she was a physical replica of everything he could possibly want in a woman. A replica he did not think could exist.

Hell. Why was it so unbearably hot? He removed his jacket again, agitated. "Let them talk. People will eventually grow wary and find some other form of gossip."

"After the legacy of your father? Unlikely." She lowered her voice, but her dark eyes became unusually bright as her lips curved into a devious smile. "I suggest we take advantage of this. You need an heir, while the girl will be in desperate need of a husband. Marry her. It is by far the best solution for us all."

"*Marry her?*" He almost choked on the words. If his mother actually knew that Maybelle was the granddaughter of a French courtesan, he had no doubt she'd faint. Then come to and faint again. For she was the most sexually repressed woman in all of London. And as her son, he hated the fact that he knew that.

Wanting to do anything but look at her, Edmund tugged on his jacket one last time. "We are talking about a misunderstanding, is all. A serious misunderstanding."

"Yes. That would certainly explain your missing gloves." She put a hand beneath the jacket he had just pulled back on and yanked the left side of his embroidered waistcoat away from his body. "You surely won't be wearing *this* particular attire again."

She released his waistcoat and looked at her hand as if she had soiled her glove. She cleared her throat, and then stared at him. "You didn't force yourself on her, did you?"

Edmund smacked the sides of his clothing against his torso. "Is that what you think of me? Christ, I barely finished a cigar when she appeared from the shadows like a she-wolf and demanded satisfaction there and then."

Her eyes widened as she huffed out, "Indeed. I've heard better stories out of your father."

Footsteps interrupted their conversation as several gentlemen, no doubt doctors, threw open the doors to the drawing room where Madame de Maitenon was and rushed inside.

The duchess paused, glanced about, and lowered her voice. "At least your father tried to be discreet."

Edmund glared at her. "Yes, insult me. It's been so long."

"My dear boy, this isn't about insults. This is about a poor girl's reputation. Not to mention whatever is left of ours." She narrowed her gaze. "I will not have any more scandals in this family. Do you understand me? You will do what is right by her and you will do what is right by me. We need an heir. And I don't care if she is the daughter of an Irish sheepherder, you will marry her and *that* is *that*."

He smirked. "Do be careful of what you ask."

"Edmund, she will suffer because of you. And I

will not have it. A woman's reputation is extremely fragile. You of all people should know that."

Edmund wearily raked his hand through his hair. Yes, yes. But how was he to protect the reputation of a courtesan's granddaughter? Duke or not, it was impossible.

The duchess smacked his shoulder with her fan. "You will see to the girl, Edmund, or I will have your head." She peered down the corridor, pointed her fan at him one last time in warning, and then disappeared into the music that played in the crowded ballroom.

Edmund blew out a breath, rubbing at his jaw, and slowly moved down the corridor. He had to find a way of bringing this business to an end. For both his sanity and his mother's. And marriage was not it.

Stepping through the now-open doors of the drawing room he paused. Madame de Maitenon lay draped across the sofa, her low-cut gown still showing off quite the cleavage, but unlike before, she was conscious. One of the two gentlemen leaned over her, checking her pulse.

Thank God. The woman was alive.

A rustle of quick-moving skirts caught his attention. "Your Grace," Maybelle's soft voice pleaded. "I appreciate all that you have done, but you really should not be here."

Edmund tried not to stare as she steadily approached. But how could he not stare at the delectable mess before him? A mess he himself had helped create. Long curling strands of blond hair, which had fallen from her chignon, decorated her bare shoulders, and the short satin sleeves of her satin cream gown were charmingly crooked. And dirty.

He cleared his throat. "I am pleased to see your grandmother is doing well."

She was quiet for a moment. "I do not know if she is at all well."

He solemnly nodded. "Allow me to call on you at a more appropriate time."

She blinked. "Call on me? What for?"

He withheld a smile, amused by her straightforward nature. "I believe you and I have a rather complicated matter on our hands. One that needs to be addressed."

She stared, apparently too abashed to respond.

"Do notify me as to the progress of your grandmother's condition. I bid you a good evening." He bowed and met her soft, blue eyes one last time.

She returned his gaze with the same intensity she had when they had first seen each other out in the lightest part of the garden. As heated as her gaze was, he was surprised at how strikingly pure it seemed, with nothing hidden or lurking beneath. And in that moment, he knew that this woman was worthy of far more than the lot life had handed her. But then, life hadn't necessarily handed him a dandy lot either.

He turned abruptly and strode out of the room. All he could look to do was set things right to the best of his ability, tell his mother who the girl really was and then walk away.

No.

Not walk.

Run.

Lesson Four

*There is no such thing as an
inexperienced woman.
Unless of course she cannot
think, see, smell, or hear.*
                    —The School of Gallantry

Two weeks later

For the first time in her life, Maybelle realized
that the life of a demimondaine was worthy of fascination. For it didn't merely consist of spreading
one's thighs apart. No. A demimondaine actually
had to be very intelligent to make her way through
the dangerous trappings of society. And required a
gut of steel.

"There is a gentleman to see you, Miss," the butler
announced from the open doorway of the parlor.

Maybelle's heart jumped. She shoved aside the
memoir she'd been reading on Sally Salisbury, the

courtesan, and rose. In her haste, she nearly knocked over several vases filled with roses, which had been set at her feet.

Damn things.

Since her grandmother's stroke, the students from the School of Gallantry had overrun the entire house with flowers. So many, in fact, that there was no other flat surface in the parlor save the floor. And that didn't include all the other flowers she'd outright tossed. Flowers which had been delivered to Maybelle by various titled men who thought that she was now on the market for hire. Market for hire, indeed. She should have foreseen all of this.

Stepping around a huge basket of orchids, Maybelle turned toward the doorway where the balding butler continued to patiently wait. "Who is it now, Clive?"

She only hoped it wasn't more flowers, or worse, another despicable offer from yet another aristocrat who happened to be at Lord Hughes's soirée; or by God, she was going to buy a dog. A very, very large dog she could set loose on every man who came to the door. Her grandmother needed rest. As did she.

Clive cleared his throat. "The gentleman refused to give his name, but claims to know you. Says there is a rather important matter to settle regarding a particular night."

Maybelle caught her breath. No. It couldn't be.

"He visited on two other occasions, Miss, while

you were at Madame's bedside, but refused to leave a card each time. Do you remember?"

Oh dear God. That had been the Duke of Rutherford each time? Maybelle glanced down at her gray lace morning gown and cringed, realizing what it was she was wearing. "I am not properly dressed to be receiving, Clive. Insist that he leave a card."

"Yes, Miss." The butler departed.

Maybelle bit her lip, wondering if perhaps she shouldn't have turned the duke away. She turned, hop-footing around all the flowers, and hurried over to the parlor window. She peered past the brocaded, green silk curtain doing her best not to be seen.

A tall man, clad in well-fitted morning attire and a top hat, came to the end of the front steps and paused. He stared somewhere out before him, then turned and slammed the black iron railing of the gate with a gray-gloved fist.

Maybelle jumped away from the window. Good heavens, it *was* him. And he seemed to be out of temper. She placed a hand to her chest and took in a shaky, deep breath, trying to ease not only the fluttering of her heart but the warmth that was spreading over her body and between her thighs. How did he find her? More importantly, what did he want? *More?*

Clive came into the parlor and looked over at her. "He refused to leave his card, Miss. Again."

Maybelle dropped her hands back to her sides. Most likely the man didn't want to add his calling card to her collection. A collection which in his mind would then be set upon a silver tray and displayed for all who visited to see. Of course, what he didn't know was that she didn't have a collection of cards, save for the few that had arrived with all the flowers. Which she'd tossed. Now as for her grandmother . . . her cards had to be kept in a basket. Several of them.

"Thank you," she finally murmured. "It is best this way." Her focus needed to be on her grandmother and only her grandmother. She quickly moved away from the window and wove through all the flowers again, still trying to control the beating of her heart.

The butler went on. "I placed today's correspondence on the desk, Miss. They are all for Madame."

"Thank you, Clive." She approached the small writing desk cluttered with roses and picked up the stack of envelopes, thankful that she had something to occupy her thoughts. "I will address these immediately."

"I'll be down in the kitchen, Miss, should you have a need for me."

Maybelle nodded and sat in her grandmother's favorite red velvet chair, busily arranging the envelopes according to importance.

Bill. Bill. Bill. Bill.

And . . .

The bold handwritten letter on one of the envelopes made her pause. It read: *Madame Thérèse's School of Gallantry* and bore the address of 11 Berwick Street. Another forwarded correspondence.

She only hoped it wasn't another letter threatening to set fire to the school. So that they all may properly burn in hell, where they belonged.

Maybelle sighed. Her grandmother was so fond of her odd creation and despite the stroke continued to correspond feverishly with all her students, promising her return. Oddly, Maybelle wanted her to. It gave her grandmother something to live for. To strive and get better for.

Maybelle took up the envelope, broke the seal, which bore the letter *R*, and carefully unfolded the correspondence. Sliding out the calling card, which had been enclosed with the letter, to the edge of the stationery, she read:

> *Madame de Maitenon,*
> *I am a man in desperate need of your advice. Please meet me at the privacy of my home when it is most convenient. Enclosed is my card. I beg for your discretion and thank you in advance.*

And nothing more. It hadn't even been signed. Maybelle pinched the card against the letter with her fingers to keep it from falling. The calling card itself was plain, with gold letters and bore an address of a very respectable residence at Park Place. Yet had no name. Who had a calling card with an address yet no name? Highly irregular and not to be trusted. At all. Nonetheless, it was addressed to her grandmother, and not her, and should be delivered as such.

* * *

Maybelle opened the door to her grandmother's bedroom and peered in. "Grand-mère?"

Her grandmother looked up from the book she was reading and smiled, the edges of her eyes crinkling. "Ah. My beautiful nurse. Where have you been all morning?"

"Reading. I wanted you to rest." Maybelle closed the door and hurried toward her grandmother. Sitting on the edge of the large mahogany bed, Maybelle set the letter and calling card onto the side table and smiled as cheerfully as she could despite her grandmother's appearance.

Those bright blue eyes looked as if they would disappear beneath their eyelids. Her sagging, sickly features asked for pity and her long silver hair lay wildly around her, in unkempt waves.

"Grand-mère, why did you undo Sarah's braids?" she gently scolded. "She spent a whole hour on your hair."

Her grandmother rolled her eyes. "Braids are only fit for horses."

Maybelle smiled and shook her head. "Allow me." She stood and hurried toward the dresser. Grabbing up one of the two brushes set beside her grandmother's bottles of French lavender oils, Maybelle made her way back to the bed, leaned in, and gently gathered a long soft handful of the silver hair closest to her.

Her grandmother frowned and swatted her hand away. "Non, non. I will do it."

Maybelle sighed and released the hair she had

gathered. Even after a stroke, the woman hated being tended by anyone and took extreme pride in doing tasks herself.

Maybelle held out the brush. Her grandmother shakily reached out and took it. Tilting her head slightly, she brushed through her long silver strands, pausing occasionally only because of how horridly her hand shook.

Maybelle blinked back tears and looked away. It broke her heart to see her grandmother in such a frail state. Yet the doctors claimed it could have been worse. She could have lost her ability to move. Or speak.

"Grand-mère," she finally whispered, glancing toward the side table. She picked up the letter and calling card and turned back to her grandmother hoping she wasn't going to be difficult about the matter. "A letter arrived. With regards to the school. You should respond to it and explain that you aren't in any condition to be making visits."

Her grandmother paused and set aside the brush. "Who is it from?"

"It did not say."

Her grandmother's face colored for the first time since her stroke. She pushed away the book that was still on her lap and sat up straighter against the pillows.

With unexpected strength, her grandmother grabbed the letter from Maybelle's hands and snapped it open with the flick of her wrist. No sooner had her grandmother finished reading, the woman leaned over and pulled the servant bell. She jerked the red calling rope not once, but several times.

Maybelle leaned toward her. "What is it?"

The young chambermaid entered the room. "You rang . . . Madame?" she asked in between breaths.

Her grandmother pointed at the chambermaid. "Fetch Clive. Quickly."

"Yes, Madame." The chambermaid disappeared without closing the door.

Her grandmother snatched up the letter once again and after reading it, waved it thoughtfully before her. She then eyed Maybelle and mischievously quirked a silver brow.

Maybelle lowered her chin slightly. "I do not care for that particular look of mischief."

"Seeing I am bedridden, you will make the visit for me."

Maybelle felt the hairs on her arms standing on end. Although she'd been diligently helping her grandmother maintain the school without actually stepping foot into it and had even corresponded with all of her students with regards to her grandmother's progress, she wasn't quite prepared to take any more steps. Besides. One incomplete dalliance didn't even begin to qualify her for something like that.

Maybelle shook her head. Violently. "No. Absolutely not."

"Och, you are such a prude. Go and advise the man. We will bill him later."

"Bill him later? No! I couldn't possibly—"

"If he is not satisfied with your approach, I will gladly offer up a detailed letter free of charge."

"But I don't even have the sort of experience you do. All of my knowledge is . . . is . . . is *theoretical.*"

Her grandmother wagged a finger at her. "Believe me, chère, when I say that is substantial in and of itself. The women here in London are completely repressed. The men have absolutely no one to turn to. You will do just fine."

The butler unceremoniously skid into the room, causing Maybelle to turn. He paused, smoothing his livery jacket into place, and calmly approached, even though his chest still heaved from the flight he'd taken. "Yes, Madame?" he breathed out.

Her grandmother pointed at him with the letter. "Clive. My granddaughter will be conducting some business for me in a few days. You will make yourself available and chaperone her."

Clive paused, then replied, "Of course, Madame." He smiled crookedly at Maybelle, looking rather amused. And needless to say nothing ever amused the man.

Oh God no. *No.* Maybelle snapped toward her grandmother who had already comfortably settled into her pillows.

Her grandmother waved the man off. "That is all, Clive. Thank you."

Clive regally bowed and departed. With a swagger, might she add. Who knew what the man would tell the servants.

"Grand-mère," Maybelle pleaded, now altogether

hovering at her bedside. "You cannot expect me to call upon a complete stranger. The man will laugh at my advice." She snuck a glance at the door. "As will Clive."

"Oh, they will not. I have taught you everything I know. Besides, it will be good for you to leave the house. You have not left since my stroke. Now come here." Her grandmother leaned over, reached out, took hold of Maybelle's forearm, and proceeded to drag Maybelle toward her.

Maybelle stiffened, knowing full well that the woman, as always, was trying to use her charms to get her way. "I am not that gullible."

Her grandmother grabbed Maybelle's hand and placed it firmly over the silk of her robe. Right over her heart. She stared up at Maybelle with those soft, blue eyes. Pleading. The way she always did when something meant so much to her. And when she was bent on getting her way.

It was *so* unfair. Maybelle took in a calming breath that was anything but calming and drew her hands away. "I am not responsible if all of London goes down in flames."

"London could do with a bit of excitement, chère." Her grandmother grinned. "Let the city burn."

Lesson Five

There are two types of conquests:
the easy sort and the difficult sort.
Men always fool themselves into thinking
that the easy sort makes for better sport.
Yet it is without question that the latter
will ultimately result in what is
known as total seduction.
                    —*The School of Gallantry*

Edmund paced before the parlor windows, feeling as if his chest was about to explode from the frustration of it all. "What the blazes were you thinking?" he demanded, glaring at his mother every now and then. "This is my house and I refuse to be bullied into this nonsense."

The duchess swept into a plush burgundy chair and daintily plucked up the blue and white porcelain teacup before her. "You brought this upon yourself by exhibiting no self-control. Now stop grouching.

The woman should be here at any moment. Only do keep it to ten minutes, as we really should try and lull the tongues until the banns are printed."

Edmund continued trooping back and forth across the wood floor in an effort to refrain himself from roaring obscenities at his own mother. That she could sit there and drink tea at a time like this proved to him she had truly lost whatever was left of her mind. "Do you realize," he seethed through his teeth, "that if I marry the granddaughter of a courtesan it will damn well turn into the biggest uproar London has ever seen?"

She took several quiet sips from her tea, then set it onto the polished surface of the table before her. "No, dear. The biggest uproar went to your father."

Edmund came to an abrupt halt and turned to stare at her. "You are poisoning not only your life but mine. I have given you all the support a son can give and this is how you choose to repay me? By forcing me into a marriage so far beneath me I cannot even see the bottom?"

"Edmund, we need an heir."

He groaned and threw back his head. "*This much?*"

"You have outright rejected every respectable woman in London who might have married you. What options do you have left?"

He leveled his head. "I need someone who will help me rise above scandal." He waved his hand toward his mother. "Not *add* to it. For all we know this woman might be touched in the upper works.

Need I remind you, she hunted *me* down in that garden? What is worse, her grandmother is running a school for Casanovas. *Casanovas.* How much lower do you intend to sink us in the name of an heir?"

"Edmund." The duchess leveled a dark gaze at him. "Have you considered the possibility that she might already be with child? Unlike others in the *ton* who have no qualms about turning away from their transgressions, I will not cast away an innocent grandchild."

Edmund opened his mouth to respond to that, but quickly clamped it shut, not wanting to damn well go into any more detail than he already had. This was his mother, for pity's sake, how much more was he to disclose?

She sighed. "I suppose your father would have brushed off this matter just as easily."

He stiffened as if she'd struck him. "I am nothing like the man. I face responsibility."

"As you are facing this?" She mocked a laugh. "You robbed the girl of her innocence."

Edmund pointed at her. And didn't care that he was being rude. "You tell me this. Exactly how does one rob someone of something when it is being given quite freely?"

She narrowed her gaze and lowered her chin. "Is that how you justify all of this nonsense? That she was willing? One would certainly *hope* she was!"

"I . . ." He dropped his hand back to his side. Damn her. Marriage was a very serious commitment.

Not a set of china to be bought and set out on the table. "And what about the school? You have no qualms about having our name tied to something so . . . so *ridiculous?*"

She shrugged. "With an offer of duchess, I have no doubt we can convince Madame de Maitenon to close the school. After all, you have the means to enlist Parliament if you so choose."

She rose and daintily arranged her bombazine gown. "I shall make myself useful elsewhere during the woman's visit. In the meantime, make an acceptable offer to the girl's grandmother and be done with it."

"And if I choose not to make an offer?" he challenged.

She paused and studied him for a brief moment. "After what your father did to us," she finally said in a very cool, calm tone, "I was able to gather whatever was left of my name and bring forth several proper, marriageable girls for you to consider. Yet despite all of my pride and all of my efforts, none of them ever pleased you. They were never pretty enough, or wealthy enough, or titled enough, or intelligent enough. Your list of complaints truly knew no bounds. And I, my dear boy, have had quite enough. You have no further excuses considering the circumstances, and in my opinion, it is far better to marry beneath oneself than to allow a bloodline to altogether disappear." And with that, she jutted out her chin and departed, slamming the parlor doors behind her.

Edmund blew out a breath. Perhaps he should simply look into marrying *her* off. That way, she wouldn't feel so inclined to interfere with his life and blame him for not perpetuating the Rutherford name.

Adjusting his silk cravat, Edmund went back to pacing. His boots clattered each time he stepped from the oriental carpet to the polished wood floor. Perhaps he simply needed to leave London. Disappear. Disappear somewhere where women couldn't complicate his life. Was there even such a place?

The calling bell rang, interrupting his trooping. Edmund closed his eyes and focused on calming his dizzying thoughts. Egad. The granddaughter of a courtesan? For a wife? He wouldn't even be able to take her to the park without causing a riot. And seeing he was still dealing with the aftermath of his father's death and the mess that had created, he didn't know if he could handle taking on much more.

As the sound of quick steps approached, Edmund opened his eyes and sighed. In the end, his mother was right. He and he alone was responsible for this nonsense. He needed to prove to himself and the *ton* that he was nothing like his father. That he could take responsibility for his own transgressions. And move on.

So there it was. The first Rutherford to be shackled not to a lady of gentle breeding but to the granddaughter of a French courtesan. There were worse things to be shackled to. Like an eternity of explaining to blue-blooded virgins that he would never pop off the way his debauched father had done.

Edmund shifted his jaw and turned just as the parlor room doors fanned open.

"A Mr. Adams," the butler announced, "and a Madame de Maitenon."

Mr. Adams? Now who—

A tall, balding man dressed in gray livery entered, his aged chin propped high as if he were a general of some sort. Edmund narrowed his gaze. Oddly, he recognized the man. It was the damn butler. The one who had sent him packing each and every time he'd called upon Maybelle while trying to settle all this business quietly.

A petite blonde followed a few steps behind, dressed in a high-collared, pale blue lace gown and a matching parasol.

Edmund stiffened as the familiarity of the woman's face jolted him. For it was the same body and face that had drifted in and out of his thoughts during these past three weeks.

Maybelle de Maitenon.

And the woman was even more delectable in daylight. The color of her cobalt merino and lace gown complemented her bright blue eyes and the pale creamy tone of her flawless skin. A yellow bonnet, which had been tied in place with a wide satin ribbon beneath her chin, perfectly sat atop her gathered blond curls. It framed her oval face and accentuated the graceful length of her neck.

Edmund didn't dare note the remaining inventory for fear he might grow hard there and then.

Her eyes visibly widened as she paused. "Clive," she whispered in the drumming silence of the parlor. "This must be a horrid mistake."

The servant looked toward her, then back at Edmund. "'Tis the same gentleman who called on you several times before."

"Yes." She brought her parasol close to her chest. "I know."

Apparently, this meeting of theirs was a bit of a surprise to all of them. And Edmund didn't know why, but her presence actually soothed a part of his curiosity, which had been obsessively restless since that night in the garden.

The woman's gaze suddenly paused, then to his surprise, swept the length of him. His breath hitched in his throat at the possibility that she was outright weighing whether she might like to ride *him* to Tattersal's.

He struggled to keep his voice cool and steady. "Miss Maitenon. How gracious of you to deign me with your presence. I was beginning to think I was unworthy."

She cleared her throat and met his gaze. "I apologize that you were turned away each time, Your Grace, but my grandmother is still recovering from her stroke and I simply was not taking visitors."

Now he felt like the ass that he was. "I see. How is she?"

"Better, thank you. I certainly appreciate how you tended to her that night."

Edmund nodded and they both stood in silence staring at one another. And he had to admit, it was the most awkward silence he'd ever endured in his goddamn life. All being witnessed by a rather uppity old servant masquerading as a chaperone.

She switched her parasol into her other hand and broke their gaze by glancing around. "I do not wish to be apart from her too long, Your Grace. Her condition is still very delicate. Might we tend to whatever business you have?"

"Yes. That." He cleared his throat. "Perhaps it is best I clarify this whole matter. My mother wrote that letter to your grandmother. Not I."

"Your mother?" She blinked several times in astonishment and fidgeted with her parasol. "I . . . forgive me. I don't think I understand."

Her fidgeting allowed Edmund to unwittingly note her curves. He swallowed, noticing the way her full breasts were pushed up by her corset. And how they pressed against the delicate blue lace of her gown.

An ache started to build in his body at remembering the feel of her soft breasts weighing in his hands and how she had waited for him, panting and begging. Imagine. Her. Panting. Begging. He shifted his jaw and fought from lingering on their unfinished encounter.

Certainly, marriage to Maybelle de Maitenon would be anything but tiresome. He'd have access to her body whenever and wherever he pleased. Not the worst arrangement compared to all the homely, over-bred girls his mother had tried to shuffle him off to. The woman also seemed pleasant and intelligent enough to be able to learn the ways of a duchess. And with time . . . who knew.

Edmund blew out a breath and pointed toward the cane chair beside him. "Be seated. We have quite a bit to discuss."

Her mouth dipped into a frown. "We do?"

He leaned heavily against the chair he'd offered, realizing that he was about to embark upon a very bizarre adventure. And the butler who continued to stare blankly at him wasn't going to help matters either.

Edmund smiled. Tightly. "Might we speak in private, Miss Maitenon?"

She flushed to the tips of her ears. "Despite what you may think, Your Grace," she said, her blond curls quivering from beneath her bonnet, "I intend to keep this visit respectable as I have no intention of gathering any more offers from your peers. I assure you that whatever is said before Clive will be kept in strict confidence."

Edmund inwardly cringed at the thought of proposing before a servant. A male one, at that. He pushed himself away from the chair. Perhaps he ought to change the subject for a bit of time and come back to the whole shackling of the leg bit later.

He eyed her. "Seems your grandmother's school

is gaining vast popularity. I cannot seem to go any-where these days without reading or hearing about it. Even all the clubs of Pall Mall are placing bets, guessing at to what goes on inside."

Maybelle lowered her chin and tartly stared at him, clearly displeased with their line of conversation.

Damn. Perhaps a compliment should alter that. "Your grandmother must have quite the experience to undertake such an endeavor." He paused and only then realized that had not come off quite as he'd intended.

Maybelle narrowed her gaze and pointed her blue parasol at him as if it were a sword. "You are being an ass, Your Grace. Is this what I was called here for? To be insulted?"

Edmund pulled in his chin. Nobody had ever called him an ass before. Not to his face anyway. He held up a hand. "I apologize. I didn't mean to offend. I simply—"

"No. No one ever means to offend." She lowered her parasol and snapped it back to her side. "I think it best I leave."

Her lips tightened as if she were withholding from spitting something besides words out. She glanced toward the butler. "Come along, Clive. Our business here is done."

It was obvious he'd better get to the matter at hand. Even if he had to do it in front of the damn butler. He was a man, after all. A man capable of not only taking responsibility for his carnal actions, but also his duty to sire an heir.

Which is why he finally blurted, "Miss Maitenon. Upon serious reflection and consideration, I have decided to offer for your hand in marriage. I do hope that you will stay long enough to consider my offer of matrimony and what that will entail."

There. Now he could begin regretting his words for the rest of his life.

Lesson Six

A man in need is a man indeed.
                    —*The School of Gallantry*

Maybelle froze in the doorway of the drawing room, her heart momentarily freezing along with the rest of her. She couldn't possibly have heard right. The Duke of Rutherford had *not* just asked for her hand in marriage. Did he?

"Ehm." Clive leaned in from behind. "Shall I excuse myself, Miss?"

Maybelle glanced over her shoulder toward Clive. She'd almost forgotten the man was in the room. She passed her parasol into her other hand and sighed. She supposed she could handle this on her own. Although she'd never dealt with having to reject a marriage proposal before. "Yes, Clive. Thank you."

"I will be outside the doors. Should you need me." He quickly departed, closing the double doors behind him.

The dark paneled drawing room suddenly became quiet. Unnervingly quiet. Maybelle slowly turned to him. Judging the man's tiger-like stance, she realized that he was quite serious about his proposal. So why in heavens did he seem so displeased?

Perhaps she should sit and give him a moment to explain himself. Before she outright rejected him.

As calmly as she knew how, Maybelle breezed past him, clutching her parasol as tightly as her gloved hand would allow, so as to squeeze away every bit of her nervousness. She sat in a plush burgundy chair, the farthest one she could find from him, and waited for him to say something more on the matter.

When the large walnut clock on the other side of the room chimed four times and hummed back into silence, and no words had been exchanged, Maybelle glanced toward him.

To her surprise, she found him staring at her quite intently. With those piercing, obsidian eyes. His lean square jaw was tight, as if he were holding words between his teeth.

"Yes?" she prodded.

He crossed his long arms over his chest, the fabric of his gray morning jacket straining against his muscles. "What do you think of me, Miss Maitenon? Aside from our unfinished business out in the garden."

An unexpected shiver shot through her. He was rather to the point. As always. She wet her lips, knowing she had to guard herself well. "I do not

know you well enough to comment, Your Grace."
Which wasn't entirely a lie.

The duke lifted a dark brow. "You have no opinion of me whatsoever?"

She stiffened. Of course she had an opinion. She
simply chose to keep it to herself. For once. "No.
None."

"Regardless of the fact that you called me an ass
only a few moments earlier?"

She lifted her chin. "I do not take kindly to being
insulted."

"Understand that it was not my intent to insult
you." He blew out a breath. "Perhaps it is best we
commence with pleasantries from the beginning.
Allow me to formally introduce myself." He bowed,
his black combed hair falling forward onto his forehead. "I am Edmund Richard Worthington, the
sixth Duke of Rutherford, and I am very pleased to
make your acquaintance, Miss Maitenon."

Maybelle gripped her parasol hard and eyed him.
Why was he doing all this? He was a duke, for
heaven's sake, and she was too many classes below
him to count.

He put his hands behind his back, his chest muscles visibly stretching against his gray morning jacket
and vest. "I have come to the conclusion that I have
wronged you by exhibiting no self-control. I also
have no doubt that you require protection against
the multitude of complications that surround your
grandmother. Our marriage will not completely

shield you, considering I myself am not in good standing, but that is simply the way of things."

He cleared his throat. "So here is my offer. Upon matrimony, you shall receive the title of duchess, along with a townhouse and the generous sum of five thousand pounds a year to do whatever it is you please with. Any other outstanding expenses you should incur need only be forwarded to me. In return, you will see to the permanent closure of the School of Gallantry. You will make it your primary focus to produce an heir. However long that may take."

Maybelle froze. Setting aside that the man wanted to snatch every last bit of her independence away, and engage her in some bizarre matrimonial courtesanship, the man was also demanding that she close the school? Was he mad?

The duke paused. His gaze drifted from her face down to her neck and farther down to her breasts, making her full aware that he had not forgotten what had passed between them. He quickly met her gaze again. "Until an heir is born, you will have no other in your bed but me, as I am not one for raising bastards. That is my offer. I do hope that you find it to be fair and generous."

Fair? *Generous?* She couldn't believe that he'd actually related so much intolerable information with such stoic sincerity. What made him think that she was going to sit around in some townhouse playing the part of a snob only to then open the door from time to time to let him crawl into her bed? For what? A title and a dribble of respectability that wasn't guaranteed? And of course, he failed to mention that while she played the role of a dutiful and faithful wife, he would damn well frig anyone he pleased. Why, she was better off being a full-fledged courtesan!

Maybelle popped up from her chair and waved her blue parasol at him. "I could damn well get a better offer from any one of your peers, Your Grace. Now despite what you and the rest of the *ton* may think, I am not interested in marriage. At all. So please. Whatever you do, do not call upon me again. For *your* sake. Good-bye." Fighting the heat rising into her face, she hurried past him. Never in all her life—

"You will not walk away from me or my offer," he snapped after her.

"Oh, but I will," she flitted over her shoulder, marching her way toward the door. "Observe."

"Damn it all." The duke swiftly came in from behind and grabbed her arm, forcing her to not only stop, but to also turn and face his dense, muscular body.

Maybelle froze as the scent of sandalwood, one she remembered all too well, surrounded her. Every bit of her body blazed beneath his powerful stare and for one crazed moment, she actually wondered what it would be like to be at his command once again. With his hands on her body. His length deep within her, making her feel wanted, needed.

He slowly released her but inched closer, bringing in more of that sandalwood, which was sensually tinted with the heat of his body. "Your grand-mother's school is going to complicate your life in a manner you aren't even prepared for. Admit it. My offer is a good one."

Finally grabbing hold of her wits, Maybelle stepped back and crossed her arms, her parasol sticking out to the side. "Oh, is it?" She tilted her head slightly. "You might say I'm a bit concerned about being deprived. On every possible level."

He stared at her for a long moment, his dark eyes slowly turning into a smoldering invitation. "I would never deprive my wife of *anything.*"

"Oh, really?" She quirked a brow. "I don't know about you, Your Grace, but that one night in the garden left me *completely* deprived. Based off of that alone, I am somewhat concerned."

His mouth visibly twitched as he struggled to hold back his obvious amusement. "I assure you, there is no need for concern, though it pleases me to no end that you think about that night so often."

Her eyes widened. The arrogant puff! Yes, well, enough was well enough. "Good day and good-bye!" She spun on her heel.

The double doors to the parlor banged wide open, startling Maybelle into a frozen stance.

"I have had quite enough," a woman drawled from the doorway. "Must the entire household listen to this?"

An older woman clad in a bombazine gown breezed into the parlor. The woman quickly turned, closed the doors on Clive, who was peering in on the commotion, and turned back. Her overall posture was very stiff, yet very elegant, and her sharp dark features resembled those of the duke. There was no mistaking those eyes.

"Might I introduce my mother," the duke muttered, "the Duchess of Rutherford."

Maybelle felt the room shrinking. For the rules had officially changed. She was now in the presence of what society defined as a real lady. A lady of first quality, which Maybelle knew she'd never be, even if she accepted the duke's offer.

Maybelle curtsied humbly. "How do you do, Your Grace?"

The duchess nodded in turn, and slowly approached Maybelle, a questioning look on her face. She paused an arm's length away. "Why did your grandmother not come, child? The letter was intended for her."

For all the gossip that went around, not enough of the proper sort seemed to reach ears. "She is still recovering from a stroke, Your Grace."

"Ah, yes. Yes. I apologize. I trust she is better?"

"Yes. She is. Thank you."

The duchess paused and tilted her dark and silver streaked head, as if taking in her features. "You are certainly prettier than my son had described. Far prettier."

"Why are you here, Mother?" the duke interjected, sounding unusually exhausted. "I am more than capable of negotiating my own marriage."

"Is that so?" the duchess snapped. "By offering

the poor girl a separate townhouse? How do you expect that to result in children?"

Maybelle bit back a smile as the duke sank into the chair, grumbling. Why is it the man was so rebellious and unyielding to the world, yet one word from his mother and he became the saint she wanted him to be? It reminded her a tad too much of her relationship with her grandmother. Which couldn't be *all* that bad. It meant the man had a heart somewhere in that broad chest of his.

The duchess brought her dark eyes back to Maybelle. "I know full well who you are. I also know who your grandmother is and how she, like so many other women, steals our sons and husbands from beneath our respectable noses. But considering your age, I was utterly surprised to learn of your innocence. It means that despite your upbringing, you have a sense of morals. I pity you. Greatly. After all, you were born unto terrible circumstance that is by no means your fault."

Maybelle felt her cheeks flushing. This woman pitied her. *Pitied* her.

The duchess turned slightly and looked at Edmund with what appeared to be admiration, despite her earlier treatment of him. "Setting aside some of his shortcomings, Miss Maitenon, my son is a good man and would make for an excellent husband. Please. Reconsider his offer. I promise you will not be ill treated. You will be family. Something Edmund and I have little of."

Maybelle's brows rose. After the way this woman's

husband died, one would think she'd be set against having a courtesan in the family.

The corner chair creaked in protest as Edmund finally rose from his post. He strode toward them, paused beside his mother, and leaned toward her. "I will see to this. Go."

The duchess sighed and eyed Maybelle. "I assure you that he will make a better offer." With that, the woman turned and swept out of the room, shutting the parlor doors on herself and Clive, who still lingered just outside.

In that moment, Maybelle didn't know what to think anymore. She sensed desperation. As if the granddaughter of a courtesan was their last resort.

Oh, this was not good.

Edmund stepped toward her and said in a low, smooth voice, "My mother refuses to let this matter go for reasons that go beyond the humanity of anything I will ever know."

The duke stepped closer, his broad chest now blocking her view of the room. Maybelle swallowed and wanted to step away, but knew her knees would buckle from beneath her if she dared to even move.

"Now as for me," he murmured, tilting his dark head and openly admiring her lips, "I admit to being rather curious as to what more I can expect from you. Oddly, you fascinate me. In so many ways."

Maybelle felt as if the floor were now swaying beneath her. "Kindly step away." She would have moved away herself, but didn't trust her legs to step in the proper direction.

He didn't move and his gaze remained steady. "I am certain we can come to a mutual understanding that would ultimately benefit us both." With that, he reached out, took hold of her shoulders, and dragged her toward him.

Shocked by his forced closeness, her body went numb and the parasol she'd been clutching slipped from her gloved fingers, clattering to the floor. She could now feel the heat of his hands sinking through the shoulders of her gown as he stared down at her and rubbed his thumbs in small, seductive circles.

"Clive is waiting right outside those doors," she warned, trying desperately not to think about how amazing his large hands felt.

"Inform me when I have overstepped my bounds, Madam." He paused, his eyes searching her face as he lowered his face to hers. His hot breath grazed her forehead. Goosebumps feathered her body and she felt herself melting.

He lowered his head farther, his parted lips now hovering over the bridge of her nose. Her pulse leaped when his lips paused just over hers. A mere breath away.

Yet . . . he did not kiss her. Instead, his hand trailed up the side of her corseted waist and possessively found her breast.

He cupped it. Hard.

Maybelle sucked in a sharp breath and stilled against his aggressive touch. A part of her desperately wanted it, while another part of her fought not to give in. And she couldn't decide which part she should listen to.

The duke continued to watch her face as his fingers slowly circled the lace of her bodice and the breast beneath it. Her nipple hardened beneath his playful and delicate touch as wonderful sensations fluttered across her chest and tingled the pit of her stomach.

"Are you enjoying this as much as I am?" he murmured, his lips still lingering a mere breath from hers.

Oh, yes. Very much so.

Not breaking her gaze, he grabbed her gloved hand and pressed it down against the front of his trousers. Firmly.

Her eyes widened and her breath caught as her palm met the length of his large erection. It was the first time she'd ever touched a man down *there* with her hand. Even if it was only through trousers.

The intensity of his dark gaze along with her own curiosity made her curl her fingers around the pulsing heat of his hard length. She held it tightly through the wool.

A muscle flicked in his jaw as his nostrils flared. "Now." His voice was low, his gaze steady. "Allow me to see to your needs. Whatever they may be."

She swallowed, still holding onto his erection, and for one crazed moment, she actually contemplated flipping her skirts up for the bastard. But if she gave in to this man every time he had a fancy, she knew he'd come back to haunt her and claim her again and again and again. Without any offers.

Maybelle moved her hand and shoved at him, scrambling outside the circle of his embrace.

There was only one way to end this. "*Cliiive!*" she belted out.

The doors to the parlor immediately swung open. Clive jumped back as though he'd had his ear pressed to the doors. He scrambled in, his chest heaving and his face a bright, crisp red.

Perverts. The world was infested with perverts.

"I wish to leave, Clive," she announced. "My business here is done." She cheered inwardly at her strength and smiled tightly at the duke, who stood quite stunned.

At last, *she* was in control. And that is exactly how she wanted it to be.

Lesson Seven

When all else fails in your efforts to seduce,
simply make use of all your resources
and try, try again.
—The School of Gallantry

When the granddaughter of a courtesan refused a
Rutherford, his days were numbered. Considerably.

Disoriented, Edmund grabbed for a chair and
sat. He was still trying to understand what had actually occurred. In mere moments he'd undertaken
everything from proposing to outright trying to
seduce the woman in his own parlor. Although his
erection had subsided, it still ached like the devil.
Ached to finish what always seemed to commence
but could never quite end.

Edmund leaned far forward, blew out a harsh
breath, and rubbed at his temples, trying to relax.
He was coming to the realization that he had a serious problem. He bloody wanted to bed Maybelle

de Maitenon. Again. Although that first time didn't truly count, did it?

"She departed rather quickly," his mother commented from the doorway.

Edmund looked up and lowered his hands, placing them heavily onto his knees. "I take it you listened to the rest of the conversation."

"What sort of woman do you take me for? I was merely glancing through all of your correspondences."

He wasn't even going to dignify that with an answer.

She sighed. "You could have at least tried romancing the girl. She might have been more willing."

"I've never engaged in the notion of romantics and I am not about to begin." He stood and slowly shook his head. "I offered to the best of my abilities and have absolutely no intention of dealing with that woman ever again. It is best we move on."

"Edmund, please." His mother brought a hand to her throat. "Can we not make a better offer? Can we not—"

"Not *we*. *Me*." Edmund pointed to himself, making sure she understood what it was he was saying. "Whatever takes place from here on will take place because *I* say so. I do not want any more of your ridiculous notions about what I should or should not do."

She lowered her hand from her throat and moved toward him, a questioning look coming over her face. "So what will you do?"

"Nothing."

"*Nothing?*" she demanded.

"Yes, nothing. Believe me. She would make for the worst duchess and I for one have enough responsibilities without taking on one more."

"Come now. All she needs is polish. I can assist her with that."

He snorted. "The trouble with that logic, Mother, is there is no silver left in her drawers to polish. Quite literally."

His mother reddened and huffed out, "Well, I liked her. She was quite pleasant."

"Tart best describes her."

"She was also exceptionally beautiful for a common girl."

"Yes, I will grant you that."

"And clearly, has no hidden motives."

"All women have motives. Yourself included."

She placed her hands on her hips and stared him down. "Edmund. Admit it. You and she are one of the same when it comes to reputation. Yet she wants absolutely nothing from you. Despite the fact that you have robbed her of her innocence. Does that not move you to at least try and understand her? Obviously, she is not a fortune hunter."

Yes, but if Maybelle de Maitenon wasn't a fortune hunter, what the hell was she then?

"Find a way to win her heart," she softly pleaded, stepping closer. "Before I pass from this life without ever looking upon the angelic faces of my grandchildren. Edmund, please. It is all I will ever ask of you. Do not rip away my last hope of ever finding joy. I deserve to be happy after all that has come to pass. I deserve a family. Do I not?"

Why, oh why, did he have to care? Edmund sighed heavily and glanced around the parlor. Yes. If there was one thing his mother deserved it was happiness. Especially after their very name had been completely destroyed by his father. Clearly, his mother refused to let this matter go and it was up to him to create a new family for her. Even if it wasn't going to be a proper one.

In the end, he supposed he could scrounge up a better offer for Miss Maitenon. Although he doubted the woman would ever see him again.

His mother gently grabbed hold of his arm. "You can be quite charming when you apply yourself appropriately."

"Thank you. Really."

"Please, dear. Help her. Help her before her only option is to become a courtesan. Or worse yet, a teacher for her grandmother's school. Could you imagine?"

Edmund paused. The school. Of course. The school. Why hadn't he thought of that? Maybelle had been rather quick to defend the School of Gallantry. So quick, in fact, he had no doubt he could use that to his advantage.

He eyed his mother and patted her hand, which continued to cling to his arm. "I think you've given me an idea."

The duchess paused and took back her hand,

looking quite pleased with herself. "I am so happy I inspire you from time to time. So tell me. What exactly did I inspire you to do?"

"Enroll."

Her dark brows popped up. *"Enroll?"*

He slowly started walking backwards, toward his desk. "Yes. In the School of Gallantry. I cannot coerce the woman into marrying me. But I can coerce her into seeing me in class." He grinned. "With time, I have no doubt I can make a respectable duchess out of her. And I promise to do all of this for you. Remember that."

His mother gasped and smacked a hand over her mouth. "By becoming a rake?" she cried through her clamped hand.

"Oh, come. It isn't the worst thing a Rutherford has ever done." And as a student, he'd be able to better exploit the school and shut it down before it further interfered with Maybelle's reputation. Or his own. He'd also get a chance to make the woman writhe. Writhe in a way she'd made him writhe today. And that night. Oh, yes. By the time he was done with the woman, *any* offer would do.

Edmund turned and strode over toward the gilded secretary. He snatched up a piece of embossed stationery and the quill set next to the inkwell. "I think it's damn well time I put my title to use. People seem to think it doesn't mean anything anymore. Oh. And another thing." He pointed the quill in his mother's direction. "Invite her to that upcoming ball of yours.

I need to know how capable she is of handling the pressure of the *ton.*"

"Heavens above! Edmund, no!" His mother rushed toward him, her black skirts bustling all around her. "This is not the way I envisioned your courtship to proceed. Surely there are other ways to—"

"Do you or do you not want grandchildren?" he drawled.

She froze, wide eyed, and for the first time in a long time, actually did not have anything more to say.

He nodded. "Have the invitation ready. I shall include it in my letter to Madame de Maitenon."

Lesson Eight

The greatest test of one's passion
lies in the price one is willing to pay.
—The School of Gallantry

"How dare he!" Maybelle exclaimed, restraining herself from altogether stomping her foot against the floorboards like a child. "How dare he threaten us like this!"

Her grandmother sighed, folded the letter the duke had sent, and set it neatly onto her lap atop the white linen gathered around her. "Despite his reputation, he is still a duke. If we do not enroll him, as he wishes, he will enlist Parliament and close the school. What is worse, he expects class to be in session next week. Rather serious, if you ask me."

That good-for-nothing bastard. He couldn't get her to flip up her skirts in his parlor or be his pot-flesh of a wife, so he went and used the only thing he did have. His title. Well, she might not have a title, or a reputation for that matter, but *she* would ultimately win this battle. Not him.

Her grandmother tilted her silver braided head and eyed her for a long moment. "You must have terribly wounded his sensibilities, chère. A duke would never offer lightly on women of our caliber."

Maybelle hurried toward her and leaned against the side of the four-poster bed. "The man is full of himself. Utterly full of himself. '*I am not one for raising bastards*,' says he. Indeed. *And I am?*"

Her grandmother laughed and sat back against her pile of pillows. "Oh, I would have loved to have been there!" She shook her head, lowered her gaze, and poked at the letters still on her lap. "It would seem, Maybelle, that my little school rests entirely in your hands. Whatever shall we do? Allow a man to govern us?"

Maybelle narrowed her gaze. No man would ever govern her. Ever. Especially for his own gain. She pointed at the duke's letter and the invitation he sent along. "You tell that bastard that school shall commence this Monday. If need be, I will personally oversee all classes and will even take up his silly little challenge of going to his mother's ball. If the Duke of Rutherford ever thought he knew the meaning of scandal, I am about to redefine it not only for him, but for all of London."

Her grandmother's silver brows rose, her eyes brightening. She excitedly clapped her hands in glee. "At long last! My granddaughter has officially arrived into the wonderful world of scandal."

* * *

Four days later, evening

"Where is she?" Maybelle demanded, after peering into the parlor and finding it empty. "Where is Mrs. Williamson? She was supposed to arrive an hour ago."

Clive, who lingered before the staircase, blinked back at her, confused. "Madame ordered your chaperone away the moment she arrived."

Maybelle turned to him completely. "Ordered her away? Whatever do you mean?"

"Madame intends to escort you herself to the Rutherford ball."

Her grandmother was bacon brained, to be sure. She marched up to Clive. "Escort me? The woman hasn't been out of bed in weeks. I'll not run the risk of her suffering another stroke."

Clive shrugged knowingly. "That is what I said, Miss. But as you know, a butler can only do so much."

"Yes, well, I intend to put an end to this nonsense. At once." Maybelle gathered her emerald silk skirts to head up the staircase, but paused at discovering her grandmother at the top of the stairs, leaning against her gold and black ivory cane.

Her grandmother stared her down with firm, blue eyes that clearly stated "*I am going.*" Dressed in a lilac satin gown which was cinched tightly at the waist with dozens of small diamond brooches, she was quite splendid to behold. Her thick, silver hair had been parted and arrayed with perfect ringlets, making her look unusually young and vibrant, considering her state of health. It would seem the woman had planned to attend all along.

"You should be in bed," Maybelle scolded up at her. "A crowded ballroom will be the death of you."

Her grandmother tapped her cane, sending an echo down the staircase and across the corridor. "If I am going to die it will be amongst people. Not alone in my room."

"But you cannot possibly be well enough to go."

"Tosh. It is only one night. You will need me, chère, and I refuse to be left out of all the excitement."

Maybelle shook her head, knowing the woman couldn't possibly be prepared for a long night on her feet. The doctors agreed that she needed to remain bedridden for at least a few more weeks. "You suffered a stroke, Grand-mère. Be sensible."

Her grandmother tapped her cane again and set her chin, demonstrating she was not about to retreat. "If I do not go, *you* do not go. Comprenez-vous?"

Maybelle sighed.

It was going to be a long night.

Allow me to survive this, Maybelle silently pleaded as she and her grandmother were formally announced. Side by side, they entered the large, ornate ballroom.

An endless array of lit candles flickered from the

solid gold sconces attached to the paneled walls. Gilded crystal chandeliers graced the high, arched ceilings. Every flame from every candle glittered and multiplied within the mirrors which decorated the ballroom.

Despite her rising nervousness, Maybelle managed to appear aloof. She held her coiffed head steady as she walked past an endless parade of wide-eyed staring faces and overdressed, stiff postures.

And although the merry strings of violins fluttered in the background, there might as well have been a world hush. For everyone looked utterly abashed at seeing her and her grandmother whisk into the ballroom. Several chaperones outright scrambled to usher their girls back and away, scolding them for even peering in their direction.

Ah, yes. The *ton*. They all appeared the same—arbiters passing death sentences. Instead of the women having judgment mallets, they held colorful, delicate fans, which they incessantly waved before their rouged faces, hiding what it was they thought. While the men? Well. The men did not have mallets. They had their cocks to judge by. And so theirs was always a very different verdict.

Moving farther into the ballroom, Maybelle glanced toward her grandmother for reassurance, only to find the woman grinning and nodding to the people gawking at them. It was as if she was thrilled to be out among the living again and causing the latest scandal.

"We are finally done with appearances, chère."

Her grandmother pointed her black ivory cane toward an adjourning room serving refreshments. "That is where you will find me."

"Do try to rest."

"Oui. Oui. Go. Play."

Maybelle smiled as her grandmother sashayed away, her cane more of an ornament than an instrument to walk with. At least she didn't have to worry too much about her grandmother. The woman appeared to be getting around quite well. Too well, actually.

Alone for this first time since her arrival, Maybelle snapped open her fan and eyed the crowd, knowing it was only a matter of time before the duke found her. Strangely, a part of her couldn't wait to see if he still had the ability to send her pulse flying, while another part of her simply couldn't wait to make the bastard miserable.

"Madam. What an unexpected pleasure."

Ah. The devil was officially at hand.

Maybelle dropped her fan, letting it dangle from her wrist, and turned sweepingly to the Duke of Rutherford. And damn it all, her heart almost leaped out of her rib cage at seeing him. As always.

His black hair was fashionably swept back, and he looked very much the picture of when she first saw him, dressed in a black formal suit and a high, white starched collar and cravat, which framed his shaven square jaw.

He grinned down at her. The most perfect god-like grin. The damn bastard. He knew full well how alluring he was. And was using it to his advantage.

"Why, if it isn't His Grace," she retorted, turning away slightly to keep him from witnessing the color in her cheeks heightening. She fanned herself to keep the flush down.

He glanced around and lowered his voice. "And where is your chaperone, Miss Maitenon? A lady of quality should never be left unescorted."

Lady of quality, indeed. "You and I both know that appearances are of little consequence to a person who has no reputation to uphold."

"Ah, but I have the ability to change that for you." His eyes traveled down the length of her emerald silk gown, which she had the modiste pucker at the waist with a veil of thin gauze for more allure. He paused and lingered at the top rounds of her exposed breasts. As if they were his to admire.

After a few lingering moments, he decided her face was worth looking at again. "Honor me by putting my name on your dance card."

The way the man continued to stare at her made her realize that dancing wasn't at all what he had in mind. His eyes still clung to her body and seemed to slowly strip her naked, casting aside every bit of clothing she had on, including her stockings.

The man really had no shame.

Yes, well, neither did she.

She lifted her left hand, drawing up the white card that dangled from a piece of red ribbon. Holding it before her, she read the dances listed for the night as if they were the names of dance partners.

Her card was empty, of course, but she wasn't about to inform him of that.

"I do apologize," she casually flitted. "It seems my dance card is already quite full. Perhaps another time?"

A baffled expression passed over his face and before Maybelle could decipher his intentions, he leaned in and whisked the card from her, jerking her wrist toward him. "Your Grace!"

"There isn't a single name written here." He continued to look at the empty dance card, then cocked his head. "I suppose I can write myself in for the quadrille."

"How utterly rude!" She snatched back her wrist and card. "You take too many liberties and seeing you will soon be a student of mine, I shall gladly issue your first lesson. Never touch a woman without her permission."

He coughed, although she could have sworn it was more of a laugh. "But you gave me permission that one night. Remember?"

"Yes. Once. I was deeply disappointed and shall not give it again."

He winced playfully. "We'd best work on your manners first."

"Despite what you and the rest of the *ton* may think, I am rather pleased with my position in life. I am permitted to go and do as I please without male rule."

"Yet you and your grandmother are still financially

dependent on all of us men to survive. The school being a good example of that."

Maybelle smiled even though she felt like smacking him. "Which leads me to the point of why I am really here, Your Grace. I am trying to encourage more business. For the school."

He paused.

"As you know, I am not at all interested in marriage, but I am interested in finishing what was started between us. It would certainly make me and the school all the more popular knowing that I have entertained the scandalous Duke of Rutherford. Which is why I have decided to offer you one night."

Edmund's face clouded and a muscle flicked in his jaw. He glanced around, as if only now noticing there were people around them, and then grabbed hold of her arm with his gloved hand. The next thing she knew he was rudely leading her toward the back wall and into the farthest and darkest corner, away from everyone around them.

He paused but didn't relinquish his firm grip. "Never offer a Rutherford something you cannot afford to give," he growled down at her. "You might find yourself at a loss when he chooses to collect."

She yanked her arm away and took several steps back, toward the wall. "I assure you my offer is quite sincere, Your Grace. Although I highly doubt you can afford it."

His expression grew taut and derisive. "How much?"

He said it as if there wasn't a price he couldn't pay. Which sent her pulse galloping. She cleared her throat knowing she was about to slam the door on his face. Once and for all. "One hundred thousand pounds. For one night."

He paused, and if he was in any way astonished by the sum, he most certainly did not show it. Instead, he narrowed his dark gaze and leaned in close. So close he broke every social rule that was supposed to exist in public. And clearly, he did not seem to care.

Her chest tightened as she continued to boldly hold his gaze. For all that mattered was the end result. Getting rid of him. Once and for all.

After a few moments of hovering silence, he finally retorted, "Permit me three days to produce the sum. I do hope that banknotes will be acceptable."

Although Maybelle tried to hide her shock, her lips parted and she couldn't help but gawk at him. Was the Duke of Rutherford truly worth that much? Impossible.

Edmund stepped back and bowed, his haunting dark eyes never once leaving hers. He then straightened and drew out his large white, gloved hand. "Now. To seal our agreement, I ask for this dance."

Maybelle struggled to keep her thundering pulse in check as she unwittingly extended her hand and allowed his warmth to surround her gloved fingers. What on earth was her grandmother going to say? The woman had insisted that no man would be willing to pay such an outrageous sum. Not even for the most exquisite of demimondaines.

"At such a lofty price, Madam," the duke drawled as they made their way to the dance floor, "I expect every breathing moment to be well spoken for."

As they arrived onto the dance floor, Maybelle struggled to throttle the dizzying current that assaulted her body in response to his words. She could only fathom what a night with him would entail.

He gripped her gloved hand tighter, quite possessively, and together they moved in time to the music down the line. As they passed each couple, Maybelle was painfully aware that all eyes were on her and Edmund.

For the first time in her life she was truly mesmerized. By a man. Something she never thought possible. Each time his dark eyes met hers from across the line and the short distance they stood apart, she wondered why she felt so light and giddy when only a moment ago she wanted to beat him at his own game.

Each time he bowed during their dance and took her hand to whisk her down the line, she seriously wondered why he would agree to such an outrageously expensive night. If it was sex he was looking for, he could have damn well gotten it anywhere. For free, no doubt.

After a single dance, she was surprised to find the duke already escorting her off the floor. "You will now take leave of me, Madam."

He brought them both to a halt, released her hand, and bowed. "Despite our *unconventional* agreement,

I am taking it upon myself to ensure that you publicly adhere to the rules of the *ton*. Now find your chaperone, Miss Maitenon, and enjoy the rest of your evening. It was a pleasure."

With that, he turned and strode away.

Maybelle blinked. That was it? She frowned and couldn't help but feel . . . utterly disappointed. This had to be some sort of game. She was certain of it. And she didn't even want to think about what that could possibly mean.

She quickly turned and whisked herself off in the opposite direction, keeping her chin set high should anyone be watching. When she was far away enough, she paused and drew in a shaky breath. Then several more. Heaven help her. She'd actually sold herself off to the duke for one hundred thousand pounds. Without meaning to.

"My, my," a man drawled, grabbing her waist and drawing her toward him. "If it isn't the delectable granddaughter of Madame de Maitenon. How are you?"

Maybelle gasped at finding herself tightly bound against a young blond male who was apparently drunk out of his trousers. "Sir! I ask that you release me! At once!"

"Oh, come now. I hear you're good for a dance . . . or two . . . or three." He guffawed and leaned toward her, trying to yank her closer. The stench of stale sweat and cognac overwhelmed her. "Are you in the market? I'd rather fancy knowing what my money can buy."

Maybelle swallowed back the sensation of spiders crawling into her throat, knowing exactly what the man wanted. She shoved hard at him, but his drunk arms weighed too heavily on her and her body was once again pressed against his. "Release me," she growled out. "Or I'll bloody—"

"One dance is all," the man continued to blubber. "I'm certain you've given more than that."

The bastard! Gritting her teeth, Maybelle forcefully freed her right hand, fisted it, and bopped him in the nose. Hard. So hard, her hand actually stung.

Yet the alcohol must have numbed his senses for the man only blinked in response. His face slowly twisted in anger as he seized both of her wrists, causing pain to shoot up the length of her forearms. "I'll damn well teach you to—"

"*Wharton*," Edmund said sharply, now stepping into view. "What the devil are you doing?"

Seeing Edmund actually made her weak with relief. His tone alone implied he wasn't any more pleased than she was.

"Your Grace." The drunk tightened his hold on her wrists, causing her to wince. "I was merely asking for a dance."

Edmund drew close and leaned in. So close all three of their bodies were practically touching. "Her dance card is quite full, I assure you."

Maybelle's heart jumped at being scrunched between two men who appeared to be out of their minds.

Edmund continued to glare down at the man.

"This lady does not deserve your degrading advances. Leave her be."

"Lady indeed." The blonde snorted. "You've rather lost your mind."

"Miss Maitenon is officially under *my* protection," Edmund seethed through his teeth. "Now release her, Wharton. I'll not ask again."

Maybelle blinked in astonishment. Edmund looked almost crazed, his dark features dangerously fixed on the man who continued to hold her wrists. Imagine. The Duke of Rutherford claiming her. Clearly, he'd been serious about marrying her all along.

"You intend to publicly defend a whore?" the bastard scoffed, still not releasing her wrists.

Edmund snatched the man by the collar, yanking him off of her completely and with one full swing smashed his gloved fist upside the man's head.

Maybelle scrambled back and away. She felt her slippered heel catch on the hem of her skirts, and though she desperately fought to balance herself with her arms, she tipped far backwards and braced herself for the fall.

She would have fallen, too, if it weren't for a gentleman who had swiftly swooped in from behind. She froze as she was lifted back to her feet. The tantalizing scent of lemon and leather floated around her.

The stranger continued to hold her tightly with muscled arms, pressing her backside firmly against the length of his heated body. She could feel his chest rise and fall. And if she didn't know any better, his cock was rather hard.

She inwardly cringed. "Thank you," she whispered, quickly yanking herself away.

She turned and blinked. A tall, good-looking man with striking green eyes and swept-back bronzed hair grinned down at her rather saucily.

He quickly adjusted his evening jacket in an effort to cover his faux pas and drawled, "A pleasure." He reached out, grabbed her satin-gloved hand, and kissed it before turning and walking away.

Maybelle blinked down at her gloved hand in astonishment. Seems her plan to drum up scandal was working.

She cleared her throat and turned back to Edmund. She paused, realizing that the blond man who'd tried to grope her was now unconscious on the ballroom floor, his legs spread apart and his mouth open wide.

Edmund continued to tower over him, opening and fisting one of his gloved hands, as if making certain the man remained on the floor.

People started gathering around them, their fans flickering, their lips whispering, and their bodies leaning.

This would certainly make the papers.

"His lordship is foxed, is all," Edmund muttered at those around him.

His lordship?! Oh do save her from the humiliation of it all. Did the man have to be titled?

The duke turned and strode up to Maybelle, curtly

commanding, "Madam. I ask that you follow me at once."

As if she had a choice. He was her rescuer *and* her host. She followed him off to the side.

He paused and leaned toward her, his dark eyes searching her face. "Did he hurt you?" he whispered.

"No. I am well, thank you." She nodded, unable to push away the feeling that he was genuinely concerned for her well-being. It touched her, actually. No man had ever publicly stood up for her honor. Ever. And there had been a few occasions in which she could have used such protection.

He lowered his voice. "Allow me to be your protector until you and I can come to some sort of an agreeable conclusion."

Maybelle didn't know whether to be pleased or offended. "I prefer to keep our relationship to the standard one night, thank you."

The orchestra ceased, as if she had cued it to cease with those very words. The supper bell sounded, calling the guests to indulge.

She curtsied, turned, and then hurried away before she altogether changed her mind. For strangely, she was beginning to wonder what it would be like to be under the man's protection. At all times. Clearly, the man had a disturbing and unsettling effect on her. One that made her want to give up all control and sensibility.

A rude laughter chimed out from a group of women Maybelle had passed. Instead of ignoring it, as would have been the proper thing to do, Maybelle turned and readied herself for another battle.

The tall, dark-haired woman in the center of the group paused, surprised that Maybelle would be so bold. "Do find a better chaperone," the woman chirped. "For you are making quite a fool of yourself."

Although the words stung Maybelle's pride straight to the core of her soul, she bit down on her tongue and turned away before she did something she'd regret. Like wallop the smirk off her face. But she was a representative of her grandmother's school and, as such, refused to add brawling to her list of credentials. Which is why she simply breezed out of the ballroom and into the refreshment room, determined to hunt her grandmother down.

Soon enough, she found her grandmother. At the center of male attention. As always. Maybelle inwardly groaned. Her grandmother was talking quite enthusiastically to Lord Hughes. As if the night had barely commenced.

Glancing around, Maybelle hurried toward them hoping she wouldn't have to explain before the man why it was time to leave.

Her grandmother must have noticed her approach, for she leaned toward Lord Hughes and uttered something that made him quickly bow and depart. Her grandmother set her chin and then walked toward her, her cane following each elegant movement.

When they were within an arm's length, her grandmother eagerly eyed her, awaiting the news.

Maybelle flicked open her fan, covering the lower half of her face, then leaned toward her grandmother and hissed, "The duke intends to pay. With banknotes, mind you. And what is worse, only moments ago, he rendered a man senseless on my behalf before all of London. Now I suggest we leave. Immediately."

"The duke rendered a man senseless on your behalf?" A small smile touched her grandmother's lips as she glanced around. She then whispered back, "We leave after supper."

Maybelle's eyes widened in disbelief. "But—"

"Tut-tut." Her grandmother held up a gloved hand. "You have a new reputation to uphold. It is not every day the *ton* publicly fights its own. We must revel in it."

Maybelle clamped her mouth shut, knowing there was no sense arguing. She supposed this was damn well part of redefining scandal.

Lesson Nine

Do not question the heat involved in passion.
Instead, question what more you can do
to ignite the flame.
                                   —*The School of Gallantry*

One hundred thousand pounds. His mother was going to have a fit. And rightfully so. But hell, she wanted grandchildren, did she not?

Edmund shook his head and tugged on the cuffs of his sleeves. Here he was trying to publicly clean up Maybelle de Maitenon's name only to end up muddying his own. By knocking out an earl. Before all of London, no less.

He glanced around. It was time to find the woman again and make certain no other arsy-varsy was trying to mount her. He'd expected a frigid reception, and wanted her to know what the *ton* was capable of, but didn't realize it would get this out of hand. God knows what the woman dealt with on a daily basis. The very thought sickened him. It was no wonder she always seemed ready to battle.

Edmund nodded his pleasantries toward a passing couple and strolled into the formal dining room, searching all of the occupied white linen–covered tables.

He paused at seeing Maybelle.

She was intently exchanging words with her grandmother while seated at one of the tables. The strands of pearls that had been perfectly weaved into her gathered blond curls glistened as she leaned toward her grandmother. Her off-the-shoulder gown tightened around her breasts whenever she moved, the thin outside gauze shifting against the silk beneath as it emphasized the top rounds of her generous breasts.

Maybelle, not to mention her grandmother, momentarily paused from their involved conversation. As if he'd outright called out their names from across the room, they both turned their heads toward his direction and stared.

Edmund offered a gallant nod in their direction.

Madame de Maitenon briskly patted Maybelle's hand, whispering something into her ear, and stood. Rounding their table, the Frenchwoman slowly made her way toward him with the help of an ivory cane. Her sharp blue eyes were fixed on him the entire time.

This promised to be entertaining.

Soon, Madame de Maitenon stood before him in all her elegant splendor of lilac satin and diamonds.

She quirked a silver brow at him and motioned toward the doorway with her cane.

Edmund swept a hand toward the doorway. "After you, Madame."

She breezed past.

Once outside the dining room, Madame de Maitenon fully turned, her skirts sweeping the marble floor of the corridor. She observed him pensively as if trying to understand something.

Edmund placed his gloved hands behind his back. "Yes?"

A devilish gleam appeared in her blue eyes as she lowered her voice and leaned toward him. "Less thoughts of poom-poom, oui? My granddaughter already gets enough of that."

Edmund blinked, not knowing what he was supposed to say in response. *Poom-poom?* Did that mean what the hell he thought it meant?

"Edmund." The duchess marched on toward them from down the corridor in all her black splendor. "Did you actually assault one of my guests?!"

"This is not the time, Mother," he said tightly. His eyes went back to Madame de Maitenon. He leaned toward the woman and drawled, "What do you suggest then, Madame? For I am genuinely hoping to make your granddaughter my duchess."

She lowered her chin slightly. "Are you incapable of understanding that independence is her only lover, Your Grace? Maybelle is not like the women of the *ton*. She is intelligent. Sophisticated. And has interests that lie in things like Voltaire and Egypt.

Everything she could ever want she can easily receive from five others without a single form of commitment. Perhaps it is best you move on, oui? Save your money. You will need it."

Edmund knew not why, but the woman's insolent words bothered him. That there were others. And that his money and title were not enough. Because in reality, he had nothing else to offer. Involving more meant involving emotions, and emotions only damn well destroyed everything. Made people do things that they normally wouldn't think to do. Like commit suicide.

His mother hurried over to him. "Edmund, for heaven's sake, are you listening? I—" She paused beside them and gawked at Maybelle's grandmother. And then at him.

As if the conversation weren't awkward enough. "Mother. I need a few moments to finish this conversation."

Dark eyes pinned him with a crushing stare. "Perhaps you need a few moments to tend to Lord Wharton. You promised to keep things respectable." The duchess turned and smiled genuinely at Madame de Maitenon, then turned back and glared at him. "I will talk to Madame de Maitenon. Perhaps we women can come to a better understanding. Yes?"

Edmund stared at his mother in disbelief. She was going to converse with Madame de Maitenon? In public? Seemed her intent to marry him off was officially out of hand.

Madame de Maitenon tapped the side of his lacquered shoe with the end of her ivory cane. "My granddaughter sits alone, Your Grace. Inform her that I shall be joining her shortly, oui?"

"Of course." He bowed to both women, not wanting to even think about the conversation he was about to leave behind, then turned and strode into the dining hall.

He glanced to where he'd last seen Maybelle and froze. A dark-haired gentleman leaned toward her, a viscount of some sort, and was saying something that looked rather involved. Maybelle, in turn, smiled up at the man from her seat and simply listened.

In that very moment, a jealousy he damn well had never felt seized not only his brain but his entire body. He balled his fists. He didn't like seeing her with other men. Mostly because he knew what it was they wanted. The same thing he did. But at least he was trying to make something respectable of her. A wife.

Edmund set his jaw and headed toward her just as the viscount bowed and moved on. Yes. Keep walking, bastard. Keep walking.

Edmund didn't pause in his stride until he was at Maybelle's side. "Good evening. Again. Might I join you?"

She turned, clearly startled, and looked up at him from where she was sitting. And quickly looked away. The napkin she clutched fell into her lap, which gave him a detailed view of her cleavage set just below her diamond necklace.

He sucked in a quick breath at seeing the soft dip

between those full, smooth breasts and cursed himself for being a man.

She must have noticed where his eyes had drifted for she immediately snatched up her napkin and firmly pressed it against her bosom. "I think it unwise that we be seen together anymore tonight." She leaned toward the empty chair beside her and with her other hand rudely pulled it in, dragging it toward herself. "Furthermore, this seat belongs to my grandmother."

Now how was he to be a gentleman after a retort like that? He took hold of the chair, forcefully prying it away from her hand, and sat. "Thank you for the chair," he said dryly. "Now. Perhaps you'd best be aware that there is something rather serious going on out in that corridor."

The napkin Maybelle had been covering her bosom with slipped to her lap. She glanced toward the entryway, then back at him, and lowered her voice. "Whatever do you mean?"

Oh, yes. Let her think that she was outnumbered and that he had others working for his cause. That there was no escaping her fate. "Your grandmother and my mother are chatting away. Very much like old friends. What do you make of it?"

She stared at him. "Taradiddle, you say."

"'Tis true. And although I have no idea how your grandmother feels about the matter, I do know that my mother is still very intent on having us married. Something to do with grandchildren."

"God forbid they should fall upon the subject of

grandchildren." Maybelle smacked her napkin onto the table and snatched up her gloves from beside her plate. She yanked them on rather violently, then scrambled up out of her chair, but in her haste stumbled and lost her balance. She tipped far forward against the small table.

Although Edmund jumped up and caught her arm to keep her from altogether falling, her body and full skirts still managed to send the table, and everything on it, crashing forward to the floor.

Edmund froze, as did Maybelle, realizing that everyone was gawking at them. Bloody hell.

On cue, three male servants swarmed in. One stomped on the end of the tablecloth that had caught fire from the burning candle. Another promptly picked up pieces of crystal and china, while another collected the flowers that had decorated the table.

Whispers rumbled around them as couples stood to leave. It was time to officially escort her out of the room and out of the public's eye.

"Come," he muttered, grabbing her hand and quickly leading them toward the doorway.

"What do you think is worse?" she hissed, trying to keep up with him. "Overturning a table? Or an earl?"

Edmund bit back a laugh, despite everything. The woman's tongue truly knew no bounds and together, there was no scandal they couldn't conquer.

When they arrived out in the corridor, he released her arm and paused, surprised to find that neither his mother nor Maybelle's grandmother was in sight.

It was as if they had both up and disappeared. They were no doubt plotting in private, out of the eye of the *ton*.

Good. At least they knew how to be discreet.

Edmund looked over at Maybelle and was about to say something with regards to the matter but froze at realizing the entire front of her emerald and gauze gown had been splattered and streaked with wine. "Uh . . ." He gestured toward her gown.

She looked down at herself, let out a small laugh, and commenced brushing at the stains. She shook her blond head. "Why is it, Your Grace, that my gown is forever being soiled whenever it comes into your presence?"

He grinned, strangely enjoying the playful lilt in her voice. How did she do it? How did she so easily scoff at dire circumstances? It was indeed something to admire.

"Your Grace." A male servant held up a means of cleaning her. "Someone insisted the lady was in need of a basin and a towel."

Ah, yes. This is where they disappeared and finished off a bit of business in private. And perhaps a bit more. "Thank you."

Edmund grabbed the dry towel from the servant and draped it across his shoulder. Taking the small porcelain basin from the servant's hands, Edmund turned and cocked his head toward the direction he wanted Maybelle to go. "Madam. If you please. The second door on your right. Before anyone sees you."

She gawked at him. "I would prefer one of your servants tend to my dress, Your Grace."

"What better servant than I, Madam?" He grinned. "Besides, you and I have yet to arrange a date and time for a rather important event."

She sighed, as if thoroughly exhausted, looked toward the dining hall and then at the servant, who was still watching them with rather large eyes. Without sparing him another glance, she gathered her skirts, set her chin, and breezed down the dim corridor toward the second door on the right.

Edmund grinned at her duchess-like departure and followed her. When he reached the doorway of the room where she had disappeared into, he paused, and wondered if it was wise to proceed any farther. For there, in the middle of the study, away from all the activity that dwelled within the house, stood Maybelle. Waiting for him.

The candles lighting the room made her pearl-strung golden hair and pale skin shimmer. The diamond necklace around her throat brightly winked at him, accentuating the soft curves of her throat.

He shifted his jaw. This was fatal. It was as if he could not force himself to think rationally when in her presence. What was worse, he didn't want to think rationally. It was unlike any lust he'd ever experienced in his life.

He slowly entered the study, the only sound being that of the water whisking inside the porcelain basin. As he drew closer, their eyes met and the attraction he felt for her exploded. That familiar, glorious ache filled his groin.

Pausing a few feet before her, he set the basin down on the wood floor and tried not to grab for her then and there. He stood. "Allow me to tend to our privacy first, as we have drawn more than enough attention to ourselves tonight."

With that, he turned, made his way back across the room, and shut the doors into one another, turning the key in its lock. As he withdrew the key, he turned and tucked it into his inner vest pocket. Her blue eyes watched him with a raw, sensual intensity he wanted. The sort of intensity he needed.

"After we tend to your gown, we can finalize the details of our night." He strode toward her.

"Being locked in a room is not what I agreed to when I decided to meet you here."

He paused before the basin, half smiled, and waved her over. "If you promise to be a lady, I promise to be a gentleman."

"I am not a lady and you are not a gentleman," she snapped.

"If at any time you become concerned, Madam, you know where to find the key." He patted the front of his vest pocket. "All you need do is fetch it." He eyed her. "That is, if you care to wander that close."

She bit her bottom lip.

"Do allow me to tend to your gown. It is the least I can do considering how the evening turned out."

"No. I would rather you not. You'll ruin the silk." She shifted from foot to foot, then sighed. "Let us simply get to the matter at hand. The matter you called me in here for."

"Of course." He glanced toward the settee placed in the middle of the room and gestured toward it. "Shall we be seated?"

"Yes. Thank you." She hurried over to the sofa and set herself on the farthest end.

Edmund ignored her obvious attempt to put space between them and decided to sit beside her. He blew out a breath, trying to release the tension in his body. Of course, the only reasonable way any man could release *this* amount of tension was by doing the obvious. Though he was not about to set a bad example.

"So where is it to take place, Your Grace?" she finally asked, breaking the awkward silence. "The sooner we agree on the terms, the sooner I can leave."

If there was one thing he admired about Maybelle de Maitenon it was how she always seemed confident in whatever it was she was saying and doing. A confidence that even he, as a duke, lacked from time to time. "You decide the terms, Madam."

She was quiet for a long moment, then said matter-of-factly, "Your bed will more than suffice. Send word as to when and I will come to you."

Hearing those seductive words from her lips made his pulse throb and his blood warm. He turned to her, wanting to ask her what it was she really wanted out of a man, other than the emotional rubbish every woman expected, but paused upon noticing something on her neck, right above her diamond necklace.

He leaned in, causing her to stiffen. "I believe a bit of wine spattered on your skin." He grinned. "Or let us hope it is wine. I don't think I sprayed blood when I removed Wharton from your person."

A laugh escaped her. She swiped at her neck and eyed him. "Is it gone?"

He glanced at the skin beneath her necklace, which was still tinged with droplets of dried wine. "Uh . . . no."

She swiped at her skin again. "What about now?"

"No."

"Oh, for heaven's sake. Can you be trusted not to overstep your bounds?" With that, she tilted her head slightly, offering the length of her neck to him.

Control yourself, man. You can do this. "Of course."

Edmund cleared his throat, removed his gloves, and set them aside. He then wet his finger with his tongue, leaned toward her, and dipped his moist finger into her skin, gently rubbing at the smidge of dried wine from the hollow of her neck.

As her smooth, velvet skin heated his finger, he realized not only did he not want to stop touching her, but the bit of wine seemed to have stained her skin. He leaned closer in and rubbed at it one more time, trying to ignore the fact that he was still touching her. But it was like trying to convince a dog that it was a cat.

Although she didn't move beneath his touch, her chest seemed to rise and fall a bit more unsteadily, as if she were having difficulty breathing. Her pink lips parted ever so slightly as she stared ahead.

Edmund paused, removing his finger from the warmth of her skin, but continued to hover over her, wondering if in fact she was as affected by his presence as he was by hers.

He stared down at her moist lips and though he tried, hell how he tried, he could not refrain. Using his hand, he gently nudged her face more toward his direction, leaned down, and brushed his mouth against her soft, full lips.

She closed her eyes, but otherwise did not move.

He pulled his mouth away from hers and whispered hoarsely, "I thought you should know that I cannot be trusted anymore."

"Go on," she breathed, her eyes still closed, and her warm breath coming in short, quick takes. "I will tell you when I have had enough."

Feeling as though his chest would explode from her seductive invitation, he lowered his face to hers and pressed his mouth more forcefully against hers, parting her lips. Their hot tongues met, gliding against one another, and in an instant his entire body hardened. His cock throbbed as it expanded, demanding he take her. He fought to remain in control and sucked on her tongue, pulling it into his own mouth.

Maybelle leaned into him and slid her arms around his shoulders.

It was all the encouragement a man needed.

His bare hands rigidly traced her slim profile,

moving from her soft shoulders to her back. He slid his lips down the side of her throat, savoring the sweet flavor of her smooth skin.

"Yes," she whispered, raking her gloved hands through his hair.

Edmund leaned her farther back and slid off the sofa, kneeling completely before her. She watched him through heavy lids as he dragged her skirts up to her slim thighs, pushing her chemise up and out of the way with them. He trailed his hands up the entire length of her silken limbs, savoring every soft, warm inch of her.

Her breaths were growing heavier, steadier.

He raked his gaze across the length of her shapely stockinged legs. Stockings that were held in place by white lace garters. He paused at seeing the patch of tight blond curls nestled between her thighs. His breath hitched in his throat and his pulse thundered as he nudged her legs apart, realizing he'd never had a chance to really look at her. To really look at her.

Her pink folds were lush, visibly wet and ready. And he had no intention of stopping this time. He gripped hold of her thighs and forced his mouth down onto her.

She gasped and quivered against him as he suckled on her nub. The sweet taste of her wetness filled his mouth. Although the tip of his cock was beginning to bead in anticipation, he refused to settle for anything but her climax. He licked her and then sucked, licked her and then sucked, refusing to pause even for a moment.

"Oh God," she panted, reaching down and pulling him harder against her. Her hips moved up and down, up and down. "Edmund. Yes. Yes."

Intent on making her come on his command right there and then, he licked her faster and harder.

She cried out and her thighs tightened, enclosing him against her softness. Her wetness met his tongue. Though he knew she was climaxing, he refused to stop until he had taken every wave of sensation from her core. She squirmed and then finally stilled, her thighs relaxing.

Lifting his mouth from her wetness, he straightened and undid his trousers. It was damn well time to claim her and make her his. Here. Now.

A banging on the double doors startled him from his intent haze.

Maybelle sat up, pressed her thighs shut, and froze before him, her gloved fingertips digging into the couch. Her eyes widened.

"*Edmund?*" The doors rattled against their hinges. "Edmund Worthington, open these doors!"

Christ. It *would* be his mother.

Maybelle frantically pushed herself up. She shoved at him, sending him fumbling back, and arranged her skirts down over her legs. She quickly rolled off the sofa, her bum wiggling and brushing past him.

His cock throbbed, reminding him that he would have to wait for God knows how long. Bloody no.

Edmund grabbed her waist and tightened his hold. "The doors are secure," he growled out, trying to yank her back toward him. "And our night has yet to begin."

Maybelle smacked his hands away and glared down at him from where he was on his knees. "I believe you have received more than your share of handouts, Your Grace, and I certainly don't see a hundred thousand pounds sitting in your lap. Now. Open the door."

Edmund threw his hands up in the air and let them drop back down to his sides. Bugger. She was right. What was worse, he was bloody losing sight of what he was supposed to do. Make a lady out of her.

He slowly rose to his feet and grumbled as he put himself away and fastened his trousers back into place. Adjusting and readjusting his cock, he winced and felt as if he was going to damn well burst. Which at this rate, he most likely would.

He shook his head and eventually made his way toward the door, withdrawing the key from his vest pocket.

"Edmund," his mother hissed from the other side, still knocking. "This is not the way to go about making her into a duchess. Do try and remember that we have guests to tend to!"

Yes, and you'd think she would keep her voice down because of that. "Coming, coming!" he yelled out.

Pausing at the doors, he glanced back toward Maybelle to ensure her appearance was intact. To his surprise, Maybelle had not only pried open one of the farthest windows of the study, but was hanging onto the frame with both gloved hands pulling herself up onto the windowsill. She winced and dragged herself and all of her heavy skirts up with whatever strength she had. She then popped her slippered feet out through the window. As if she did this sort of thing all the time. Her gown billowed up all around her elbows as her bottom wiggled around to get out.

All of London was getting an amazing show. At no cost at all. While he was damn well paying a hundred thousand pounds for it. "What the blazes are you doing?" he hissed from across the room.

"I'd rather not face your mother. Do inform my grandmother that I will be waiting in the carriage. Good night." With that, she completely slid out of the window and disappeared for a brief moment outside. She then popped back up, slammed the window shut, and disappeared into the night.

Gone. Just like that. The disappointment that met his gut was overwhelming. Not to mention unexpected.

His mother pounded on the doors again. "Edmund!"

He blew out a breath, shoved the key into the lock, and clicked it open. His mother was one sure way to get rid of the damn bulge in his trousers.

Lesson Ten

Lewd and erotic thoughts
are a very necessary evil
when it comes to the art of seduction
because they will ultimately prepare you
for what is most important. Reality.
                    —*The School of Gallantry*

Maybelle slowly sat on the edge of her grandmother's bed, folded her hands, and patiently awaited the set of instructions promised. The set of instructions that would propel her into the world of educating men on the art of seduction. Needless to say, she was nervous. Incorrigibly nervous.

In a single day, she would take the role of headmistress at the School of Gallantry. And she had absolutely no idea what that entailed.

She'd already read and reread all four of the applications which had been originally submitted to the school, and was shocked to discover that one of the students—the Earl of Brayton—was actually a thirty-one-year-old virgin. Now *there* was a story.

Her grandmother leaned toward Maybelle and tapped the bottom lobe of Maybelle's ear to ensure she was listening. "I have several rules, chère," she announced in a rather serious tone. "No one, not even you, is allowed to be seen going in or out of my school. It marks our exclusivity and more importantly protects my étudiants. After all, no man wants to advertise that he is in need of lessons."

"So how do they get in?" Maybelle smirked. "Or out?"

"Ah." A mysterious smile tilted her grandmother's lips and her blue eyes sparkled. "There is an underground passage that connects from one of the neighboring townhomes to my school. I have been most fortunate to have procured it at no cost by its owner, Lady Chartwell."

"Lady Chartwell? You mean the widow you earlier spoke of?"

"Oui. Though I suspect you will not have that many chances at meeting her. She is very occupied with several worrisome prospects both in and out of the city. Now. This passage. Lady Chartwell disclosed to me that it had once been used by her family's great grandfather, who frequented his mistress almost a hundred years ago. Quite appropriate, oui?"

Maybelle pinched her lips together. Yes, and who knew how many other such tunnels existed beneath the streets of London. Men digging in the name of lust. She only hoped that the Duke of Rutherford wouldn't start digging a tunnel to her room. She certainly wouldn't put it past him. He was intent on making her writhe.

She swallowed and tried not to linger on the incredible pleasure he had bestowed upon her with his mouth. She hadn't even told her grandmother about it. Mostly because her grandmother was a firm believer that a woman's body was a form of business. Handing out free goods, as she liked to call it, was horrible business, because then customers expected free goods all the time.

Her grandmother leaned back against her pillows; smoothed the crisp, white linens around her waist; and sighed. "The tunnel will take you below the school and from there, Harold will escort you up into the classroom."

Maybelle realized she wasn't listening. "I'm sorry. Harold?"

"Oui. He is the gatekeeper, of sorts, and ensures that everyone goes where they are supposed to. He will be waiting for you at the end of the tunnel."

Impressive. "I have to say, I am quite astonished as to the amount of thought you've put into this. How long have you been considering this notion of a school?"

"For years, chère. Ever since I became a demimondaine in France. Now. You are in possession of some very private and delectable details with regards to each étudiant. Be certain to keep those details private as they prefer their matters to be tight-lipped, for obvious reasons. I have also sent each of them, including His Grace, a detailed letter informing them how and when to arrive at the school. They will each deliver a nightshirt for you to examine."

Maybelle pulled in her chin, her heart pounding. "Their nightshirts? Whatever do you mean?"

Her grandmother chuckled, reached out and patted her hand. "They will not be wearing them. They will merely be presenting them to you as part of your first lesson. Try to remember. You are there to offer these men the psychology of an experienced woman they do not usually have access to."

"And their nightshirts have to do with . . . ?"

"Your opinion. As you know, you will be addressing bedside manners before and after an encounter. And a man's nightshirt very well includes that. Och, why I remember back in Paris a very rich and very titled man offered that I share his bed at a price I could not resist."

Maybelle inwardly winced. Her grandmother had a tendency to divulge much more information than was really necessary.

"So I agreed. Until I saw him in his nightshirt." Her grandmother rolled her eyes and clucked. "A man must know how to present himself in the bedroom or he shall find himself at a complete loss. Which is why you must advise these men as to what you find attractive and what you do not. Right down to their nightshirts. Easy, oui?"

Maybelle half nodded. She supposed there was no chance of getting out of this now.

"Ah, yes. One other matter. Do try to touch upon the subject of flowers in the next few days. Explain to them that delivering funeral flowers to a lady is not acceptable and that too many flowers is rather obsessive and disturbing. Between all four of my students, I should not have received more than two hundred."

Maybelle grinned. "You expect me to nag them for you?"

Her grandmother wagged a finger at her. "Of course not. Always be tactful. And do be wary of Lord Hawksford. He has quite the reputation."

Hawksford? The one obsessed with conquests? Maybelle leaned toward her grandmother. "Shall I bring a pistol?"

"Your intelligence is the only weapon you will need against them. And that I know you have. Arrive early tomorrow morning. Before seven. It will allow you enough time to conduct class and have the men out of my school by ten. That way, the men are able to abide by their daily schedules without drawing any attention to their activities."

"Absolutely brilliant." Oddly, Maybelle meant it.

Her grandmother smiled. "Merci. Now. Like you, all of my girls will be arriving for the first time tomorrow. They all know to be there before you and the men arrive. It has taken me a bit of time to find the right girls for the pleasure room, but I am certain the men will be more than pleased."

Maybelle leaned toward her. "*The pleasure room?*"

"Oui. It is where the girls will be staying. They have strict orders to remain there at all times while school is in session. Until they are called upon by you. They also know there is to be no dallying with the men, as it is a school, not a bordello. Harold will ensure everyone is adhering to my rules."

Clearly, this was becoming rather complicated. Maybelle cleared her throat and leaned away. "Now these girls. What would I need them for? Exactly?"

Her grandmother frowned and waved a hand toward her. "They are for the classroom, of course. You do not intend on using yourself to demonstrate techniques, do you?"

Maybelle gawked at her grandmother. A raging blush took over her entire face. "Of course I don't intend on using myself."

"They are paid very well and will do whatever it is you ask them to. Be sure to introduce yourself to them before you start class. Harold will escort you to where they are." Her grandmother pointed past her, toward the dresser on the other side of the bedroom. "Now fetch that book for me."

Dread was beginning to ebb into every part of her being. She simply couldn't imagine herself positioning any woman, dressed or not, before an entire group of men. Or Edmund.

Maybelle rose, drawing in a shaky breath, and made her way toward the dresser. A large, black leather book of about five hundred pages of bound parchment sat on its corner. Maybelle took hold of it, its massive weight surprising her. She returned to her grandmother's bedside. "What is this?"

Her grandmother patted her lap. "Set it here."

Maybelle leaned toward her and set the book gently on her lap, curious as to what this was all about.

"Now." Her grandmother opened the large book and paged through it, pausing every now and then to read her own perfectly scribed writing. "Read as much as you can. It will educate you all the more on the subject of what men like to do in bed."

Her grandmother flipped a few more pages and then stopped and pointed to one of the four columns that divided each bound parchment. "Disregard the names and money received. Instead, read my notes. It is in French, but I know you can translate very well."

With that, her grandmother turned the book toward her. "Read this one."

Maybelle tilted her head to one side and slowly translated aloud: "The man prefers to talk of dirty things rather than actually doing them. 'If given a chance you would lick my wife's—'" Maybelle's mouth dropped open as she stared at the rather dirty French word.

"Go on," her grandmother insisted, tapping at the page. "Go on."

Maybelle cleared her throat, knowing modesty was not something she could hold on to anymore. "'You would lick my wife's *cunt*,' he says. 'Yes, I would,' I say. And so on and so on as he joyfully masturbates. The man is not actually looking for sex as much as self-gratification. And for it, I like him. There is less work on my part."

Maybelle looked up. "What on earth is this?" she demanded.

Her grandmother shrugged. "Detailed notes on every client I have ever entertained."

Maybelle's eyes widened. "You retained notes on every man you ever bedded? Why on earth would you do that?"

"First and foremost I am a businesswoman. I must always have a form of blackmail. Payment is not always guaranteed."

"And the purpose of showing this to me is . . . ?"

"It is important that nothing astound you as you will be getting all sorts of questions from your étu-diants. Share your findings with them and tell them what you find attractive and what you do not." Her grandmother closed the book and pushed it toward Maybelle. "Take it. All I ask is that you protect its contents. Do not ever let it leave the house."

Maybelle bit her lip, eyed the big black book, and wondered if she was treading on dangerous territory. By the looks of all the filled pages, there must have been at least a hundred clients listed. Which meant there were at least that many sexual encounters to read. Dear God. This sounded rather like work.

"That is all, chère." Her grandmother sighed, tilted her head back against the pillow, and closed her eyes. "I am tired and admit the Rutherford ball took more énergie than I had expected."

"Which is why you will not be leaving bed again

anytime soon." Maybelle snatched up the book, leaned over, and kissed her grandmother's smooth cheek. "Rest. I will manage." Somehow. Some way.

"I have no doubt you will. Now go. Read. Enjoy."

Enjoy? Enjoyment isn't what she had in mind, though she supposed there were worse things than reading about her grandmother's sexual experiences.

Like instructing a room full of men on the art of erotic love. Oh what, oh what had she gotten herself into?

Lesson Eleven

*Surprise yourself by opening
your mind up to the possibility
that seduction is not merely good
for one's body, but also for one's soul.*
　　　　　　　—*The School of Gallantry*

11 Berwick Street . . . or rather, beneath it

The dank smell of earth and dry rot filled May-belle's nostrils. She wrinkled her nose, trying to keep herself from brushing up against the moss-ridden slate walls, and held up the lantern to see how much farther she had to go. To her relief, in the far distance, she could make out a rough oak door. The door that was to mark the end of her journey. She still couldn't fathom why anyone would make this sort of effort day in and day out. Especially her grandmother.

Maybelle gathered her cloak and morning skirts in

one hand and hurried toward the end of the corridor, trying to keep the glass lantern steady. When she finally reached the door, she released her hold on her cloak and skirts, took hold of the rusty iron knob, and pulled. Only it refused to open. So she pushed. But it still would not open.

Oh, no. She was *not* going back through the tunnel and into Lady Chartwell's rather desolate townhouse, where no doubt ghosts resided alongside the servants.

Placing the lantern in her other gloved hand, she pounded her fist against the door. "Hello?" she called out, her voice echoing all around her and fading into the distance. "Hello? Is anyone about? Hello?"

A loud clank vibrated the door as someone unlatched it from the other side. It creaked open. A massive, heavyset man with a mop of curly brown hair and sharp brown eyes peered down at her. His hand alone was large enough for him to grab her by the head and lift.

The gatekeeper. She smiled feebly up at him, hoping he knew who she was.

His eyes widened and he yanked the door farther open. He bowed from his place beside the door, showing off his dark blue livery, which must have taken more yards of material than two ballroom gowns. "Madam." His voice rumbled out deep. "A pleasure. Everyone is waiting."

Everyone? She swallowed. She thought she was arriving early. Why, it wasn't even seven o'clock. Maybelle hurried in through the door and into a small, candlelit passageway where a set of rough stone stairs spiraled upwards. She pressed herself toward one of the nearest walls as it seemed the large man beside her took up most of the small space around them.

"You must be Harold," she offered, trying to make pleasant conversation. Albeit short.

"Yes." He closed the door, the cool breeze from the tunnel trying to push through to the end, and latched the iron rod across the door. He turned back toward her, towering over her like the giant he was, and pointed at her lantern. "Allow me."

She quickly handed it to him, not wanting to argue with anything the man said. "Thank you."

"This way." He quickly mounted the stairs, each large step rising over three full stairs. Quite easily.

Maybelle gathered up her cloak and skirts and tried to keep up with him lest he disappear with all the bright light. The stairs continued to spiral upward for several more feet until they finally arrived at another door. Harold pushed open the door with a large paw, flooding the staircase with natural light. He stepped into the corridor, hanging the lantern on a hook just outside the door, and waited for her to pass.

Maybelle hurried up the remaining stairs and stepped up into what appeared to be the corridor of a townhouse. As Harold closed the door and latched it behind them, Maybelle paused and glanced toward the front of the house, where a grand foyer awaited.

"Your cloak and hat, Madam."

"Oh, yes." She undid the clasp, stripped the cloak from herself, and handed it to him. Untying the lace ribbon from beneath her chin, she carefully removed her blue silk bonnet so as not to ruin her chignon and held it out, noticing that her gloved hands were shaking. And she didn't know if it was because of him or because of the fact that she was inside the school.

Fortunately, Harold didn't seem to notice as he took her bonnet from her hand. Instead, he stalked with her belongings over toward the coat stands and hat racks set against the far wall, off to the side.

Five male cloaks and five horsehair top hats ornamented the stands and racks.

Long cloaks, mind you. Which meant they were all tall. God help her, how was she to handle so many men towering over her?

Harold, not included.

She bit her lip and wandered toward the foyer, pausing just beneath a large, crystal chandelier lit with dozens and dozens of candles. Silence drummed as the scent of melted wax and flowers permeated the warm air. The foyer walls were painted a soft powder blue. Gold-framed mirrors were scattered along its length, illuminating and reflecting a brilliant amount of light that created a sultry, yet glittering environment.

Surprise didn't even begin to describe her reaction to her surroundings. She didn't know what to expect, but it most certainly wasn't this. It was all so . . .

elegant. Respectable. There wasn't a single nude portrait hanging anywhere. Which one might expect. Obviously.

"This way, Madam," Harold rumbled from behind her. "Your students await."

Startled, Maybelle turned toward him and realized his large gloved hand was gesturing toward the mahogany staircase and its red-runner stairs. Upstairs. Meaning, the bedrooms. Of course. Where else was one to educate rakes?

She drew in a shaky breath, trying to calm herself, and gathered up the skirts of her light blue muslin gown. She'd been mentally preparing for this and yet at that moment she realized no amount of preparation could possibly ready her to face a room full of men. A chaperone would have been rather nice.

Harold's heavy steps shook the staircase as he followed her.

She quickened her pace. When she reached the landing, Maybelle glanced down the corridor and noted one of the doors leading into the bedrooms was wide open. Low, male voices came from within. Those deep masculine tones unnerved her. One of them, she knew, belonged to the duke.

Oh God. Oh God. Could she do this? Could she stand before a group of men and pretend she knew everything there was to know about sex? No. She couldn't. She simply couldn't.

Harold loomed at the top of the staircase. Adjusting his large jacket, he gestured with a gloved hand toward the open door just a few feet from them.

The girls. Her grandmother had insisted she meet the girls. "Harold? Could you please take me to the pleasure room before class begins? My grandmother insisted I introduce myself to the women."

"Of course." He moved past her, in the opposite direction of where the male voices were coming from, and approached a narrow door set in the corner just off the stairs. One leading to the floor above them, which usually served as the servants' quarters. How . . . *fitting*.

He opened the door wide and stood waiting for her to enter. She didn't know why she was nervous. They were only women. Maybelle walked past him, gathered her skirts, and went up the narrow flight of stairs. The scent of lavender overwhelmed her senses.

Maybelle paused at the top stair, her eyes widening. The walls and floors were draped with colorful silk scarves and velvet tarps. Without a doubt, it was a sultan's harem. Glass lanterns were hanging throughout the room, softly lighting the sloped walls, which were generously adorned with silks and velvet.

Leather trunks of all sizes were scattered everywhere. And from where she stood, she could make out the contents of a good many. One revealed stacked books. Others revealed clothing, glass jars filled with unidentifiable substances, horsewhips, shackles, chains, gloves, feathers, fur mitts, fur rugs, paddles, canes, candles, and . . . dildos. Dozens and dozens of dildos. And that did not include even half of the inventory laid out before her.

Soft laughter caught her attention, making her

turn her head. There, among all the colorful and naughty splendor were four absolutely beautiful voluptuous women. All dark haired, all with rich, olive skin, and all of them dressed in identical red brocaded robes. They were lounging on a large settee, on the far side of the room, giggling amongst themselves as they hovered over what Maybelle might have guessed to be a pornographic book.

Maybelle made her way toward them. "Good morning."

The women looked up.

Maybelle blinked. All of them appeared to be somewhat similar. Not identical. But similar. Which would certainly explain why it had taken her grandmother so long to put together the small group. For all of them had black eyes; long, thick black hair; and sensual full lips. It was as if her grandmother had been specifically searching for olive-skinned beauties who denoted far more romantic lands. Exotic lands.

The women shoved the book aside, and elegantly rose, their red robes shifting around their slender long legs and dainty, slippered feet.

They all curtsied.

The one on the far left, who bore a small birthmark on the upper corner of her sensual lips, stepped toward her. In a heavy, Italian accent she said, "Madame requested that we not disclose our names or speak in the presence of her students. For more allure."

Oh, her grandmother was a genius. No wonder men were paying one hundred pounds per week. It was certainly more entertaining than going over to some boring brothel.

Maybelle smiled and nodded in their direction. "I am Maybelle de Maitenon, her granddaughter, and will be the headmistress of the school until she is well enough to return."

Another woman with doll-like features eyed her and asked somewhat eagerly, "Will you be calling upon us today, Miss? We have yet to meet the men."

Maybelle paused, not knowing how she was to answer that. They did know there was no dallying, right? "Uh . . . yes. I will see to it today's lesson includes all of you." That is if the lesson wasn't a complete disaster.

Not knowing what more she could possibly say to these beautiful women who continued to stand before her, she quickly said, "Lovely to meet you all. I must see to class. Good day."

She then turned and tried to walk toward the stairs as elegantly and calmly as she could. She was, after all, the headmistress and had to set a good example.

Once she made her way down the narrow stairs, leaving behind the scent of lavender, and stepped back out into the world of the school, she glanced toward Harold, who was still waiting for her by the door. "Thank you."

He nodded, closed the door to the pleasure room, and directed her toward the classroom once again.

She smiled shakily, nodded, and headed toward the room. Without giving in to thinking anymore about it, Maybelle swept into what appeared to be a large bedroom, its walls draped with brocaded red velvet.

But instead of a bed or any other furniture associated with a bedroom, there were five leather wing-backed chairs set in a semicircle. With a grown man sitting in each one. A red velvet upholstered chair and a letter-writing desk which was piled with night-shirts had been set across from all the men, indicating where her place was to be.

Her heart jumped as she paused just inside the room.

Conversations faded and all five men rose to acknowledge her. Every single one of them was meticulously dressed in his finest morning clothes. Maybelle tried to remain calm as they stared at her in complete and utter silence.

Whatever composure she did have at that moment felt under complete attack when her eyes unexpectedly met those of the man on the far right. The Duke of Rutherford. His black eyes pierced the distance between them.

Her stomach fluttered at the thought of his hot, wet tongue stroking her and his tousled dark hair between her thighs. Calm. She needed to remain calm and focus on why she was really here.

Maybelle averted her eyes, counterfeited a confident smile, and forced herself to scan the faces of the other four men, who continued to silently observe her, each in his own, domineering way.

They were all surprisingly fit, well muscled, and

good looking. Men you wouldn't expect to be in need of lessons. And even though there was only one blonde amid all of them, their hair tones varied from deep, rich brown to almost bronze.

Edmund stepped forward and bowed. "Madam."

She inclined her head toward him. "Good morning, Your Grace."

The man standing beside Edmund also bowed, albeit a bit more sweepingly, causing his unruly, wavy blond hair to fall across his forehead. Lush, chocolate brown eyes met her gaze and a half-smile tilted his lips. "I am Lord Caldwell, at your service."

Ah, yes. The one who was so intent on seducing the American woman who had caused an uproar a few weeks back by wearing trousers and pistols in public. To each his own. "Good morning, Lord Caldwell. I have heard so much about you."

Lord Caldwell's half-smile broadened, exposing a perfect set of white teeth. "I am quite certain you have."

The brown-haired gentleman with the startling, deep blue eyes standing beside Caldwell stepped forward and bowed curtly. Though he met her gaze head-on, there was a sharp aloofness and distance not only in his stance but in his eyes. A long jagged scar trailed from the left side of his ear down to the bottom front of his square jaw. No doubt a blade having met it.

"Lord Brayton," he said coolly, introducing himself. Although the man's voice was courteous, it sounded rather patronizing. And unlike Edmund or

Lord Caldwell, his full lips were set in a grim line as if he were not at all pleased to be in her presence.

Brayton? The virgin? Rather dark for a virgin. "A pleasure, My Lord. Are you always this cheerful? Or is it the early hour?"

Caldwell grinned and smacked Brayton hard on the back. "From what we have gathered, this is as cheerful as he will ever be."

One of the men at the end coughed, disguising a laugh.

Brayton shifted his scarred jaw, placed his hands behind his back, but otherwise remained quiet and detached despite the stab at his honor.

Despite his being a virgin, Maybelle sensed that this man was not someone to be trifled with. "Any other man would have been quick to draw blood on less. It seems you have a talent for self-control, Lord Brayton. I have no doubt it serves you and your lady well."

Lord Brayton met her gaze and for a fleeting moment she sensed there was a new approval lingering in his blue eyes.

Maybelle eyed the bronze-haired gentleman beside Lord Brayton. "And you are?"

The man instantly caught her gaze, a mischievous light dancing in his green eyes.

She froze, wondering why he seemed so familiar. It was as if . . . *no*. It couldn't be. Oh God. It was. The man who'd kept her from falling that night during the scuffle at the ball.

He strode toward her, slowly, his large, muscular

frame moving with suave, steady intent. Everything about him, from his perfectly swept back bronzed hair, right down to his polished boots reeked of arrogance and wealth. He stopped not even a foot away, bringing with him the seductive scent of leather and lemon she remembered all too well. Reaching out, he took hold of her gloved hand and brought it up toward his lips, his eyes never once leaving hers.

He paused, the heat of his breath lingering above her glove, and answered indulgently, "I am Lord Hawksford." Although he kissed her hand once, his thumb traced her knuckles the whole while. "You shall have my undivided attention. At all times."

Hawksford? Oh well, that certainly explained everything.

Maybelle drew her hand away. According to her grandmother, Hawksford was obsessed with unattainable conquests and had no morals whatsoever. And coming from a courtesan that was a very serious charge. "Try not to overdo the kissing of a lady's hand, My Lord. It leads a woman to think that you are desperate and we all know a man should be anything but."

The men behind Hawksford refrained from laughing, several of them opting to clear their throats instead, while Edmund looked as if he were about to trounce the man.

Lord Hawksford didn't seem to be in the least bit affected by her curt words. He merely nodded in her direction, a smile tilting his lips, and stepped back toward his seat. "Some see it as desperation; others see it as adoration."

Maybelle ignored him and decided to move on to the next. With Hawksford's introduction being over, the only one left to be made was from none other than Lord Banfield. A man intent on seducing his own wife. A wife who interestingly enough refused to be bedded by her husband for reasons that were not stipulated on the application.

Lord Banfield stepped forward and bowed. Unlike the rest of the men, whose hair was short and swept back, he had long golden-brown hair, which he neatly tied. Though a queue went out of fashion years ago, it rather suited him and showed off his sharp features and soft brown eyes. Maybelle couldn't begin to imagine why his wife would refuse such a good-looking man.

"I am Lord Banfield," he said in a low, steady voice. Although he acknowledged the fact that she was a woman by sweeping his gaze across the length of her body, he quickly took to looking straight at her face. "An honor. How is our Madame? Is she feeling better?"

"Yes, My Lord. Thank you. Depending on her progress, you can expect her return sometime in the next two months. Now please, if you would all sit, I'd like to commence."

She smiled, still in disbelief as to how calm and collected she appeared even to herself.

Everyone, including Edmund, sat without further ado.

Maybelle paused, noting how quickly they had all obeyed. That's when it occurred to her that she rather liked this whole idea of commanding so many good-looking men about. Especially Edmund. He'd been rather difficult to manage from the moment she'd met him. And needless to say, she planned on taking advantage of her position of power. In every way imaginable.

Drawing in a calming breath and slowly letting it back out, Maybelle folded her hands before her and eyed all of them. "I believe my grandmother requested that you bring your nightshirts to class. Did you bring them?"

Edmund cocked his dark head and pointed in her direction. "Behind you, Madam."

"Thank you, Your Grace." Maybelle turned and walked toward the small mahogany table piled with nightshirts. She plucked up the first, turned, and held it out before her. It was so big it looked like a wrinkled white cotton gown. What was worse, it had been ripped around the collar and appeared to have a few off-white stains. You would think at a hundred pounds a week, a man could afford basic upkeep. Or a maid.

Maybelle brought the material toward her and sniffed. The familiar scent of leather and lemon drifted toward her. But of course. She quirked a brow and found all of the men intently observing her with marked curiosity. "Lord Hawksford, the only pleasant aspect of your nightshirt is the way it is scented. It is wrinkled, disturbingly tattered, and has unidentifiable stains. How do you think a lady will respond when she sees you in this?"

Hawksford smirked. "Unfortunately, love, I am unable to keep up with all the demands. And as for the stains, I think they speak for themselves."

Edmund let out a laugh and shifted in his chair.

Maybelle tossed aside the nightshirt, thankful she was wearing gloves, and glared at Edmund for laughing.

Edmund cleared his throat and put up a hand in apology.

Maybelle snapped her attention back to Hawksford. Her grandmother had warned her about him. "If you intend on making life difficult for me, My Lord, I assure you that I will see to it *your* life becomes difficult."

Hawksford's green eyes slowly and seductively raked over her. "I rather fancy the sound of that."

She pinned him with a hard stare. "If you do not intend on taking these lessons seriously, I will see to it that Harold escorts you out of the school. Through the front door. London will no doubt have all sorts of questions for you."

The gleam in Hawksford's eyes faded, though not entirely. "Point well taken. My apologies." He was quiet for a moment, then pointed toward his nightshirt. "Please. I am rather curious to hear about my nightshirt."

"Above and beyond all else," Maybelle drawled, trying to maintain her composure, "do try and maintain basic upkeep. *Especially* after an encounter.

Otherwise you will be giving away your history, when in fact a lady prefers mystery. On to the next."

She only hoped Hawksford hadn't set the tone for the entire lesson. She sighed, turned, and picked up another nightshirt.

It was also white and made out of cotton. However, unlike the last, it was not only devoid of stains, but it appeared to be so white and so perfectly pressed that the cotton appeared to glisten and glow. She brought it to her nose. It smelled of soap and too much starch.

Maybelle held out the shirt for all to see. "And who does this belong to?"

Lord Banfield shifted in his seat, put up his hand, and then lowered it back onto the armrest.

Ah, yes. The man who was having trouble bedding his wife. "Suffice it to say, there is nothing wrong with your nightshirt, My Lord. However, I admit that it does not even appear to have been worn."

"It has," Lord Banfield growled out. "It simply hasn't seen the amount of use Hawksford seems to get out of his."

Hawksford waggled his brows at Maybelle and caught his tongue between his teeth.

Maybelle ignored him. "My advice, Lord Banfield, is that you personalize this. Do you wear cologne?"

Banfield shrugged. "From time to time."

Maybelle lowered her voice and stared him down, trying to exude a flare of drama. "Find a seductive scent you think would appeal to her and wear it as often as you can. Whenever she finds herself alone, she will come across your scent and be forced to think of you. Forced to linger on your very presence. A man's scent is as important as anything else when it comes to seduction."

Lord Banfield leaned forward and eyed her, as if contemplating her advice.

She smiled, folded his nightshirt, and turned back to the table. Setting it aside, she picked up the next.

She held it up and paused. Unlike the other two, it was made of a simple thin white muslin. She blinked at it and slipped one of her hands between the fabric. Sure enough, she could see her hand. As clear as day. Dear God it was fascinating to think that a man would dare to wear something of this nature.

She slipped her hand back out and looked up at Edmund but just as quickly looked away before their eyes could meet. No. She wasn't going to even think about it. "And this one?" she ventured, trying to keep her voice steady.

The dark and ever-so-serious Lord Brayton raised his hand and lowered it just as quickly.

What an unexpected surprise. The virgin had rather erotic taste. "I find this rather attractive," she admitted, "and it allows a woman to see the journey she is about to embark upon. I like it."

Brayton gave a curt nod, but otherwise didn't respond.

Caldwell quirked a brow. "Yes, but is it not possible that a man such as Brayton could actually frighten a woman by exhibiting a bit too much too soon?"

Everyone burst into roaring laughter except for Maybelle and Lord Brayton, who rolled his eyes.

Edmund leaned forward in his chair, threatening to altogether roll off. He shook his dark head as several tiny laugh lines crinkled the edges of his eyes.

It was time to set this childish teasing straight. Her grandmother wouldn't stand for it, and she sure as bloody hell wouldn't either. "Lord Brayton is a *very* attractive man," she called out above all their guffaws. "And if he were to ever wear this in my presence outside the bounds of this school, I would bed him. Repeatedly. Until I was unable to walk."

The laughter faded and everyone stared at her, not knowing if she was serious.

Lord Brayton's straight brows rose a fraction and a small tremor, which might very well have been a smile, touched his lips.

Maybelle sensed Edmund's burning gaze digging deep into her but didn't dare to even acknowledge it. For acknowledging it meant that in some way she was giving him permission to be jealous. And she was not about to hand over that sort of control.

Instead, she glanced around at the other faces and calmly retorted, "So try and remember that I may not represent every female view, but there will be others who will share my tastes."

Maybelle met Brayton's dark blue gaze and held up his nightshirt. "Promise you will never take advantage of my weakness for muslin, My Lord."

Brayton inclined his dark head in deep gesture. "Never."

"I thank you." She folded the nightshirt, turned, and set it aside.

Maybelle plucked up the next one off of the mahogany table, held it up and sighed, noticing that the sleeves on the nightshirt had been sheered off. Or rather ripped off. "Now who on earth does this belong to?"

Lord Caldwell shifted in his chair. "Mine. I despise sleeves on my nightshirt. They're a damn nuisance."

Maybelle lowered it and tsked. "If the sleeves bother you, My Lord, then I would advise that you have them removed by a seamstress. Otherwise a woman might think you're rash. Or without funds. Or worse yet . . . *both.*"

With that, she turned, set it aside, and was about to reach for the last nightshirt when she noticed that there were no more left on the table except for those she'd already gone through. She hesitated, then turned back. She eyed the only person left. Edmund. "Did you forget your nightshirt, Your Grace?"

Edmund pointed to himself and looked around. "Me? No. I simply have nothing to present."

She blinked. "Why ever not? What do you usually wear to bed?"

He shrugged. "Nothing, actually."

Maybelle's eyes widened. "Nothing?" she repeated in disbelief.

"Nothing. I sleep in the nude."

Maybelle bit her lip hard trying not to picture his naked, muscled body draped across his bed with all the linens tangled around his thighs.

She blew out a quiet but shaky breath and placed a hand on her hip, trying to keep herself from outright fanning her neck and cheeks, which were growing hotter by the moment. She had to admit that the idea of wearing *nothing* to bed was rather appealing. For any man capable of sleeping in the nude exhibited a comfort level with his body that could only lead to more fascinating avenues.

"Well . . ." She cleared her throat and noted that all the men were waiting for her opinion. If she fibbed about this, it would show not only in her face but in the tone of her voice. For she wasn't a good liar.

Damn. She hated admitting even to herself the effect Edmund had on her. "I must say, Your Grace, that I find your approach most provocative. Daring. I like it." There. She admitted it.

Although she expected the duke to smirk haughtily in response to her admission, instead, he leaned back in his chair and rubbed at his chin looking rather surprised.

She cleared her throat again, paused, and looked about. "Any other questions before we further our discussion on bedside manners?"

"Yes." Hawksford raised his hand. "What is your opinion of orgies?"

She gawked at him, lowering her chin slightly, and realized that the man was quite serious.

Edmund glanced at her and froze.

"Is that not off topic, My Lord?" she forced herself to ask.

Hawksford shrugged. "You wanted to know if there were any questions. That is a question, is it not?"

Maybelle inwardly cringed knowing that although he was being a complete ass, such questions were inevitable. She had to prove that she was open to every topic.

Orgies. According to her grandmother's black book, the woman had attended several in her lifetime. And despised each and every experience. For she had always felt neglected by the others.

When in doubt, use Voltaire. "As Voltaire once said in response to an invitation to an orgy, after having already attended one, 'Once: a philosopher; twice: a pervert.' And I agree with him."

"So you have been to one?" Hawksford pressed.

Edmund leaned toward the side of his chair closest to Hawksford and glared at him. "Do you need to be throttled? Is that it?"

Maybelle bit back a smile. It seemed the duke knew what a man's limit should be. "Thank you, Your Grace, but I believe I have no trouble answering his question."

She averted her gaze back to Hawksford. His green eyes continued to observe her in a rather dark, almost provocative way.

"No, I haven't attended an orgy," she flitted, pleased with how nonchalant she sounded. "And because of my inexperience on the matter, I'll not further comment. If that ever changes, however, you will be the first to know."

Hawksford folded his hands behind his head, leaned back, and grinned. "Pleased to hear it."

God help her. She had to do this day in and day out? She would never survive. At least not for very long.

Lesson Twelve

Be creative.
Be very creative.
                    —The School of Gallantry

There was only so much more Maybelle could possibly discuss on the topic of bedside manners. After a very long, very detailed dissertation that addressed everything from hygiene to bed linens to lighting and so on and so on, it appeared by the dead and blank faces of her students that it was time to change the subject. At once.

Which meant she might as well return to a topic no man would ever bore of. Sex. "That concludes my overall dissertation on bedside manners before and after an encounter. Moving on to the last topic evolving around the setting of the bedroom. Would one of you please define the purpose of a dildo and why a man should consider keeping one at his bedside at all times?"

Life seemed to stir once again amongst the herd. Edmund snapped his gaze back to her face.

Hawksford cleared his throat and raised his hand.

Of course. "Yes, Lord Hawksford?"

The man leaned forward and set his hands onto his knees. "I am of the opinion that they should be banned."

She eyed him. "Really? Why so?"

He shrugged. "If a woman is in possession of a dildo, what need is there for us aside from our seed? I understand a woman needing to pleasure herself, but I want the focus to be on the length I have to offer. Not the length an inanimate object has to offer."

Edmund sat forward in his chair and eyed him. "I for one, Hawksford, would rather have my woman pleasure herself with a dildo than with another man."

Maybelle coughed, trying desperately to conceal a laugh. She never realized Edmund's thinking was so forward. She winced and then asked, "Have you ever handled a dildo, Lord Hawksford?"

"Why should I?" Hawksford grinned and patted the space between his legs. "This is about all I can handle."

God forbid. It appeared the man had penile jealousy. Which, according to her grandmother, was quite common amongst men. This should be rather entertaining. At the very least. "*Harold?*" she called out, hoping the man was still within earshot.

Within moments, heavy footsteps came down the corridor toward them.

Edmund, Brayton, Caldwell, Banfield, and Hawksford all sat up ramrod in their chairs and eyed the door, not knowing what it was she had in mind.

Harold appeared in the doorway, his massive body eating into the space. He glanced at the men and then at her. "Yes, Madam?"

"Do you know where my grandmother keeps all the dildos?"

Harold stared at her for a long moment and then cleared his throat. "Yes."

"Wonderful. Fetch five, please. Oh, and inform all the girls to make an appearance in about five minutes. We will be commencing demonstrations."

Harold drew his brows together, nodded, then disappeared.

"*Demonstrations?*" Banfield demanded, staring her down.

Brayton didn't say a word, only sat back, rubbed at his scarred jaw, and kept his eyes trained on the door.

Hawksford sat far forward in his wing-backed chair, bracing his elbows on his knees. "*This* is what I am damn well paying for."

Caldwell raked his hands through his blond hair, blew out a breath, and let his hands drop back into his lap, as if preparing himself mentally and physically.

And Edmund? Edmund simply grinned. As if he were thoroughly in control of the situation.

Yes. But for how much longer?

Within moments, Harold came in with a hatbox, stalked toward her, and shoved it into her hands. "The ladies will be down shortly." He then left the room, wiping his gloved hands briskly onto his trousers.

Maybelle turned toward the small writing desk, set the hefty box on it, and removed the lid. Inside were about a dozen perfect, hard leather dildos with a carved wooden handle on the end of each one. She scooped up five and turned back toward the class.

Stepping toward them, she tossed the dildos, one by one, onto all of their laps. They froze and simply stared down at what she had given them.

Maybelle folded her hands before her, already pleased with their response. "In Latin, *dilatare* translates to open wide. Hence the origin of the word. Dildos have had various uses throughout the centuries, including ancient rituals and ceremonies whose one of many purposes was to deflower virgins, and were once known to be made of stone and wood. A few splinters and bruises later, a woman demanded a little more satisfaction. The result is what you have in your lap. As you might imagine, the upkeep of a dildo is quite important. Especially after each use."

She paused, eyeing them. "Would any of you gentlemen care to demonstrate to the rest of the class as to how to properly handle a dildo?"

"*No,*" they all said in firm unison.

Maybelle bit back a grin. Men were so easy to agitate. Any thought of competition, including that of an inanimate object, and they were predictably upset. "We will leave that to our ladies, then."

As if on cue, one by one the four models swept in through the door, their red robes flowing around their slim bodies and long legs like the goddesses that they were. Their long, dark hair had been let loose and brushed against the fluid movements of their thighs and buttocks, which were outlined by their clinging brocade robes. They all settled standing perfectly in a row before all the men, each setting an elegant right hand onto her hip. As if trained to do so. Which most likely they were. By her grandmother.

Banfield sat frozen, dread overtaking his rugged face.

Caldwell sank farther back into his chair and appeared to be in agonizing, yet blissful pain.

Hawksford grinned like the devil that he was, his green eyes roving over each woman, no doubt coming up with all sorts of ideas.

Brayton crooked a dark brow and scrutinized them. As if they were displays at the museum.

While Edmund? He scratched at his shaven chin and appeared to be somewhat occupied with a thought. Though only God knew what thought.

Maybelle gestured toward the women. "These beautiful women will be demonstrating the dildo." Maybelle paused, only now realizing there were four ladies and five men. Her grandmother hadn't planned for Edmund.

She eyed the duke, who was now cocking his head and openly admiring the women. She fought the twinge of jealousy that overtook her. She needed to stay focused. She had a class to conduct.

Maybelle pointed each beauty toward Caldwell, Banfield, Brayton, and Hawksford. She then met Edmund's dark gaze. "Seeing there are only four women for the demonstration, Your Grace, I shall have no choice but to be the fifth."

Edmund cleared his throat, grabbed up his dildo from his lap, and shifted in his chair, eyeing her.

Maybelle tried to calm the fluttering in her stomach at his apparent eagerness and instead took to instructing the class. "An experienced and generous lover learns to keep a dildo at his bedside so that he can offer it to his lady whenever she pleases. The objective is to be creative. The more creative you are, the more pleasure it will result in. And as my grandmother always proclaims, 'A woman has more than one entrance to occupy a man's time.'"

"I'd say." Hawksford stuck the end of the dildo into his mouth, waggled his brows up at his model, and said through the dildo, "Do you think a woman will still respect me in the morning?"

Everyone started laughing.

Maybelle rolled her eyes, hurried over to Hawksford, and yanked the dildo out of his mouth using the wooden handle. Passing it over to the model, who looked rather flushed, Maybelle glared at Hawksford. "This is a classroom, My Lord, not a circus-minded bordello. Allow me to demonstrate one proper use." Maybelle took in a calming breath and told herself she could do this. She could.

Casually making her way back to Edmund, she leaned toward him and took his hand, which still held the handle of the dildo. Gently, she repositioned his fingers around the wood handle. She tried hard to ignore the warmth of his fingers and how his large palm seemed to swallow the length of the dildo.

Knowing that she was about to set a precedent her grandmother would no doubt be proud of, Maybelle lifted the dildo to her mouth, parted her lips, and gently slid it into her mouth. As far as it would go. Toward the back of her throat.

Edmund sucked in a harsh breath, his firm grip on the handle tightening all the more. He stared at her mouth and clearly seemed to note how deep it had slid inside.

Silence drummed within the classroom.

Although she knew every single man and woman was watching, the only eyes that mattered at that moment were Edmund's. His gaze seemed to darken with an intensity that had yet to match anything she'd ever seen before in his eyes. His jaw tightened but otherwise he did not move.

Guiding his large hand, Maybelle slid the dildo gently in and out, in and out, the taste of the hard leather tingeing her lips. With each steady stroke, a strange boldness overtook her. She wanted to prove to Edmund right here, right now, who was really in control. Did he want a duchess who had no qualms about swallowing a dildo in public? She somehow doubted that. And regardless, she was certain that she had made her point.

Maybelle slid the dildo out completely, straightened, and calmly turned back to face the class. "Your purpose is to deliver pleasure. Being creative is always helpful with regards to this aspect. For in the end, it does not matter where this instrument goes, but whether your lover is receiving pleasure."

Brayton, Caldwell, Banfield, and even Hawksford gaped at her. Banfield's dildo slipped from his hand and down onto his lap. He quickly snatched it back up and cleared his throat.

Maybelle smiled. "There is no reason to be shy," she prompted. "If you can find it tolerable to insert a dildo into the lips of a complete stranger, I assure you, you will have no trouble inserting it into any part belonging to your lover. It is your duty to ensure that she is thoroughly sated."

All of her students eventually turned their gazes to the women before them and now appeared quite serious about the topic of the dildo.

Maybelle turned to Edmund, who continued to stare up at her from his chair, his jaw tight.

Oh, yes. It was time he recognized who was really in control of this game. She smiled at him, leaned over, and patted his knee. "You were ever so brilliant, Your Grace. Do you require another demonstration?"

"No," he growled out, his thumb circling over the tip of his dildo, where her mouth had been. "Thank you."

Maybelle tried to ignore where his thumb was or what he was insinuating. For one brief moment, she actually wondered what it would be like to place *him* into her mouth. She wet her lips, which still tasted of salted leather, and quickly snapped her attention back to the rest of the class.

The men were naturally enjoying themselves, mesmerized not only by the closeness of their beautiful models but by the way the dildo went in and out of their open mouths.

The clock in the far corner of the room chimed ten times before clicking back into silence, reminding her it was time. "Ladies, you may return to the pleasure room," she announced. "Thank you for the marvelous demonstration. I am certain the men appreciated your participation."

Each woman slowly slid her dildo out, some of them revealing very wicked grins. They then straightened, and one by one whisked out of the room.

Maybelle exhaled and glanced around at the serious, flushed faces of all the men, who were still holding on to their dildos. With white knuckles. "Are there any questions before we end class today?"

No one said a word. Clearly, the lesson had been a success.

She smiled. "Seeing there are no further questions, I will leave you all to discuss this amongst yourselves. It was a pleasure spending the morning with you. Tomorrow, as part of our lesson, I am asking that each of you bring a gift for a would-be lover. There is a reason I am not giving you time.

Producing gifts for your lover with little time is a difficult endeavor. Do remember that the way you present your gift will be just as important as the gift itself. Have them ready for presentation tomorrow in class. Any questions?"

The men still said nothing.

She nodded toward them, rather pleased with how things had turned out. "Good day, then. Until tomorrow."

With that, she turned and sashayed her way toward the doorway, still in disbelief that she had actually kept herself afloat. Or at least she thought she had.

"Madam!"

Maybelle paused and turned to find all five men, including Edmund, standing in honor of her departure, the dildos still in their hands.

Lord Caldwell intently made his way toward her, toting along his leather dildo.

She lowered her chin slightly and tried to remain serious despite the all-around display of dildos. "Yes, My Lord?"

Caldwell paused before her and shoved several blond strands of hair out of his eyes with his other hand. "I am hosting a gathering tonight. Though I confess it is a bit . . . *risqué.*"

Risqué? Oh, her grandmother would be jealous. "Are you asking me to attend, Lord Caldwell?"

"Yes. I think you would add immense flavor to the evening."

Immense flavor? How quickly one became popular

when open to the subject of sex. Maybelle glanced over toward Edmund and realized the duke was frowning, tilting his head, and inspecting the dildo in his hand. As if he weren't even listening.

Maybelle didn't know what came over her at that moment, perhaps she had inherited too much of a naughty nature from her grandmother, but she knew that there was only one way to go about responding to something as delicious as this. "If all of my students will be in attendance, My Lord, then so will I."

Edmund glanced up, as if now realizing what was going on, and stared at her.

Oh, yes. His mother, along with the rest of the *ton*, would no doubt *love* that.

Caldwell snapped back toward the men, pointed with his dildo and said, "You are all going," then turned back toward her and bowed. "We look forward to seeing you tonight. I shall have an invitation delivered to your door immediately."

Maybelle bit back a smile, inclined her head toward him, then turned and swept out of the room. This whole improper education was rather quite fun. Especially knowing that Edmund had no choice but to tag along.

Her grandmother was going to be understandably upset at not having been invited.

Edmund shoved the sizable leather dildo into his vest pocket and glanced at the other four men, who continued to blankly stare after Maybelle long after she'd gone. He was seriously contemplating shutting down the school. Immediately. Before these classes got any more out of hand.

Hawksford eyed Edmund. Holding up his dildo he slid his forefinger alongside the length of it and drawled, "Did you enjoy yourself, Rutherford?"

Edmund shifted his jaw and snapped his frame toward the bastard. "I take it you only come for the entertainment."

Hawksford snorted and shoved his dildo into one of his pockets. "It is entertaining, but I admit that I am not here for that. Hell, I doubt if any of us are here for that."

Hawksford turned to the rest of the men, who were standing around listening. "Banfield? What are you here for?"

"I am not professing shit to you, Hawksford." Banfield put up a hand and made his way out through the door.

"Probably a virgin." Hawksford smirked. "What about you Brayton? What are you here for?"

Brayton blew out a breath and shook his dark head. "I do not know. I really do not know." He then strode out of the room and disappeared.

Hawksford was making every man scatter one by one. Which is why it didn't surprise Edmund when Caldwell quickly put up a hand and jogged out of the room right after Brayton.

Hawksford shrugged. "I won't even bother asking why you're here, Rutherford. It's not like anything can help your reputation."

Edmund strode up to Hawksford and tried to remain calm. Crossing his arms over his chest, he growled out, "I am here to see to Miss Maitenon's safety and ensure a sense of respectability. She deserves better and I have very specific plans that do not include you or this goddamn school."

Hawksford's brows rose. "You mean to . . . ?"

Edmund narrowed his gaze and gave him a grudging nod.

Hawksford groaned, then chuckled. He reached out and jabbed Edmund playfully in the arm. "Remember that women of her caliber never play by the rules. Believe me. I should know." And with that, he walked past and out of the room.

Edmund dropped his arms heavily to his sides and tried not to give in to the sinking reality of what he had gotten himself into. Because the bastard was right. Maybelle was not like other women. And certainly not like the *ton*.

As he continued to stand in the silence of the classroom, Edmund seriously wondered how things between them would ever become tolerable. For a woman of her upbringing and tastes *would* get restless.

Oh, but the possibilities. They were endless. With a woman like her, he'd never have a reason to wander. With a woman like her, he'd never *want* to wander.

Hell. It appeared a new strategy was in order. One that required him to get creative and walk over to *her* side of the world. That way, she could see what he was capable of and that when it came to the realm of the bedroom, he could damn well care less what was respectable or not. Once he'd shown her that he had no objections to her world, he'd be able to eventually drag her over to where she belonged. With him. And not with a classroom full of other men.

Lesson Thirteen

If you are going to wear your heart on your sleeve
do remember not to wear it out in public.
                    —*The School of Gallantry*

That evening

"Presenting Madame de Maitenon!"

Maybelle smiled and curtsied to Lord Caldwell, who was at the door greeting guests. Caldwell looked very much the part of a gentleman. His evening attire was well fitted to his large frame and his wavy blond hair, which had been so unruly earlier in the day, had been smoothly swept back with tonic.

Maybelle politely held out her gloved hand. "My Lord."

Caldwell took her hand and tightened his gloved fingers around hers. "You honor me with your presence, Madame."

Using his hold on her, he drew her close, forcing her to lean toward his muscular body.

"You look exquisite," he whispered, ardently kissing her hand. He met her gaze. "And if it weren't for the fact that you were already spoken for, I believe you'd find me a nuisance."

Maybelle blinked up at Caldwell, retrieved her hand, and stepped away. Seemed Edmund spared no time cozying up to the boys.

Lord Caldwell grinned, then turned away and gave his full attention to the next guest, leaving her to guess as to how much he really knew.

Maybelle shoved the thought away and headed toward the receiving room. She was going to thoroughly trounce Edmund for wagging his tongue with all the details. Trying to remain calm, she mentally perused her surroundings, knowing Edmund was no doubt somewhere in the building.

Although Caldwell's townhouse wasn't very well lit, the sparse candlelight lent a sense of intrigue to the surroundings as shadows and light shifted across the dark red walls and wood floors. She paused and noted all of the people gathered in the parlor.

Everyone stood intimately close to one another, not at all adhering to the arm-length distance that governed the Season. Women were eagerly leaning toward men and men were eagerly leaning toward women, all blithely laughing and chatting as if they were in the privacy of their own homes.

None of the men were dressed in the usual black

evening formal attire. Shockingly, none of them were wearing jackets. Only trousers, vests, and shirts, which displayed each and every cut of their bodies.

While the women . . . the women wore traditional evening gowns, but with *very* daring, Parisian flare. Their curved necklines dipped much lower than what was considered acceptable. So low, in fact, that some emphasized not only the top rounds of their breasts, but in some cases, the hint of nipples.

Maybelle glanced down at her modest lilac lace neckline and quickly looked up again. It would appear she was the only woman in the room who had her breasts covered. Why was it that no matter where she went in London she couldn't ever seem to fit in?

A very lush, chestnut-haired woman dressed in a shocking black velvet gown that provocatively clung to her sizable breasts and small waist made her way toward Maybelle. A cigar was tucked between her raised bare fingers.

The woman paused, lingering before Maybelle, then drew in a long puff from her cigar. Cocking her head, she set her red painted lips and blew out a tuft of cigar smoke in Maybelle's direction. Smoke the woman apparently wished to share with her.

Maybelle coughed.

The woman smirked and pointed her half-smoked cigar at Maybelle's neckline. "Why, if it isn't Miss Pious. Will you be attending church come morning?"

Miss Pious, indeed. Usually she wouldn't even dignify answering, but she had the school's reputation to uphold. Maybelle turned away and adjusted the front of her bodice, trying to maneuver her corset in a way so as to shove her breasts up even more. She hesitated, peering down at what she'd done. Perhaps a bit too much.

Ah, well. She turned back and pointed a gloved finger to the top rounds of her breasts. "Why, I never miss church. After all, every Sunday, all the men dutifully pray to these."

A slow smile spread across the woman's lips. She crinkled her nose. "I do believe I like you."

The woman sidled in closer, wrapped a slender arm around Maybelle's waist, and yanked Maybelle against her, draping their front sides seductively together.

Maybelle froze, not being able to suddenly breathe, and stared back at the woman, who was now openly admiring her lips and delving in for a kiss.

That is precisely when Hawksford chose to appear. He wrapped his muscled arms around both their shoulders and gathered them toward his wide chest. "Is there adequate space for one more?" he drawled down at each of them, grinning. "I brought my dildo."

Maybelle scrambled out of both their embraces, smacking his muscled arm hard. She pointed rigidly at Hawksford, warning him, yet couldn't seem to utter a single word in her defense.

Hawksford laughed, smacked his bare hands

together, then turned and swaggered down the corridor. Clearly pleased that he had for once silenced her.

Why was he even enrolled in the school? The man put the very word *cock* into cocky. Maybelle drew in a shaky breath and nervously eyed the chestnut-haired woman. "I apologize. Truly. And although you are very beautiful, I confess that I am not one to indulge in . . ." What was the word?

"No worries, darling. I completely understand. Do remember to keep those men on their knees every Sunday." The woman winked, placed her cigar between her lips, and sashayed away toward a group of men and women on the other side of the room.

Maybelle blew out the breath she'd been holding. Welcome to the world of the wild and wicked.

"My Lady," a low, husky voice whispered into her ear from behind. "Already popular with the masses?"

Goose bumps frilled her body as she sucked in a sharp breath. She didn't have to turn to know it was Edmund. She lifted her chin, but otherwise didn't move. "Your Grace. I am rather astonished you came."

Edmund rounded her and then stepped before her, grinning. "Indeed. So am I."

Edmund paused, cocked his head slightly to one side, and let out a low whistle.

Heat splashed over Maybelle not only at his obvious attempt to disarm her, but at realizing he wasn't wearing a jacket. Only a shirt, cravat, vest, and trousers and a pair of lacquered boots. His broad shoulders appeared seductively wider and his muscled legs looked longer. A red silk cravat had been casually tucked into his fitted black vest. It was like witnessing him in the privacy of his home. And she rather liked it. A lot.

"Might I say that is quite the cleavage," he commented, flicking his dark eyes over her breasts. "Do you intend on making this evening difficult for us?"

Maybelle knew by the look on his face that he actually meant it. And strangely, for the first time since their meeting, she genuinely felt comfortable standing before him as a woman.

A part of her reveled in the idea that this man seemed so physically affected by her. She smiled flirtatiously. "Your Grace is far too kind."

He leaned in and placed a bare forefinger across her lips, startling her. "Call me Edmund," he whispered, his eyes meeting hers. "You and I have shared more than enough to warrant some familiarity."

For a moment she could do nothing but correlate that warm finger to when he had spread her on the sofa and touched her very core with it.

"Edmund it is," she whispered against the warmth of his finger, not being able to move or think.

"Good." He slowly removed his finger from her lips and stepped back.

Maybelle swallowed and glanced toward the other side of the room, wondering if she should find someone else to pass the evening with. Before she ended up with her skirts up again in some back room.

A yearning heat rose within her. The one she always felt before giving in to him. "Do you intend on following me about all night?"

"Yes. I do."

He was certainly to the point. "Perhaps you would care to share what it is you've been telling Caldwell and the rest of my students about us."

"Nothing too involved," he said matter-of-factly. "I was merely hoping to ensure that the evening didn't turn into a goddamn orgy. Although I didn't realize it was the women I should be more worried about."

Maybelle burst into laughter, slapping a hand over her mouth to keep herself from snorting. "You noticed, did you?"

Edmund also laughed and shook his head. "Perhaps I should be the first to inform you as to what we can both expect this evening."

He cleared his throat and gestured toward their surroundings. "According to Caldwell, there are only three things allowed to occur in this house. Drinking, gambling, and sex. Since you do not come across as the drinking sort, that leaves us with either gambling or sex. I will be more than happy to escort you to whatever activity you are most interested in. Of course both will be done with me and only me."

Maybelle's eyes widened as she lowered her hand back to her side. What happened to keeping to respectability? He'd become rather nonchalant about all this.

"Sex is it?" he asked, sounding strangely hopeful.

Her throat tightened. One night with the man was probably about as much as she was going to be able to handle. "I would rather gamble, Your Grace."

Edmund drew closer and wrapped an arm around her shoulder. "Spoken like a duchess. This way."

Spoken like a duchess, indeed. Is that what he was up to? Maybelle dipped away from his arm, knowing the more she kept her distance the better off she'd be.

Edmund clearly had other plans. He grabbed for her hand, the warmth of his large palm encompassing her own, and led her out of the crowded parlor. Slowly, he led her through the corridor and toward the back of the house.

Though the back of her mind screamed as to whether she should be trusting him, her body didn't seem to object to his lead.

As their surroundings grew all the more dim, with only a lone candle on the wall sconce burned halfway to its stub, Maybelle noticed three shadows lurking in one of the corners off to the side. Shadows that were jerking feverishly into one another against the wall, thud after thud resounding all around them.

Maybelle's eyes widened and her heart almost stopped at the realization of what she was seeing. One man stood behind a half-naked woman gripping her shoulders while another man stood in front of her gripping her waist, both of them having their way with her as she writhed with pleasure between them.

Edmund squeezed her hand and hurried her

onward, leaving the three shadows to continue their business.

"More," the woman panted, the thuds against the wall growing louder and more frantic. "Yes. More."

More? Maybelle quirked a brow and glanced back. For heaven's sake, how much more did the woman want? Maybelle stumbled as Edmund hurried them on.

He eyed her from over his broad shoulder, his shadowed features hidden by the darkness of the corridor. "Quite the gathering."

"Yes. Quite."

They soon reached the end of the corridor. The duke finally paused, released her hand, and threw open a door leading into a walnut-boarded room. "After you."

Maybelle hesitated, then stepped inside. The room was noisy and very crowded. It had countless three-cornered tables set about wherever there was space. And except for one empty table, all of the dozen or so tables were occupied with both men and women.

All of them held cards. And some of them were dressed and some of them . . . *not.* Maybelle tried not to stare at a voluptuous blonde who was down to her chemise, corset, and white silk stockings. Apparently, clothes were being laid for wagers. Although there were coins and paper notes set in the middle of most tables.

Maybelle coughed as thick cigar smoke filled her eyes and nostrils. So this is what it was like to be a man and enjoy a night of debauchery. She didn't know whether she liked it or not. She coughed again.

Edmund touched her arm. "Perhaps we should find another room. One with less smoke."

Her eyes watered, but she rapidly blinked to keep her vision focused. "No, no. This will do. However, a drink would be lovely."

"Are you certain you wish to stay here? Because—"

"Of course I'm certain."

He nodded and after scanning the room pointed to a corner. "That table there. Once we claim it, I'll go fetch a drink for you."

There was certainly no need to drag her this time. Maybelle quickly followed him straight toward the table. Being the refined gentleman he was, he pulled out a wooden chair and gestured toward it. Probably the only man in the room to do so for any of the ladies.

"Thank you." She sat and arranged her lilac gown.

"I promise to return shortly." Edmund strode to the other side of the room and disappeared.

A booming laughter from beside her made her glance toward a rowdy group of men and women who apparently had only started their card game.

Maybelle shifted in her seat and found herself wishing that Edmund would return. Before anyone noticed she was sitting alone and thought she needed company. Needless to say, she rather preferred his company over those around her. And she honestly didn't know if that was something that should be of concern to her.

"Here," Edmund offered, finally coming around and placing a glass before her. "Apparently, the sherry and port won't be available until later. My apologies."

Maybelle stared at the wineglass filled with a yellowish murky substance. Gin. "I've heard very bad stories about gin."

Edmund paused, then reached over and snatched up the glass. "I will find something a bit more respectable."

"No, no." She quickly took the glass from his hand and cleared her throat. "Gin will do. Really." Her throat desperately needed something. Anything, really.

"If you say so." Edmund seated himself diagonal to her and leaned back in the chair, watching her.

"Cheers." Maybelle lifted the small glass to her lips and tossed as much as she could into the back of her parched throat. She gagged, the harsh, stinging liquid rushing down into her throat and up toward her nostrils. She could feel it seeping into every crevice of her stomach, causing an inferno to burn within. Ugh. And she thought cognac was deplorable.

Edmund quickly rose to assist.

Although her eyes were watering and she continued to gasp for soothing air, she waved for him to sit down. She most certainly wasn't about to admit to him or to a room full of gamblers that she couldn't handle a bit of gin. They'd all think she was a ninny. "I—I swallowed it wrong, is all." She pushed the remainder of the glass toward him. "Perhaps . . . you should finish it."

He shook his head and pushed it off to the side. "I've already had more than my share, thank you." A small smile now played at the corners of his mouth. "Shall we play?"

"Yes." The fiery sensation the gin had caused was finally dwindling. Now, a different sensation was taking over—that of excitement. For she was actually going to play cards. With Edmund, no less. She had never played cards with anyone else other than her grandmother.

Edmund picked up the stack of faded cards that lay waiting on the table and separated them into two piles. He zipped them together with his thumbs.

"Would you prefer to do it?" he asked, watching her. "I may not be that trustworthy. Here." He patted them into a pile and pushed the deck toward her.

Hesitantly, Maybelle extended her hand to claim them.

That is when Edmund reached over the table and caught her wrist. "I want you to do something for me."

His strong hand continued to hold her as if he had no intention of ever letting go. She looked up at him. "Whatever could you want now?"

He arched a brow, as if taking the challenge. "I don't believe I've ever seen you without your gloves. Indulge me. Only this once."

Maybelle could now feel his finger tracing the edge of the glove near her wrist, daring her to take them off. The night had hardly begun and he was already trying to get her out of her clothes.

She yanked her hand away and snatched up the glass of gin, to give her something to do. She swallowed the remaining stinging liquid and set it aside, shoving her hands into her lap. "Perhaps you should deal."

"I will take that to mean my request has been denied." With that, he swept up the deck set before him and shuffled.

Maybelle eyed him and hoped to change the subject. "So what are we playing?"

He shifted forward in his seat and continued to shuffle. "Écarté. Do you know the rules?"

She slowly grinned. "Quite well. It was the first card game my grandmother taught me when she came over from France. Why, I remember—"

A brocaded vest flew through the air and plopped onto the table between them.

Maybelle stared at it for a stunned moment and then burst into laughter. "Is that your wager?"

Edmund laughed, shoved the vest off their table, and shook his head. "I only wager what I can afford."

Shuffling the cards a few more times, he grinned and passed them out. "Two for you. Two for me. Three for you. Three for me." He paused, interrupting the deal, and slapped down the remaining cards in his hand onto the table. He eyed her.

"What is it now?" She tried to ignore that danger-ous gleam that now appeared in his eyes. What was worse, she started to feel a bit of a haze coming over her. As if the gin was already taking full effect.

Edmund leaned toward the table and quirked a dark brow. "Speaking of wagers, what is to be yours?"

The haze started mixing with a bit of panic. "Mine? I am expected to wager something?"

He tapped the cards before him. "Playing cards merely to play is not by any means gambling. Gam-bling is when you play cards *and* wager." He leaned into the table and deviously observed her. "I shall wager a score of five before you can."

"Wagering what?" she cautiously returned. "Be-cause my clothes stay on."

"Damn." He chuckled. "All right. How about you wager anything you want against something I want?"

"Anything?"

"Anything."

Maybelle wondered whether she should even con-sider taking up that sort of challenge. It wasn't that she was scared of losing; she was actually very good at Écarté, but she didn't like the way he said "some-thing I want." That something could very well be anything. And "anything" wasn't something she could afford to give to a man she had already given too much to. "What exactly did you have in mind?"

"You first."

Fully aware that he was already challenging her, she finally said, "I shall wager to score five more than you." She'd never lost a game of Écarté once she'd learned the rules. Not even to her grand-mother.

"*And?*" he prodded.

"If I win, you will immediately withdraw from the school and refrain from ever enlisting Parliament. And put it in writing. The school requires quite the protection and I have learned, Your Grace, that I cannot entirely trust you."

His dark eyes momentarily clouded, as if a storm had descended into his thoughts. Then, just as quickly, it lifted. He shifted in his chair. "If that is the sort of wager you wish to make."

"Good." She tipped unexpectedly toward the table and caught herself. Damn. She knew she should have never finished that glass of gin.

What was worse, her skin felt unbearably hot all of a sudden. No doubt the gin. It had been a rather large glass. She fanned herself. "So what is your wager?"

He leaned back against his chair, his eyes intently watching her the whole time as if expecting her to flee at any moment. "It is more of an offer than a wager, really."

"Oh?"

He cocked his head slightly and lowered his voice. "Instead of one night for my hundred thou-sand, I want an entire week. Without any rules."

Maybelle bit her lip, not wanting to even think about what *that* would entail.

He paused and stared her down, a strange inten-sity and need overtaking his sharp features. "And should you become pregnant as result of that week, you will marry me."

Maybelle gaped at him as a flicker of apprehension coursed through her. She suddenly felt not only sober, but as if that world had snapped sharply back into focus.

Why was it that he, like the rest of the *ton*, was incapable of opening up to the possibility that despite her reputation, she not only had feelings, but a heart? A heart that refused to bring a defenseless child into this world and force it to suffer the same way she had growing up. In the same way her father had growing up.

Maybelle stripped both of her gloves from her hands, tossed them aside, leaned toward him, and held out a hand. "Give me your hand, Your Grace."

He glanced at her hand. "Why?"

"Because I am asking it of you."

He hesitated, then reached out and covered her hand with his. Maybelle brought her other hand onto his and clasped it tightly, allowing his warmth to seep into her own. Trying to make him feel that she was made of flesh and blood, as was he.

Through the cigar smoke, and the groans of loss and cries of wins, and the gin that clouded her judgment, she desperately tried to pretend that his touch did not affect her. Oh God how she tried, but all she could think about was how intimately involved they already seemed to be.

"Edmund." She tried to keep her voice steady and calm. "Do you even realize what it is you are asking for? A child born unto us would be forever unhappy. Trapped between your world and mine. Never knowing where to turn. Is that what you want? For your child to be ridiculed? Scorned? Unhappy? Because that is what you will be sentencing your child to. That is why I intend to only give you one night, and mind you, that night will be conducted in a way so that your seed does not threaten my womb. Do you understand me?"

His questioning gaze turned strikingly dark and serious. And cold.

He slipped his hand out of hers and drew it back and away. He stared off to the side and shifted his jaw. "I suppose you think I have absolutely nothing to offer a child."

Hearing the hurt and bitterness in his voice unexpectedly twisted her gut. "That is not what I meant."

He shifted in his chair again but refused to look at her. "I know full well what you meant." He rose. "Good night."

Maybelle scrambled to her feet, grabbed his arm, and held him in place to keep him from going anywhere. "Edmund, it was not my intention to upset you. Understand that I am merely stating my belief. Am I not entitled to that much?"

He glanced at her hand still holding his arm and quickly looked away. "Release me," he murmured.

"No. I will not permit you to leave my presence while in a bothered state."

He glared at her. "Do you not understand that when it comes to you, I am forever in a bothered state? But then, I am learning that you thrill in that. It is your trade, after all."

Her lips parted in astonishment, a crippling sensation she was not used to feeling sweeping through her. She didn't know why she felt as if he'd stabbed at her heart. At her soul. Her heart didn't usually respond to men in the way it was responding to him right now. Throughout her life, others had said far more cruel things to her. Yet for some reason . . . this hurt. Horribly.

She released his arm and stepped back. This dalliance was over. There was no choice in this. "I have no trade, Your Grace," she coolly stated, meeting his dark gaze head-on. "Perhaps you need to understand that a whore has no choice but to take everyone's money, while a demimondaine has a wealth of choices. I, Your Grace, am neither, as I am choosing to be independent of you and of all men. Which is why I am terminating our night. If you dare to come near me or the school I will see to it you are immediately removed. I also dare you to enlist Parliament."

With that, she turned and walked through the spaces between the crowded tables. Although she wanted to altogether run to keep his continual stare from burning into her back, she kept a slow, steady pace, one that exuded calmness. Control. Something she certainly did not feel.

When she finally made it into the dark and quiet corridor outside of the gambling room, Maybelle paused and tried to force herself to breathe again. She momentarily closed her eyes and wished to God that she'd never laid eyes upon him. Wished to God that she'd never tried to claim him in that garden. For he belonged in a world she couldn't even touch.

A hand suddenly pressed to the small of her back, then two. Startled, she opened her eyes and before she could respond, she was spun and set against a neighboring wall.

Edmund towered before her. He placed both hands on the wall, just above her head, and leaned toward her, his massive body blocking her in. She froze, suddenly not being able to breathe.

"Forgive me," he softly whispered down at her, his dark eyes searching her face. "I had no right saying what I did."

Maybelle stared at his lower jaw and felt herself growing fainter by the moment. She didn't know why his apology meant so much to her. All she knew was in that moment, she wanted to yank him close. So close that their lips would collide and in that instance they could forget who they were and what their separate worlds expected of them.

His lips brushed against her forehead, bidding her to escape somewhere exotic with him. "Understand that I must have you. At least once."

Maybelle closed her eyes. Oh God. A part of her wanted to be in complete control. And independent. It was all she'd ever known. All she knew she could count on. Yet another part of her wanted to give in to this blind passion and see where it could possibly lead to. One night. It was only one night.

It wouldn't change anything. She was the one in control.

She opened her eyes, trying to keep her breathing steady, her thoughts rational. "I promised one night, Your Grace, and as such, you shall receive it. The conditions, however, have changed. It is I who will inform you as to when I am ready to receive you. Though it may be in a week or it may be in a year."

With that, she ducked, slipping beneath his muscular arms, and hurried away. She wished she could blame her rattled thoughts on the gin, but knew something else was happening to her. Whatever it was, she didn't like it. Not one bit. She felt as if she was losing her sense of confidence and her direction in life. And control. One she had been taught to always maintain impeccably by her grandmother.

It was time to leave. She needed time to herself to clear her thoughts. Time to think about what had just occurred between her and Edmund, what it was she was feeling and what it meant.

Maybelle headed into the foyer, set on leaving the entire night behind, when she heard a man call out, "Madame de Maitenon!" from the open doors of the parlor on her left.

She froze and inwardly cringed, recognizing the voice. She slowly turned, hoping she appeared calm.

Lord Hawksford casually stood in the middle of the crowded parlor, his white collar completely stripped, exposing a solid and very attractive neck. His bronzed hair was in utter disarray, as if he'd been rolling around. He grinned from across the room, those playful green eyes clearly bidding her to join him.

Oh God. She hurried over to him, paused, and set her hands on her hips. "Do not make life difficult for me."

"This'll only take a moment. I assure you." Hawksford grabbed her waist and yanked her toward his hard, muscled body. "I am in need of advice," he drawled down at her, shifting. *"Female advice."*

Cognac tinted his warm breath and his eyes appeared unusually heavy and hazy. Was the man inebriated? He had to be.

Quickly taking hold of his arms, Maybelle tried to ease out of them. "I do not think my advice will do you any good, as clearly, you won't be able to remember a thing come morning."

He wrapped his arm heavily around her shoulder and swayed as he tried to look down at her. "Does love truly exist? Or is it something we . . . want to exist?"

Maybelle froze against him. Love? She didn't know Hawksford had even heard of the word. "Really, My Lord, this is far beyond my level of—"

His arms and his body suddenly grew heavier. Hawksford slumped toward her, his bronzed head sagging forward.

Her heart jumped as she grabbed for him and staggered, desperately trying to hold his massive body up.

"My Lord?" she demanded, feeling as though the

very bones beneath her skin would snap beneath his dense weight. Her legs started to shake and although she should have dropped him, she was scared she'd end up hurting him or cracking his skull.

"I hereby claim any and all wages!" a man boomed from somewhere behind. "As I said, Hawksford wouldn't last past twenty!"

Lovely.

Absolutely lovely.

Lesson Fourteen

What happens to a man
who begins to compromise what he wants
in the name of passion?
It's a delicious case of total seduction.
Better known to the world by its devious
alter ego as love.
—The School of Gallantry

Edmund hung his head, his hands still firmly pressed against the wall. "I have completely lost my mind," he muttered, staring down at the wood floor beneath his feet.

What was worse, he had this nagging feeling that by accepting that night in the garden, he'd handed over not just his goddamn body, but his goddamn soul. For nothing had been the same since. Nothing. He was losing sight of what his title expected of him. Of what his mother expected of him. Of what the *ton* expected of him.

And being with Maybelle tonight only confirmed what he experienced in her presence each and every time. Not only hard, savage lust, but complete and total fascination. More and more he wanted to know who she was, what she thought, what she wanted out of life, and what she wanted out of a man. Out of him.

He drew in a deep breath, then pushed himself away from the paneled wall. The reality was Maybelle de Maitenon would never fit into his world. She was too wild. Too free-spirited. So unlike him. So unlike the *ton*.

And despite the fact that he was going to crush his mother's dreams of having a family, he knew that after his night with Maybelle, he had no choice but to let her go. For he had no intention of forcing her into a world she clearly didn't want to be a part of. Or a world she didn't even belong in.

Edmund made his way to the end of the corridor and eventually paused in the walnut arched doorway of the receiving room, the noise and chaos drumming against his ears.

He froze and stared wordlessly at what was going on. In the middle of the crowded parlor, Maybelle struggled to uphold what appeared to be a very drunk Hawksford. Her blond pinned curls had come undone and were coiling down to the side of her waist, waving back and forth as she desperately tried to balance herself and Hawksford.

Although the unfamiliar faces around them appeared to be laughing at the whole matter, Maybelle looked quite distraught, her limbs shaking.

What the devil was going on?

He strode toward her, only now realizing Hawksford was unconscious. Edmund quickly grasped the man's heavy arms and transferred his weight onto his own.

Maybelle released her grip and gasped, staggering back. "*Oh thank God*. Thank you! I thought I was going to have to drop him on his head."

"What happened?" Edmund yanked up Hawksford's body higher. The man's bronzed head rolled forward sloppily.

"One moment he was asking me an absurd question," Maybelle confessed, the astonishment as clear in her voice as it was on her face, "and the following moment, I was breaking his fall."

Edmund shook his head. "Consider yourself fortunate. I might as well take the bastard home. He is done for the night. As am I."

He shifted Hawksford into a better position, stooped, and draped him up onto his shoulder. He stood and turned about, making certain not to swing Hawksford's long limbs out at anyone.

Maybelle hurried after him. "I should go with you. To ensure that he arrives home. He is, after all, my student."

Edmund didn't want to think about what that did or did not mean. "Wave down my brougham. It should be outside."

"Of course." Maybelle hurried around them and disappeared.

Edmund carried Lord Hawksford out into the foyer and through the open door, out into the misty night. "You owe me, Hawksford," Edmund grumbled as he held the limp-limbed man in place. He made his way down the stairs of Caldwell's house and out onto the street.

Maybelle waved down the driver, who had already pulled the horses to a halt. The footman jumped down from the brougham to help. The footman opened the carriage door, and together, they hoisted Hawksford in and rolled him onto the seat, pushing him as far over as possible.

The footman adjusted his livery, then quickly scrambled back to his post at the back of the brougham.

Edmund leaned against the open door of the carriage and called out Hawksford's address to the driver. Delivering Hawksford first would ensure that he and Maybelle had more time together. He blew out a breath and stepped back down from the brougham.

"You are a good man when you choose to be, Edmund," a soft voice said from behind him.

Startled, he turned and looked down at Maybelle. Her beautiful blue eyes peered up at him, appearing gray in the gas-lit streets of London. God, how he wished she would look at him like that more often— with genuine tenderness. It was something he'd never seen on her face before. And he rather liked it.

"From time to time I surprise myself." He put out his hand and helped her up into the carriage.

Her skirts brushed past him as she stepped inside.

She seated herself opposite Hawksford and arranged her skirts into place to make room for him. When she had settled in, Edmund slammed the door of the carriage shut and took his place beside her.

Her skirts accidentally brushed against the side of his ungloved fingers. Edmund stared ahead at nowhere in particular and secretly fingered the satin material of her gown, remembering how she had allowed him to pull up her skirts that one night in the study and explore her core, her softness.

God, how he wanted her that way again. Completely.

He swallowed, slowly drew his hand away, and set it on his knee. It was foolish to think of her in any way knowing that everything she'd said earlier was true. They were of two separate worlds. She was a wild spirit who thrived on independence. While he thrived on maintaining control and trying to balance the responsibility of being a duke.

When the brougham pulled away and the horse's hooves clattered against the cobblestones, Edmund finally looked over at her.

She was leaning slightly forward, as far forward as her corset would allow, staring at Hawksford, who lay across from them, unconscious. She sighed heavily. "There are some things you cannot give advice for. Poor Hawksford."

Edmund shrugged. "Ah, he appears to have had a productive night."

Maybelle stifled a laugh with her gloved hand and shifted toward him. "Can you imagine?" She shook her head, more long, blond curls dropping loose. "Men were actually placing wagers as to how many drinks Hawksford could ingest before he collapsed. I arrived just when he had reached his limit of twenty."

Edmund laughed. Not just at the story, but at the way she said it. The way she always said things. With amazing zest and humor. So unlike the stuffy ways of the *ton*.

Maybelle's laugh eventually faded. She smiled as she tilted her blond head slightly. "You should laugh more often, Your Grace. It suits you beautifully."

"Thank you." Edmund cleared his throat and couldn't help but return her smile. In that single fleeting moment, he actually wished nothing divided them. Not their status, not their past, not the present, and not the future.

Her full lips, although still spread into a smile, slightly parted, as if she wanted to say something more.

He glanced at her mouth, and without thinking, leaned forward, reached out, and touched her lips with his thumb. As his thumb brushed across her soft, bottom lip, she stiffened.

"Kiss me," he whispered.

Her heated breath was now coming in short takes against his finger and she seemed to struggle with the idea of giving him something so simple.

"Kiss me," he repeated, urgency tinting his voice.

She glanced toward Hawksford and then back at him, her wide eyes stating the obvious.

"Where is your sense of adventure, head-mistress?" he teased, dragging his hand away from her lips and cupping the back of her exposed soft neck. He leaned in and softly kissed her lips.

He pulled away, though not completely. "Again?" She didn't respond, only kept her eyes half closed.

Edmund grabbed her waist with his other hand, digging his fingers into her corset beneath, and forced her lips apart. Her wet tongue was tinted with the bitterness of gin, but he felt as if he were tasting honey. He rolled his tongue inside her mouth, wanting to explore every bit of it.

His cock throbbed and once again he was lost in wanting her and only her. His cock sprung hard against his trousers, wanting to feel her wetness around its shaft again. Like that night in the garden.

The carriage suddenly rolled to a stop and his world of wonderful, hard bliss came to an abrupt end. She pushed at him, managing to break free, and took in several deep breaths.

No relief. As always. Edmund cleared his throat and adjusted the front of his snug trousers. He blew out a breath, looking over at Hawksford, who still lay in drunken slumber. Ignorance truly was bliss.

The door of the carriage opened and the steps were quickly unfolded.

"Pardon me," he murmured to Maybelle. "This should only take a moment." He leaned forward and yanked Hawksford into a sitting position. Pulling him onto his shoulder, Edmund stood and made his way out of the carriage.

Striding up the stairs of Hawksford's townhouse, he used his foot to bang on the door, hoping the servants were still awake. After a few moments, the door cracked open and the butler peered out.

"You may want to set a large pail beside him in the morning," Edmund commented to the man, gesturing toward Hawksford.

The man's beady eyes widened as he yanked the door wide open. "His lordship prefers the sofa when he is at his worst." He gestured toward the drawing room.

Clearly not the first time. And most likely not the last. Edmund strode toward the sofa and dumped Hawksford onto it. He smirked down at him. "Enjoy your morning, Hawksford."

Edmund made his way out, pulled the front door open, and paused within the darkened corridor, feeling as though someone was watching him. He slowly turned and glanced up at the darkened staircase leading to the second floor of the townhouse.

A brown-haired girl, of about fifteen or so, stood perfectly still atop the stairs, bundled from shoulder to feet in an exuberant amount of white linens. The sparse candlelight from the wall sconces cast long, flickering shadows across her pretty, but pale, thin face. Her silent and vacant expression was quite haunting. Almost . . . disturbing. She didn't even seem to blink.

Edmund was so moved to pity by her presence, he could not even force himself to move. From what he knew from the clubs he frequented, Hawksford was the only male in a brood of six. And this girl could have very well been part of that sisterly brood everyone always poked fun of. Though, oddly, he hadn't heard of any of them being ill.

The girl suddenly turned and stumbled away to wherever it was she came from, altogether disappearing from sight.

Edmund swallowed and continued to stand in the open doorway, though God knows for what reason. When silence still hummed, and the girl did not reappear, he stepped out and quietly closed the door behind him.

It was not his business or his right to know what went on in Hawksford's life. He shouldn't have been loitering about in the man's home. Which is why it was best he simply leave this matter be and forget what he'd seen. Out of respect for the entire household.

Calling out Maybelle's address to the driver, Edmund climbed back into the brougham and decided it was best to sit across from her. He was in no mood to further battle his emotions or his physical needs. He was far too exhausted. He needed sleep.

They rode in silence the whole while. Which was quite a long while. Edmund blankly stared out through the small window at the foggy, gas-lit streets that rolled by.

Eventually, the carriage came to a halt.

Edmund rose, stepped out, and held out his hand toward Maybelle. "I will escort you to the door."

She silently took his hand, her warmth overtaking his hand, and he guided her down the steps. The street was eerily quiet and the fog hovered, as if holding the silence.

Together they made their way up the stairs to her townhouse. The door unexpectedly opened and the balding butler, dressed in full livery, pulled the door all the way open and stepped off to the side waiting for Maybelle.

The butler bowed from his place at the door just inside the foyer. "Good evening, Your Grace."

Edmund suspected the entire household knew not only who he was but what he was after. No doubt they all thought his antics to be amusing.

Not wanting to linger, for he just might convince himself to hide somewhere in the house and sneak into Maybelle's bedroom when all had gone quiet, he inclined his head in a quick good-bye. He turned and made his way down the steps.

"Edmund?" Maybelle called after him.

He paused and turned back to her. The light that flooded the steps from the open door of the townhouse illuminated her in a soft yellow glow, highlighting all her blond, loose curls.

Her full lips curved into an unexpected smile as their eyes met. "Tomorrow," she whispered. "After the lesson."

Edmund's breath hitched in his throat. All he could manage was a slight nod. He then turned and quickly walked away before she or any other circumstance changed their set date.

He wanted to believe that she had actually conceded because she wanted him as badly as he wanted her. And not because she was hoping to finally be rid of him or collect her one hundred thousand pounds.

Either way, he had every intention of making it an affair they would both remember long after they returned to the lives that they truly belonged to.

Lesson Fifteen

Remember. The timing of your seduction is everything.
—The School of Gallantry

The next morning, 11 Berwick Street

Maybelle clutched her beaded reticule and quickly made her way up the red-runner stairs with Harold in tow, shaking the staircase as always. All she could damn well think about was Edmund. And what would happen between them today. By the dark, almost disturbed look on his face when she had conceded last night, she sensed nothing would be the same. And it bothered her not knowing what that meant. Yet she was more than ready to finish what had been started between them. So they could both finally move on.

Maybelle paused for a moment at the top of the landing and, without waiting for Harold, made her way into the bedroom, where she could hear low, almost urgent voices.

Upon entering the red velvet room, only three men rose to greet her. Caldwell, Banfield, and Brayton. Maybelle stiffened at finding two of the five wingbacked chairs empty. Hawksford's and Edmund's.

"Hawksford is still in his cups," Caldwell quickly provided. The blond stubble on his face as well as his crooked cravat indicated that Caldwell himself had trouble this morning.

Maybelle smiled tightly. "And His Grace?"

Caldwell glanced toward the two others, who in turn shrugged. Caldwell also shrugged.

Edmund was no doubt sleeping in, getting ready for the *long* night ahead. Maybelle let out a shaky breath at the very thought and moved to the middle of the room. What was she thinking?

Setting her reticule onto her small letter-writing desk, she turned toward them and tried to pretend she was not at all affected by her thoughts. "We shall proceed without them. Lord Caldwell, you may begin first. What is your gift and how will you present it to your lover?"

She quirked a brow at him, waiting for his presentation.

Caldwell reached into the inner pocket of his jacket and withdrew a flat small package wrapped perfectly in beautiful white lace. He strode toward her, paused, took her right hand setting her palm up, and gently set it on her hand, his brown eyes never once leaving hers. He then brought her other hand and set it atop the lace wrapping.

Although every movement was refined and seductive, Maybelle couldn't help but compare Caldwell to Edmund. She swallowed, glanced at the gift, and proceeded to unwrap the lace from around it.

She paused when the lace slipped from a worn, brown leather binding of a book whose gold lettering had long faded. Voltaire. She smiled and smoothed her gloved hand across its surface. "Impressive. You paid attention in class yesterday, Lord Caldwell, when I quoted Voltaire. Being perceptive will certainly endear you to the woman you are looking to impress."

He leaned toward her and tapped on the book. "Open it."

"Open it?" Maybelle opened the book and to her surprise found a faded scrawl across the yellowing, delicate parchment. Her eyes widened. Voltaire had actually written something on it.

She glanced up at Caldwell. "Where did you get this?" she couldn't help but demand.

He grinned. "It is yours, Madam."

"Oh, no, I couldn't possibly, I—"

He held up a hand. "Consider it a small token for seeing to Hawksford last night. We all had other far more pressing matters."

Maybelle laughed and shook her head. "On that basis alone, I will gladly accept it." She closed the book gently, kissed its binding, then turned and laid it on the writing desk behind her. "Thank you, My Lord. You did beautifully."

Caldwell bowed, then returned to his chair and sat.

That was certainly unexpected. Maybelle met Banfield's gaze and smiled. "My Lord?"

Banfield nodded, strode toward her, and upon pausing before her, withdrew a small gold carved box. He leaned toward her and holding it up for her to see flicked open the lid. On a small white satin pillow laid blue lapis lazuli stone carved into what appeared to be an Egyptian scarab.

Her mouth fell open but she quickly shut it. "A scarab. From Egypt."

Banfield smiled, the edges of his eyes crinkling seductively. "You like it? Someone told me you would."

Her grandmother? That woman knew no bounds. Maybelle reached out a gloved hand and ran the tip of it along the edges of the small smooth stone. "It is absolutely beautiful."

"And it is now yours."

Maybelle took it from him and slowly closed the lid. Why did she feel as if these men knew her so intimately? This was only their second class. They must have done some serious homework. "Always play into the interests of a woman's heart. It will endear you to her."

Banfield bowed and returned to his chair.

Maybelle finally met Brayton's sharp blue gaze and smiled. "All that is left is you."

"Indeed," Brayton muttered, shaking his dark head. He blew out a breath and made his way toward her, his hand digging into the inside of his jacket. He pulled out a thin long box wrapped in black satin, paused before her, and held it out, his blue eyes boldly holding hers.

Reaching out for her hand, he brought it up toward the box and used her own fingers to slowly and expertly unwrap the black satin. It was as if he knew how to flex her fingers in the right place to keep their movements firm and steady. The wrapping slipped off and still directing her fingers, he pushed open the lid of the flat, slim box, then drew away her hand.

There, on a piece of folded muslin was a beautiful gold and silver dagger. She glanced up at him.

"Every woman should possess a dagger," Brayton whispered. "To protect her virtue. But more importantly, her heart."

Maybelle pinched her lips together and took the weighted box from him. Though it was not a conventional gift or sentiment, it hit its mark, making her feel the way a woman should feel when receiving a gift. Honored. "Thank you. I shall cherish it."

These men did not need lessons in the art of love or seduction. They knew more than the average man did. So why were they here?

She nodded and turned away, telling herself she was not going to start blubbing. She set the box down on the table and stared at all three gifts. All equally worthy of praise. She couldn't possibly pick among them as they had all served the same purpose. That of the heart.

"What of my gift?" someone drawled from the doorway.

Maybelle froze and then slowly turned only to find Edmund leaning against the door frame as if he'd been there all along. He was dressed in well-fitted gray riding clothes that showed off every last inch of his muscular frame. The muddy black leather boots that reached his knees indicated he'd been riding.

She had no doubt her heart was pounding loud enough for everyone in the room to hear.

Edmund pushed himself away from the door frame and strode toward her. He moved with the fluid grace she had spied the first night she had laid eyes upon him. The room grew eerily quiet as he advanced and she knew all eyes were on her.

He paused before her, unbuttoned his tweed jacket, and held it wide open, exposing the hidden pocket within. And simply waited. As if he expected her to dig out his gift herself.

She nervously wet her lips, stepped toward him, and kept her gaze firmly on the pocket lest she got distracted along the way.

The scent of heated sandalwood filled the air around her as her fingers slowly slid into the soft and smooth warmth of his jacket. Something metallic touched the tip of her fingers. She tightened her hold around it and pulled it out.

A key. To his bedroom, no doubt.

She stared at it, deeply disappointed at his lack of tact. Then again, what was she to expect? A sentimental gift prior to giving him a night? She hated sentimental rubbish, anyway.

She fisted it and somehow could not bring herself to look at him. Heaven knows what everyone else in the room was thinking.

"This key marks the last of all the gifts I have given you today," he finally announced, his deep voice surrounding her. "Although I must confess that the whole dagger bit was more Brayton's idea."

Startled, Maybelle looked up at him. "All the gifts? Whatever do you mean?" She stepped back and glanced toward Banfield, Caldwell, and Brayton.

Brayton coughed and looked off to the side.

Caldwell was grinning, as usual.

And Banfield had a rather disgusted look, as though he were about to vomit.

"Edmund," she whispered, turning back to him. "What is this about? I don't believe I understand."

"I am bringing this session to an end, Madam." Edmund stepped toward her, that very intent marked on his face. "For I am not about to sit through an entire goddamn morning of lessons waiting to collect you."

Heat splashed her entire body. "Edmund, really, I couldn't possibly—"

"Yes, you can." He reached down and to her shock slid his lowered arm beneath the back of her knees and scooped her right up into his arms and off the floor.

She was surrounded by his muscled mass and was looking straight into his smooth-shaven face. Her pulse jumped in a similar manner as it had when she had gazed upon him that night in the lightest part of the garden.

Edmund turned them toward their audience and announced, "This concludes today's lesson, boys. And because it is Friday, do not expect her return until Monday."

Maybelle's eyes widened as she tightened her hold around Edmund's neck and the key which was still in her right hand. "*Edmund!* This is not what I agreed to! Class is far from over and these men pay bloody good money to be here. My grandmother would—"

"Do any of you mind," Edmund called out over to the men, "if I borrow your headmistress for the day? I'll gladly pay for the remainder of this month's lessons to make up for it."

"As long as you bring her back next week!" Caldwell yelled back, waving them off. He grinned. "In the meantime, we shall all occupy ourselves with the girls. They're all lonely up there and we certainly cannot have that."

Maybelle's eyes widened as chuckles rumbled within the room. Her grandmother would have a fit! She frantically shoved at Edmund's arms. He only tightened his hold. "Edmund, no! They aren't allowed to—"

"It is settled then." Edmund grinned down at her and swung them back toward the doorway. "Hold onto your key, Madam, as we will be making use of it quite soon."

And with that, he led them out into the corridor, down the steps, and toward the front door, where Harold stood gawking at them.

No! Not the front door!

"Edmund, no!" She hit his shoulder repeatedly with her fisted hand. "Not the front door. My grandmother doesn't promote anyone being seen coming in and out of the school. It marks our exclusivity!"

"Harold, open the damn door," Edmund growled out.

"Yes, Your Grace." Harold stalked forward, unlocked the bolts, and quickly swung it open.

So much for her grandmother's golden rule.

Or the gatekeeper.

Or the school.

"See to the girls, Harold!" she yelled out. "Or my grandmother will set your balls on display!"

Edmund laughed and tightened his hold on her.

Maybelle froze as he carried her out through the open door and out into the bustling cobblestone street of London. In respectable daylight!

She buried her face in Edmund's chest and didn't dare look at any of the people who were no doubt stopping to look at them. She doubted if her grandmother had ever lived through scandal like this!

A door was opened and she felt Edmund's muscles shift around her as she was hoisted up into his carriage. Only when she felt herself being set onto

Edmund's lap and the door slammed shut did she lift her face from his chest.

His arms tightened, pressing her closer. "You will remain seated on my lap throughout our short journey. To ensure that you do not abandon me." He winked, then grinned.

Maybelle felt her heart unexpectedly squeeze. Why did this no longer feel like an arrangement but a courtship? What was worse, she rather liked it. A lot.

Trouble is what this was.

Trouble.

Lesson Sixteen

*Lust certainly makes
this world spin fast and round.
But the moment you dare involve love,
know that everything will come to a complete and
quick halt. And yes, you most certainly
will fall off the planet.*
—The School of Gallantry

When the carriage finally rolled to a stop, Maybelle tightened her grip on the key and glanced up at Edmund. "Am I allowed to take leave of your lap now?" she drawled.

"No," he growled out, possessively tightening his hold. "You will stay right where you are."

As the carriage door swung open, she quickly asked, "What is the key for? Exactly?"

Without answering, he lifted her up off of his lap, tightened his hold around her, and stood. He led them out of the carriage and toward a beautiful townhouse set in one of the most exquisite parts of London. Where only the *ton* were allowed to live and breathe.

She stiffened, feeling very much out of place, as he carried her up the small set of stairs.

"The key, Madam," he murmured down at her. "In answer to your earlier question."

She released one arm from around his neck and held up the key.

"Use it." He turned her toward the door and lowered her just enough for the lock to be level with her hand.

An odd sense of excitement and anticipation fluttered inside her chest, as she realized that she had absolutely no idea what it was he had planned. She pushed the key into the lock, slowly turned it, then pulled it back out.

"Open it."

Even though she had the key in her hand, she reached out, took hold of the doorknob, and turned it. She pushed it open and Edmund carried her inside.

He set her down gently onto the floor, then using the back heel of his boot slammed the door shut, engulfing them in silence.

Maybelle glanced around, realizing that the floors and stairs had been scattered with endless orchids and rose petals. So many, the scent floated around them and filled her with a sense of longing.

As she stepped forward, cringing at the very idea of actually crushing the beautiful flowers with her slippered feet, she peered toward the parlor and realized it was void of all furniture, paintings, or rugs. Silk and lace curtains covered the windows, being the only thing to hint that someone might have once lived here.

A slow dread filled her and she wondered if perhaps this was the townhouse he had mentioned when he'd first made his offer of marriage. How she prayed it wasn't. She didn't want to ruin this moment between them.

She turned to him feeling suddenly frightened that she was going to hurt him by refusing yet another offer. "What is this place?"

He locked the door, then turned back to her and shrugged. "I bought it years ago. For the family I was to have."

Maybelle froze and sensed he was about to change something between them. And she wasn't in the least bit prepared for it. At all.

He closed his eyes for a moment, as if struggling for words. "I am certain you have heard all the rumors surrounding my family. I thought it best I share what happened. So that you might better understand me."

He opened his eyes, blew out a breath, and looked away. "Lady Anne Montgomery was her name. She was beautiful, intelligent, and came from an outstanding, respectable family. Whenever I came upon her during the Season, my adoration grew, until I knew without question that she would be my wife. After discussing the details with my parents, I bought this townhouse and called upon her parents, stating my intentions. They were pleased. Very pleased, in fact. But as for Lady Anne . . ." He frowned and shook his head.

Maybelle slowly walked toward him, then paused. She almost didn't want him to say anymore. Didn't want to further see the suffering that was etched upon his dark features.

He shrugged. "A letter arrived within the week. Lady Anne confessed that she could not marry me under any circumstance. For she had already given her heart, her body, and soul to another." His mouth grew tight and grim. "My father."

The key Maybelle had been holding slipped from her hand and clattered to the floor. She stood there in disbelief, not knowing what to say or do.

"I couldn't understand. Out of all the women my father could have chosen, why her? She was mine. He knew it." He shrugged again. "My mother was without a doubt more devastated than I. They had been happily married for so goddamn long, both she and I refused to believe it. We finally confronted him. Together. He sobbed in a way no man should and admitted to everything. Claimed it was committed out of love, not lust. I didn't care to believe a word of it."

He shifted his jaw. "My father begged for time to set it right, then that very night crawled into Lady Anne's bed and while she slept took enough laudanum to kill a dozen horses. Lady Anne's family kept everything as discreet as possible; after all it was both of our shames. So while we buried my father, blaming it on a fatal heart condition, Lady Anne's parents married her off to another man. Of course, that did not keep the *ton* from asking questions or demanding answers. How coincidental indeed that my father should die and that my engagement to Lady Anne should die along with him. My mother and I twisted the truth as best we could, but ultimately, the *ton* was set on destroying my future as a man. As a duke."

Listening to the distant, almost cold tone of his voice was too much to bear. She could only imagine the pain he and his mother had endured. It appeared life could be miserable no matter which side of the world you lived on.

His black eyes impaled her. "I have learned, Maybelle, that emotions play dangerous games with our minds. With our souls. They can lead a man to snuff everything out only because he feels he has no other choice. And so there you have it. The truth behind my scandal."

Maybelle momentarily closed her eyes, now realizing why he was the way he was. Why he offered nothing more than his body, his money, and his title. Not because of the snobby, entitled world he'd been born into, but because everything had been so viciously taken away from him. And her excuse? "Forgive me," she whispered. "Forgive me for ever judging you. I did not know."

"That is how we wanted it," he murmured. "My mother and I preferred everyone thinking that he had died in the arms of a courtesan rather than in the arms of a respectable woman. Which only now I realize was wrong. Because even the granddaughter of a courtesan is worthy of receiving respect. As you have proven to me."

Maybelle opened her eyes in disbelief and met his serious gaze. He thought her worthy of respect? Even though they stood here waiting to consummate a one hundred thousand–pound agreement?

She swallowed hard and desperately fought the sudden tenderness she felt toward him. Men of the *ton* were not supposed to say things like that. That is what separated her from the *ton*. That is what always separated them. Their respectability and her obvious lack of it.

Edmund closed the distance between them, and the next thing she knew, his muscular arms were around her. She leaned against his warmth, pressing him tightly to herself, and felt as if she had finally connected with someone. Someone who saw beyond the façade of what society saw.

He kissed the top of her head. "My mother wanted me to keep this place," he murmured. "She said it would be the groundwork for a new beginning. That out of bad would one day come good. I thought about that last night and decided that it should be yours. A beautiful and respectable lady such as yourself deserves a beautiful and respectable place."

Tears stung her eyes. And for the first time in her life she actually wished she could live up to such high praise. The reality was, she could not change the family she'd been born into. Or what she had become because of it.

Edmund released her and gently took hold of her chin, his warm fingertips feathering her skin. Lifting it up toward him, he held it in place, forcing her to look up at him.

A muscle flicked in his jaw. "Now. Give me the honor of making love to you, Madam."

If there was ever a moment to give one's self over to a man without hesitation, this was it. "I am yours tonight," she whispered up at him.

His fingers tightened around her chin as he leaned down and gently brushed his warm lips against hers. She closed her eyes and savored the softness and gentleness of that single kiss.

He slowly lifted his mouth from hers and trailed his fingers from her chin down to her throat, his touch feathery and light.

She met his dark gaze as he slid his fingers farther down to the front of her yellow muslin gown.

His fingers stilled on the lace neckline just above her breasts. His breath now came in heavier takes. "I may not be as gentle as I should be," he admitted. "I've been waiting far too long for this moment."

Her own breath now also came in deeper takes as the warmth of his hand continued to linger at her breast. "Do what you will," she whispered. "I am certain I will enjoy every moment of it."

He growled down at her as his other hand came up. His hold on the front material of her gown tightened and in one swift motion, he ripped the front of her bodice and kept ripping his way down until he had made enough room for it to slip off her arms and waist and onto the floor.

Maybelle stood only in a petticoat, chemise, corset, stockings, and of course, her slippers. A shiver shot through her as the cool air around her flecked goose bumps across the exposed skin of her arms. She could slowly feel herself growing wet, anticipating more.

Edmund stared at her for a long moment, then clamped his jaw and stripped off his jacket, flinging it off to the side. His erection was visibly pressing against his trousers.

Maybelle undid the lacing that held her petticoats in place, along with all the tapes, and let them drop from her arms and legs down around her feet with her gown, leaving her only in her chemise and corset.

Stepping outside the heap of clothing around her feet, she moved closer toward him, and grabbed hold of his vest jacket right where the buttons held it closed. In one rough, solid movement, she ripped it apart, spraying his buttons everywhere. She slid her hands beneath his vest and pushed it off from his muscled shoulders and down to the floor.

He grinned down at her. "You can damn well do that anytime you please."

"I shall remember that." She pushed him toward the wall behind him until his solid back thudded against it, then fingered his cravat for a moment, eyeing him.

"Go on," he prodded. "Do what you will."

"Gladly." She undid his cravat, stripped it from around his collar, and tossed it off to the side. She then removed his stiff collar, also tossing it off to the side, then worked open his cotton shirt. Yanking it out of his trousers, she pulled it up over his head and let it also join the rest of their clothes on the floor.

Edmund's exposed, wide, and muscled chest made her pulse thunder as she slowly leaned in and splayed her fingers over one of his hardened nipples.

He watched her the whole time, his smooth-shaven jaw tight, his eyes hooded, and his chest rising and falling as if he were struggling to breathe.

She loved having this much control over him. She smiled and dragged her hands down his smooth, almost velvet muscled sides. Toward his trousers.

Edmund caught her wrists before she had a chance to go any farther. "Is this what you want?" he quietly demanded. "Truly?"

Maybelle yanked her wrists free and stepped away from him, giving him the sultriest look she could possibly bestow on him. "It is exactly what I want. Is this what *you* want?"

"Yes. Bloody yes." He licked his bottom lip, letting his eyes travel down the length of her. "Walk up those stairs. Slowly. I want to watch the way you walk. Make your way toward the second door on your right."

Maybelle half nodded, took in a shaky, excited breath, and turned away. She set her hand on the mahogany banister and walked up the stairs, sliding her hand up along the length of the polished wood.

She could feel his eyes watching her. Wanting her. Which is why in that moment, she wanted to give him more. So much more. With her other hand, the one that wasn't on the banister, she reached up and started pulling out each and every pin from her hair and tossing it aside. The weight of her heavy curls soon gave way and they tumbled down and around her shoulders and halfway down her back.

She heard him mount the first stair at the bottom of the staircase behind her and pause.

She smiled to herself, knowing she was the one in control and despite the little watching game he wanted to play, she wanted to play something else. Maybelle darted up the remaining stairs and skidded into the corridor.

"Depriving me already, are you?!" he yelled from behind her, laughing. The staircase sounded as if it was being pounded by a herd of horses as he ran up after her.

She laughed as her chemise fumbled around her thighs and legs. She sprinted for the second door. Finding the door wide open, and hearing Edmund's running steps behind her, she darted into the bedroom.

Maybelle slid to an abrupt halt at the unexpected atmosphere. Her eyes widened and her lips slightly parted.

The entire room had been adorned in white. Pure, beautiful white. From the large four-poster bed to all the pillows and linens to the heavy curtains hanging around it. More rose petals were scattered on the floor of the room. And it was the most beautiful thing she had ever witnessed in her life. Worthy of a lady. Worthy of her.

"I have you now!"

Bare, muscular arms folded around her front side and yanked her back. Maybelle screamed out a laugh and tried to move them forward. Together they stumbled several steps toward the bed until they both fell onto the white, soft paradise.

Edmund grabbed her waist and tossed her onto her stomach. He crawled onto the back of her. "This damn corset must be removed at once." She could now feel him tugging and pulling as he worked to undo the long set of laces.

To her surprise, right before her on the linens laid none other than the dildo she'd given him in class.

"What is this?" She snatched it up, grinned, and tried glancing back at him. His muscles shifted across his wide chest and arms as he frantically worked to free her.

He glanced at what she held. "You instructed your students to keep it at their bedside. Inform me the moment you wish to make use of it."

She laughed and tossed it aside. "Not on the first try." She paused and realized he was still tugging at her corset, trying to get it off. "I would assist if I could reach," she offered playfully, shifting beneath him.

"I require no assistance in this," he snapped, tugging and pulling at her corset. "I rather enjoy unwrapping gifts." He finally yanked the corset free, causing her to take in a wonderfully deep breath that momentarily faded the room.

He tossed it toward the other side of the bed, rolled her onto her back, and pinned her wrists down just above her head, showing off the beautiful expanse of his muscled chest and well-defined arms.

Maybelle stared up at him in newfound awe. The man truly was breathtaking. A woman could not ask for more.

His black hair was scattered in every direction, some longer strands hanging into his eyes. He looked down at her, holding the biggest grin any man could hold. As if he had just conquered the world. "What shall we do now?"

"Must you ask?" she drawled up at him.

"That tongue of yours is going to cost you your chemise." He released her, reached down, and shoved her chemise all the way up her body. He yanked it over her head and whipped it off to the side.

She was completely naked except for her stockings and slippers. Which he quickly disposed of. While he, God help her, still straddled her dressed in his trousers and boots.

Her pulse beat wildly within her throat as his eyes raked over her breasts. He sat up, pinning the lower half of her body between his trouser-clad thighs. His large hands slid over her breasts, slowly, causing her nipples to harden and her body to writhe, wanting more of his touch.

She pushed herself up against his erection. "Please," she whispered up at him, squirming. "No more waiting."

Edmund grabbed hold of her wrists again and pinned them up over her head. He leaned closer and whispered back, "Tell me what it is you want."

Maybelle took in a sharp breath as he leaned farther down and gently kissed her parted lips.

"Say it," he murmured.

"Take me," she breathlessly said, wishing he damn well would.

He momentarily drew away. "I think I have a right to demand a little more from my teacher. Tell me *exactly* what you need me to do."

She gritted her teeth and struggled against him, wishing he would just take control. "Please."

"Please what?" He leaned in again and unexpectedly wet her lips with a hot, playful tongue.

She tightly shut her eyes, her world spinning out of control. Her breath escaped in panicked breaths as he licked her lips again.

"Maybelle," he murmured, his warm breath tickling the area around her mouth, "I shall gladly give you everything and anything you want. All you need do is ask."

Everything? Anything? She swallowed. What did he mean by that?

"Maybelle," he murmured, the heat of his body

feeling much closer than it ever had before. "Look at me."

She opened her eyes and gazed directly up into fathomless obsidian eyes. His nose was practically touching her own as strands of his black hair seductively feathered her forehead.

He softly caught her bottom lip between his teeth, still watching her, then released it. "Tell me what you want," he murmured.

"You. I want you." And truer words she'd never spoken in her life.

"Details, darling. Bestow upon me all of the details." He sensually trailed his lips down the bare curve of her neck. His chin nudged her every now and then. Her entire neck was now wet as if he were trying to drown her with his mouth.

"I wish for you to be inside of me," she begged.

"Inside of which part?" he dared. "There is your mouth, your cunt, and of course, your ass. Be specific."

Her breath now came in short gasps in disbelief. At how naughty he wanted her to be. "My . . . cunt."

He tightened his hold on her wrists, still keeping them over her head, and lowered his mouth to her nipple. He sucked it hard, the aggression sending her pulse racing for want of more. He lifted his lips for a moment. "Are you certain?"

Oh God, she could not take any more suffering! "Edmund, I will scream if you bloody make me wait a moment longer."

"I'd rather you scream once I'm inside you." He

released his hold on her wrists and then slid his bare hands up her thighs.

Thankful that she was finally free to touch him, she wrapped her arms around his smooth shoulders and yanked him down against her.

He chuckled as his large hands moved farther and farther up her thighs.

"Edmund," she pleaded, unable to give the required command, "why must you take so long?"

He lifted his ruffled head from her chest, his moist hands still pushed against her upper thighs, and glanced over his shoulder. "What? Is someone else waiting? Is that it?"

She laughed despite herself. "*Edmund!*"

"So damn impatient. Where do you get it from?" His hands kept trailing until finally his fingers moved between and into her wet folds. She gasped, feeling his fingers stealing into her.

"Yes," she rasped. She closed her eyes as he slowly rubbed his rigid fingers between the folds of her wetness. Her thighs quivered in response.

"Tell me you want me," he urgently said, his harsh lips moving up and down her neck.

His fingers moved faster and faster, going deeper and deeper into her, until she was gasping and squirming and wanting and yearning.

"Tell me you want me, Maybelle. I wish to hear it. I wish to hear you say it."

Feeling as though her world were about to explode into thousands and thousands of glittering shards of pleasure, she choked out, "I—I want you. Desperately."

"As I want you." He rose, withdrawing his fingers from deep inside of her and undid his trousers, leaving only cool air around her for a moment.

He removed his boots, sending them skidding across the floor. After undoing a few buttons and tapes, he stripped off his trousers and the drawers beneath. His large, solid cock sprang forth, pointing rigidly toward her as he climbed back on top of her, gloriously naked.

Maybelle wet her lips at seeing the rounded head of his shaft bead with seed.

He leaned toward her, his velvet heat spreading across her naked body. He shifted on top of her, his cock now pressing hard into her thigh.

But he still didn't try to put it inside of her.

He stared down at her for a long moment. "Do you want protection from my seed?"

She swallowed, thankful that he was able to even think for both of them. "Yes," she whispered. "Please."

"My lady has spoken." He reached down, grabbed hold of his shaft, and with his dark eyes holding hers, slid it slowly into the tight opening between her legs, pushing up against her nub. "Open more to me."

She relaxed and spread her legs open wider.

"You are mine all of this day and all of this night." Holding her gaze, he thrust into her and hissed out, "Mine."

She gasped as he slid in deeper and deeper still. A sense of complete belonging filled her very core.

He slowly worked in and out, sending jolts of pleasure throughout her entire body with every smooth movement.

"Damn," he hoarsely said. "You feel incredible. Is your body able to take more?"

"Yes."

"Good." He grabbed her waist firmly and kneeled, lifting both himself and her hips up off the bed.

Edmund clenched his jaw and began to feverishly work himself in and out of her. She opened her mouth to tell him how wonderful he felt, but could only gasp against his every thrust.

He pushed into her again and again, rhythmically showering her entire body with endless pleasurable sensations that only seemed to build more force.

Her breathing came in ragged, loud gasps as she tried to keep up. She struggled to push up against him, wanting more and more of his slick length. His shaft went even deeper, now not only hitting the core of her nub, but the very wall of her womb.

Maybelle caught hold of his waist, and refused to let him stop as that wild, mounting sensation overtook every nerve in her tightly coiled body.

"Yes," he panted, closing his eyes and tilting his dark head back as he continued to bang into her. "More. Give me more."

Maybelle moved as rapidly as she could against him, picking up more power and more force, causing him to moan so loud, she thought she would burst from the pleasure of hearing him. Just as she reached the highest level of erotic sensations she ever thought possible, her body shuddered in response to the most extreme pleasure even his mouth hadn't been able to give her. She felt herself swelling around his shaft and cried out in disbelief.

He lowered himself to her and covered both her cry and her mouth fully with his own. He grabbed her hand and forced it down hard between them. He set her fingers into a V around his thick erection so she could feel him as he continued to jerk in and out of her.

Her wetness slathered her fingers as he worked more intently. His body momentarily stiffened and he quickly slipped out of her. Using her hand, he closed all of her wet fingers around the tip of his shaft and continued pleasuring himself in her hand as he grunted into her mouth, refusing to let her lips go even for a moment.

Maybelle sucked his tongue deep into her mouth and in that moment, he tensed and his hard cock rigidly convulsed against her slippery fingers. He thrust into her hand one last time, groaning, and out poured his warm, thick seed into her palm.

He collapsed beside her and yanked her tightly against him, laying her head against his chest. As she remained pressed against his nakedness, his deep breathing and the rapid beating of his heart eventually returned to normal.

Only then did the bed around them reappear.

Maybelle slid her hands around him, toward the expanse of his broad back, and spread his seed against his moist skin, enjoying the feel of doing it. "Pardon me," she whispered, smiling shyly.

"Not at all." Edmund placed a lingering kiss on her cheek and murmured, "That was incredible. Simply incredible." He took in a deep, well-sated breath and let it out.

Heaven help her, it *was* incredible.

He leaned over her, his black strands of hair framing his face. An unexpected form of tenderness that made her heart jump beamed from his rugged, flushed face. It was as if he were a new man. Yet . . . the same.

His dark eyes searched her face, glowing with an amazing softness she'd never seen before. "You are not permitted to leave this bed until morning."

She nuzzled against him, oddly content. "I would never dare dream of it, Your Grace."

Lesson Seventeen

Only fools lead themselves to believe
that after the game is over
everything will fall perfectly back into place
as it was once before.
The only thing to ever fall into place, however,
is reality. For every conquest comes with a price.
Some simply cost more than others.
—The School of Gallantry

Evening had long been at hand, spreading cozy shadows into every corner of the bedroom. All the candles which had been earlier lit were already down to their stubs and Maybelle wondered how much longer she would last. Like the dwindling wax of the candles, her body felt thoroughly spent from all their encounters. Yet she felt so glorious. And content. Not to mention unusually happy.

Every moment throughout the day had been thought out by Edmund. In between the moments that weren't dedicated to lovemaking, large silver trays magically appeared outside their door laden with tea, fruits, tarts, cheese, pastries, and meats. And no sooner were they set back outside the door, they magically disappeared.

"I rather like this townhouse," Maybelle nonchalantly commented as Edmund strode naked toward the door to set out their empty tray. "Magical trays and all."

"The magical trays only come with me," he drawled over his shoulder.

"Drat. I thought so." She grinned and sat up on the bed to get a better view of Edmund's muscular backside, which tightened and flexed with each movement. The candlelight further shadowed and highlighted his skin in the most golden, erotic way.

She bit her lower lip. By God, he was beautiful. And thoughtful. He had tended not only to all of her pleasures but also all of her needs and comforts. For heaven's sake, if a man could go through such effort for a mistress, she could only imagine what he'd do for his wife.

Maybelle paused, realizing what it was she was thinking, and quickly shoved the thought aside. It was an impossible idea. One that did not belong inside her head.

She nibbled on her apple and paused as he opened the door and leaned over to set the tray outside, exposing an amazing view of his balls. She swallowed the remaining apple in her mouth and wondered if he was always this comfortable with the women he chose to bed.

He closed the door and strode toward her once again, his dark eyes trained on her. Stopping at the foot of the bed, Edmund grabbed hold of each end of the four-poster bed, stretching the width of his muscled chest, and stood there for a long moment watching her.

Although she wasn't particularly shy after everything that had occurred between them, the way he kept looking at her made her want to sweep up the linens around her naked body and cover herself completely.

"Toss the apple and turn onto your stomach." His voice was deep, raw. His huge erection already pointed toward her, ready.

She smiled deviously, tossed aside the apple onto the floor, and flipped herself over onto her bare stomach, stretching out for him. "What now, Your Grace?"

The bed shifted as he climbed on. "On your hands and knees, darling."

Darling. Why was it she loved hearing the way his deep voice practically growled when he said it? Maybelle slowly pushed herself up onto her hands and knees and waited. Waited for him to thrust into her and bring her to another state of mindless bliss. One she couldn't seem to get enough of.

Edmund grabbed her waist hard and yanked her entire backside toward him, pressing the length of his shaft firmly against her. He leaned forward, his velvet warmth spreading across her back, and slid his hands from her waist down under toward her breasts.

"Does my lady desire the use of her dildo?" he growled into her ear, rubbing himself against her.

"But of course." Maybelle eyed the space of the bed, hoping the dildo was within reach so she wouldn't have to leave him. Seeing the leather dildo just beside one of the pillows, she quickly reached out and grabbed for it. She held it out for him, trying to keep her breathing calm, but otherwise didn't move.

"Wet it with your mouth," he said, flicking his thumbs across each nipple. "Get it as wet as you can."

She shuddered from his touch, brought the dildo to her lips, and spread as much of her saliva onto the tip of its length as possible. Knowing it was ready, she shakily held it out for him again, desperately yearning to know what he planned to do with it.

He took it from her and using his one hand spread her cheeks apart. He gently nudged the head of the dildo into the opening of her rear.

Her eyes widened as it eased deeper inside of her and a strange new sensation took hold of her. He reached down between her thighs and rubbed at her nub, slowly but firmly. She gasped, feeling as though she could already climax. With but that single touch.

"You said to try new things," he whispered, rubbing her nub and slowly moving the dildo in and out of her ass.

She gasped again, her body wanting to shudder

from the overwhelming sensation. "It makes me want to explode from pleasure," she said hoarsely, not moving. "With so little effort."

"I don't want this to be the end of our session just yet." He slipped the dildo slowly out, taking away the heightened pleasure she'd been experiencing, and tossed it aside. Without any warning, he grabbed her waist and thrust himself deep into her wet folds, jerking her back hard several times against his length.

She cried out each time as the sensations mounted more intensely around her core and shot up through her stomach. Her breasts bounced back and forth, moving along with the rest of her body he had taken command over.

"Allow my seed to spill into you," he harshly panted, driving deeper and deeper. "This once."

Maybelle dug her fingers into the linens and pushed up against him, giving in to each and every violent thrust, her skin heating, her chest tightening. She didn't know why, but at that moment, she felt as if her climax wouldn't be complete unless he spilled every bit of himself inside of her. She wanted it. Needed it.

"Yes," she choked. "Do it."

His fingers dug deeper into her skin, acknowledging her words. He pounded faster. Never once stopping or letting her rest. As if wanting her climax to come at a rapid pace she'd not yet experienced.

She stiffened, her core already taking over her entire body. She cried out, everything blissfully and momentarily disappearing from around her, including her own thoughts.

Edmund yanked her back hard against his length one last time, holding her savagely against him, and groaned as his shaft pulsated against the walls of her womb and his seed spilled deep into her.

It was quiet now except for their ragged breaths and neither she nor he moved. Eventually, Edmund slipped out of her and turned her gently over onto her back. He lowered himself beside her, cradled her head within the crook of his long muscled arm, and kissed her forehead.

The warmth and wetness of his seed lingered between her thighs and she knew things between them had officially changed. Why had she allowed him to do it? Why had she wanted to breathe and feel every bit of him in a way she'd never thought possible?

Edmund gently brushed aside a strand of her hair which was curling around her neck and after a few moments of silence whispered, "I want more of you."

She blinked up at him in astonishment, then gurgled out a laugh. "More? You truly are relentless. You realize that?"

He chuckled and shook his head. "No. That is not what I meant. I want more nights like this. With you."

He observed her from above with that warming softness, then leaned over, snatched up the side of the linens, and swept it over them. Nesting them in white, cool softness.

As he pulled her head more comfortably into the crook of his arm and propped himself up to look down at her, she felt as if she . . . belonged. As if she belonged to this man. Completely. And it frightened her.

"Maybelle?" he murmured.

"Yes?" She anxiously looked up at him from the pillow he had made for her against his bare arm and shoulder.

He glanced down at her, then stared off somewhere to the side. "Make me an offer. Any offer. I will take it if it means having you like this."

Her eyes widened and her heart pounded. Did he want her to be his personal demimondaine? Dear God. How was that different from marriage? Both carried expectations. Commitment. And worst of all, emotional entanglement that was beyond her comprehension.

He shifted, brought around his other hand, and softly touched the side of her cheek. In a loving and gentle way that stirred something much deeper from within her.

And that is when reality came crashing down onto her. She couldn't have her independence and all of this. It was one or the other. "What more do you want from me, Your Grace?" she whispered. "Because I am confused as to what more I can give you without altogether handing over my independence."

He stiffened, his soft caress ceasing, and suddenly refused to meet her gaze.

After long, agonizing moments passed and he

still said nothing, she knew exactly what it meant. That he did not know what he wanted any more than she did.

She had to stop this. Now. Before it got any more out of hand. Maybelle sat up and gently pushed him aside. Scrambling off the bed, she hurried over to where her chemise lay and snatched it up. She wasn't even going to bother with her corset as she knew she couldn't get it back on without Edmund's help.

"I must take leave of you," she confided, pulling the chemise over her head and yanking it down over her body.

He sat up, the linens spilling down and around his naked waist. "I am willing to make concessions, Maybelle. All you need do is name them."

She turned away, keeping herself from facing him for fear she would not listen to her own sense of reason. "This is not about the concessions you must make. It is about the concessions I must make. And I will not make them. Edmund, ever since I was a girl I learned that being a wife came with too many expectations. Not to mention too many heartaches. All of which I refuse to take on."

He scrambled off the bed. "So there is nothing I can offer? Nothing at all?"

What else was there? What world existed between that of a wife and a demimondaine? There wasn't anything else. Maybelle held up a shaky hand to keep him from coming any closer. "You have already received your night from me. It is best we go our separate ways. You do not need to be attached to my troubles any more than I need to be attached to yours. Between us both, we have endured enough heartache and certainly do not need any more."

He paused, then after a few moments softly asked, "What if you are with child? What then?"

With child? Maybelle put a hand to her belly, the thought both exciting and frightening her. She still couldn't understand how she had allowed herself to compromise all of her beliefs in the name of pleasure.

She swallowed. "I will notify you of that. Now please. Do not complicate matters for me by coming to the school. And please do not use your anger by enlisting Parliament to shut down the school. My grandmother lives for her school. It is all she has left of her glory days."

Edmund was quiet for a long moment and she wondered what it was he was thinking. "I assure you I will not enlist Parliament."

She nodded, though strangely, the weight she felt inside of her remained unchanged. "Thank you, Your Grace. Understand that this is our last encounter."

"I understand." His voice now sounded distant. As if his mind had drifted somewhere else. "There is a carpetbag in the corner. Take it. As part of our agreement."

Maybelle struggled with the reality of what she was about to do and what it very well could mean. But there was no other way around it. Taking the money didn't feel right. She felt as if receiving his body had been payment enough. "Give it to charity, My Lord. I have no use for your money. I cannot accept this townhouse either. I respect you too much and have no intention of taking advantage of your generosity."

After a moment of prolonged silence, he murmured, "You may go now. If you must."

"Thank you." With that, she hurried past him and out of the room, not daring to look at him.

How had she fooled herself into thinking that she could hand over her body to him for a night and then walk away from the experience untouched? God help her, she had somehow lost herself to him without meaning to.

She used to be content with her way of thinking, her approach to life, her claim to independence. And now? All she wanted was this unfamiliar, aching pain within her to go away. To go away so she could return to the way things were. Untouched.

Long after Maybelle had departed, Edmund continued to simply stand naked in the middle of the bedroom feeling as though he'd been stripped not just of his clothes, but of his very heart. How? How had it happened? How had he allowed himself to fall in love with her?

He gritted his teeth, made his way toward the nearest wall, balled his hand into a fist, and slammed it against the paneling. The muscles in his arm jumped back as he savored the stinging throb in his knuckles, wanting to feel anything but this . . . this loss of control.

He wanted her. Wanted her so damn much that he didn't care anymore that she was merely the granddaughter of a courtesan. Didn't care if she ever learned the ways of a duchess or if the *ton* turned their backs on them completely. What was worse, he'd almost told her that. Almost admitted that he was in love with her.

But somehow, he couldn't force himself to do it. It remained buried deep inside, where he'd always kept his emotions under strict command. He simply could not force himself to let go and trust that she wouldn't abandon him in his time of need. Abandon him for her real lover—independence. For if his own father could betray him on every level, she could. And she would. The only difference here was that she at least was aware of her ability to hurt him.

Edmund turned and strode toward the far corner of the room. Yanking up the carpetbag filled with banknotes, he flung it hard against the wall. The bag exploded and banknotes fluttered everywhere, twirling and scattering across the floor.

Damn her!

Donate it to charity.

Was this all a goddamn game? He should have known he couldn't change her. Couldn't make her his. She was what she was. And he was what he was.

He turned and stared at the bed, where Maybelle had laid beside him only a few moments ago. All that was left now of her was her corset, hanging pathetically half off the bed. He shifted his jaw and slowly approached it. Taking it up and without thinking what it might do to him, he drew the smooth, yet stiff contraption to his nose.

He closed his eyes, breathing in the lavender oil scent of the woman he desperately wanted and needed, and tightly pressed his lips together from the agony of it all.

"Leave her be," he muttered, crunching the corset into a fist and looking back toward the open door. "Leave her be."

It was time to recognize that just because he finally learned to wholeheartedly love a woman, it did not mean that she would ever return that love.

Lesson Eighteen

Ah, love.
Everyone eventually wallows in it.
And although many drown, some manage to survive.
—The School of Gallantry

Late morning

Footsteps from outside the parlor caused Maybelle to pause and glance up from her sewing.

Clive entered, carrying a tray laden with tea and pastries. A tray she had not requested. He placed it on the small walnut table across from her and straightened.

"Thank you," she murmured, lowering her eyes back to the needlework and pulling a needle through.

She pretended that nothing was on her mind, although every time the thread caught, which seemed to occur more and more with each passing moment, she couldn't help compare the tangled mess before her with her life.

"You haven't eaten or taken tea since you returned late last night," Clive pointed out, still lingering before her.

Maybelle's cheeks grew warm as she remembered all too well how he and two other servants had witnessed her running in through the servants' door trying to keep her ripped gown from falling off her body. God knows what the rest of London saw. "I am not hungry, is all."

"You also never sew, Miss. Should I be concerned?"

"No." The needle came up through the material and pricked her finger. She winced, brought it to her mouth, and tried to suck out the pain.

"Allow me to fetch a thimble." Clive turned.

"No need. Really." Maybelle secured the needle into the quilt she was working on and set it aside for the first time in hours. "Is Grand-mère still sleeping?"

Clive turned back to her. "Last I knew."

Damn. Which meant she had nothing better to do but keep on sewing. For it was the only thing she was in possession of that didn't relate to sex, love, or relationships. Even the thought of Voltaire depressed her. For now she associated him with Edmund and the damn book he had to go and give her. She supposed there were other ways of distracting herself. "Speaking of thimbles, Clive, would you like to hear how they came to be?"

He stared at her for a long moment, unsure as to where their conversation was heading.

"My father once told me the story," she prodded.

He crooked a bushy brow. "Oh?"

Maybelle smiled and nodded, remembering how her father's voice always lowered into a hush whenever he related the tale. As if it were some great secret. "There was once a beautiful girl named Thimbla. She was a servant to a very rich, very titled man. A man she was madly in love with. So much, in fact, that she spent hours upon hours sewing the most beautiful things for him. Her master loved her as well, but despite that, they were forced to deny their love, for he was a nobleman and she naught but a servant. In time, he was set to marry someone else. A woman of equal status."

She sighed. "Heartbroken, Thimbla sewed herself into a frenzy until both her blistered thumbs bled from the agony of it all. On the day of her master's wedding, he secretly came to Thimbla and presented her with one last gift. A token of the secret love they would always share. It was a silver covering for her thumb that would protect her whenever she sewed."

Maybelle thoughtfully traced her finger. The finger where a wedding band might have rested had she accepted Edmund's proposal. "She accepted his last gift and wore the silver covering from that day forth, like a wedding band, never once removing it from her thumb *except* for when she sewed. She wanted to remind herself that there was no greater pain in this world than that caused by a broken heart. Since then, women have forgotten all about

Thimbla. They wear their little thimbles to protect themselves from pain, yet little do they realize that only through pain and sacrifice does one learn about the true meaning of love."

Maybelle looked away, blinked back tears, and nodded thoughtfully. She never understood her father. Never understood why the fool couldn't move past her mother's death. Witnessing his emotional imprisonment to a woman who no longer existed was something she'd learned to genuinely fear. And how.

Even on his deathbed all he really wanted was to hold the lock of her mother's golden hair which she'd given him when they first married. That's when Maybelle swore to herself she'd never marry or love. For she refused to be crippled in the same way her father had been. Needless to say, her grandmother's world had made it easy for her to keep that promise. And so here she was. Caught between two worlds.

Clive cleared his throat. "Shall I go and wake Madame for you?"

Maybelle bit back a laugh and shook her head, knowing what he was getting at. "There is really no need to worry, Clive. I'm well aware of the state of mind I'm in. Or rather the state I'm not in." She set aside her sewing. "Perhaps I should see to her. She has been sleeping for quite some time."

Clive bowed, resuming his position as butler, glanced at her one last time, then hurriedly departed.

Lovely. More stories for the servants to gossip about. Maybelle shook her head and rose from her chair. She should have kept her damn mouth shut. The trouble was, she inwardly ached so much, it was difficult for her to keep anything in.

Peering over toward the tray Clive had brought, she leaned toward it and picked up one of the three warm pastries beautifully laced with berries. She stared at it, the sticky, doughy texture clinging to her bare fingertips. Though it was her favorite, and the cook rarely made it, it looked strangely un-appetizing. And she knew all too well why.

Damn the man for altogether taking away her appetite. Thoroughly frustrated, she pinched her lips and made a fist, crushing the pastry. She watched it crumble through her knuckles and back down onto the plate like clumps of wet sand.

There. Now it looked exactly how she felt.

Sucking off the remaining stickiness from her fingers, she wiped her hand into the napkin. It was time to tell her grandmother all about the mess she'd made. Not with the pastry, of course, but with her life.

Maybelle slipped in through the door of the bedroom and softly closed it behind her. Her grandmother's silver head was propped against the pillows, her eyes closed, the center of her silk robe rising and falling with each soft breath she took.

Maybelle paused, and stepped back toward the

door to leave, when her grandmother opened her eyes and turned her head to look at her. She smiled sleepily and waved her over.

"How are you, Grand-mère?" she whispered, approaching her. "I didn't mean to wake you."

"Och, you did not wake me. I was merely resting my eyes." She sat up and patted the space beside her on the bed. "Before we delve into the delectable details of your evening with the duke, how was yesterday's lesson?"

Maybelle sat and stared down at her hands. Miserably. "It was rather short. And it . . . it resulted in my doing something I probably should not have done."

"Oh?"

Maybelle cringed and kept herself from wringing her hands. "I allowed the duke to make love to me sooner than what had been arranged."

"*In the bounds of my school?*"

"No! No. What happened is . . . well . . . he took over my lesson. Against my will. Carried me out of the school. Through the front door, mind you—sorry, I tried to reason with him—and then whisked me away to this—this townhouse. Before all of London and in broad daylight! And although the townhouse was empty, it was beautiful, Grand-mère. Upstairs, there was this glorious, white bed. Fit for a lady's wedding night. It was amazing. Utterly amazing. *He* was amazing. I never knew sex could be so amazing."

Her grandmother shifted and leaned toward her, trying to get a better look at her face. "So what is the problem?" she drawled.

"Oh." Maybelle winced at the faux pas she was about to confess and felt her cheeks burning. "Well, actually, I . . . allowed him to spill his seed into me."

Her grandmother's brows went up and she slowly sat back. "I see." She hesitated, then tilted her silver head slightly to the side before matter-of-factly saying, "Your father came about that way. I know I never regretted it. After all, Henri made my life worth living and gave me so many wonderful memories before he left for England."

Her grandmother smiled warmly. "He also gave me you. Understand that there will always be moments of passion, chère, you cannot predict. It is to be expected."

"I also didn't take the money. I—I couldn't. It didn't feel right." She chewed on her bottom lip, readying herself for the whole free baked-goods lecture.

Her grandmother stared at her, her blue eyes widening. "Why, you're in love with him. You're in love with the duke."

Maybelle sucked in a sharp breath. Oh dear God. "No. I can't be. I shouldn't be."

"Denial. Och, an obvious sign." Her grandmother grabbed for her hand, shook it, and let out a small laugh. "Well. There goes your independence and your promising career with the school, eh?"

Maybelle glared at her. "Oh, for heaven's sake, be serious. This isn't love. I am simply overwhelmed by the ordeal. I've never given my body to a man before."

"Or your heart." Her grandmother puckered her lips and patted her hand. "There, there. All will be fine, I assure you. The misery you feel will pass. It is merely a matter of how you want it to pass. Naturally, with time? Or sooner, by you simply deciding to go back to the man who is causing the misery? If I were you, I would pick the latter. There is no need to make yourself or those around you suffer."

Maybelle yanked her hand away from her grandmother and tried to control the rapid beating of her heart. "I couldn't possibly go to him. I told him I never wanted to see him again. And I don't."

"No?"

"No."

"Why not?"

"Because . . . *oh because!*" Maybelle winced knowing how stupid she sounded even to herself. Where had her sense of reason gone to? "I don't know why I'm so confused, Grand-mère. I thought I was capable of playing the role of a demimondaine for one night, knowing everything I do about sex, yet I found myself unable to accept what I have done. It felt wrong taking anything from him. His body and all the pleasure he gave me was enough payment for me."

Her grandmother sat back against her pillows, closed her eyes, and pressed a hand to her lips. After a few moments of silence she whispered, "This is my fault, chère. All my fault." She opened her eyes, half nodded, and lowered her hand. "I have taught you far more about sex than I did love."

Her grandmother sighed. "I will have you know

that passion should never be feared. Only embraced. For it leads us down beautiful, unexpected paths. When I turned fifteen, Maybelle, my world changed. I blossomed. Every man in the village suddenly noticed my breasts, my face, my body, and I, of course, noticed that they noticed. And I rather liked the attention. More than any God-fearing girl should. My parents were understandably worried and before long arranged for me to marry the pastor's son. Och. Perish the thought."

Her grandmother's blue eyes lit up and her pale face visibly flushed as she leaned toward her. "One morning, three weeks before I was to marry, I was walking alongside the road heading toward the market. And that is when I came upon the most beautiful man I had ever seen in my life. Duc de Andelot. He was half French, half British. An explosive combination. Andelot rode toward me upon his horse. When he came upon me, he slowed. Then completely stopped."

Her grandmother glanced lovingly up toward the canopy of the bed as if he were there now. "Our eyes met and suddenly, I was swept upon his horse and into his life. Nothing mattered. Nothing. I fled everything to be with him. Andelot introduced me to a violent passion I never thought possible. A passion that is still with me to this day. I would have married him, chère, but I was naught but a thimble on his thumb. I was but his Thimbla."

Maybelle's lips parted as her eyes widened. Thimbla? Like the story Papa had told her? Impossible.

Never would she have connected it to her grandmother. Ever.

A tremor touched her grandmother's lips and
she shook her head. "When I became pregnant
with Henri, that is when everything changed. Andelot had me swear that I would never reveal to the
world Henri was his. And though it assassinated my
soul, I understood. He gave me a generous settle-
ment, a beautiful house and told me when Henri
was born I should try to lead a respectable life.
Without him."

Her grandmother was quiet for a long moment,
as if reminiscing, then cocked her head and
grinned. "Respectable, indeed. After the passions
he had introduced me to, I had acquired an insa-
tiable thirst for sex. After several unsatisfying experiences as a demimondaine, I started thinking
about creating a school to better educate men. And
so here I am with you and my wonderful School of
Gallantry."

Maybelle swallowed hard, struggling against tears
that were now blinding her. For she finally knew. Finally knew why her grandmother was what she was.
"Why did you never tell me?" she whispered, grabbing her hand and squeezing it. "I would have been
more understanding. More supportive."

Her grandmother reached out her free hand and
gently patted the side of her face. "I did not think it
necessary to burden you with my past. At twelve, you
were already cynical about men and relationships.
I did not want to add to it by making you think a

man made me into what I am today. It would have destroyed any possibility for you to enjoy men."

Taking back her hand, her grandmother settled against the pillows once again and whispered, "Allow me to give you advice, Maybelle. The only advice I can give you on this very complicated subject matter. Tell him how you feel. If he feels the same, you may have a different ending from mine. Unlike my Andelot, who could not get past our differences, this one is willing to offer you marriage. The question is, what are you willing to offer up in return?"

Maybelle choked in unexpected sentiment. Sentiment she never knew she was capable of. Swiping away tears, she scrambled off the bed. "No. I can't. I can't crawl back to him after what I said. He will think I'm a complete want-wit. Confused. Mad."

"Pride has no place when it comes to love, chère." Her grandmother waved her off. "Go. Tell him how you feel."

"But if I tell him how I feel, or rather what I think I feel, and he doesn't feel the same, he will take advantage of me. I know he will. He enjoys sex far too much."

Her grandmother eyed her, that playful glint now returning. "Is he any good?"

Maybelle's mouth dropped open. She pointed at her. "I am *not* disclosing any details. That is rude."

Her grandmother shrugged. "Perhaps I am pushing too hard. Give it time. Think about what I have said." She leveled her with a soft gaze. "Now be honest with your grand-mère. How concerned should I be?

Will this affect the school in any way? Should I be acquiring another teacher? Or getting out of bed?"

Maybelle dropped her hand back to her side and blew out an exhausted breath. "No," she grumbled.

"Good. Because it is supposed to be a school that teaches men the art of seduction. Not the art of misery. Take a week off to clear your mind, oui? I will inform everyone that you are ill and pull together some of my own lessons for them."

Ill.

Right.

That certainly made her feel better.

Lesson Nineteen

Games can be delicious.
Games can be divine.
But when they go wrong
remember, 'tis your fault, not mine.
                    —*The School of Gallantry*

Five days later, late morning

A curt knock sounded on the bedroom door. Maybelle set aside the lesson plan she'd been tediously working on and rose from the writing desk set against the window. "Yes?"

"Lord Hawksford to see you, Miss," Clive called out from the other side of the door.

Maybelle froze before she could get to the door. What on earth could Hawksford possibly want? She was planning to attend school tomorrow.

"Shall I tell him you are indisposed?" Clive prodded from the other side.

Drat. No doubt all of London already knew her business. She had to face this. Head-on. "Tell him I will be down shortly!"

Maybelle hurried over to her mirror set in the corner of the room, leaned toward it, and checked her face. Why did she look so pale? She pinched her cheeks. Smoothing out her full indigo skirts, she stepped back and set her chin. She would face whatever Hawksford had come to say. With dignity.

Rushing over to the door, she threw it open and quickly made her way down. When she reached the bottom stair of the foyer, she took in a deep calming breath and then breezed into the parlor.

Hawksford rose from the sofa. His green eyes met hers as he gave a small bow. "Madam."

"My Lord." Maybelle smiled, suddenly feeling a return of her old self. And it was nice for a change. "It pleases me to see you walking on your own again."

He chuckled. "I was rather disappointed you didn't choose to take advantage of my condition."

She smirked. "In your condition there was nothing to take advantage of."

Hawksford grinned and put up a gloved hand. "I confess I have not come here to duel." He strode toward her, quickly closing the distance between them. He paused only an arm's length away, his lemon and leather scent teasing her.

After eyeing her, he said in a low, devious tone, "Caldwell is hosting another one of those infamous gatherings. I was rather hoping you'd join me."

Maybelle's eyes widened and heat spread across her face as she remembered the last time she went. "Although I am . . ." Oh dear God, what was the right word for this situation? "*Honored* that you'd think of me, I regret to inform you, My Lord, that I am not available."

Hawksford's green eyes sparkled with mischief. "Ah. Now what if I were to tell you that we both stand to benefit from going tonight?"

She pulled in her chin. "Benefit? From what? I don't know what the devil you're up to, My Lord, but I have absolutely no—"

"*Rutherford will be there*," he sing-songed, raising both brows. "The poor man is only attending because Caldwell told him you'd be there. You wouldn't want to disappoint Rutherford, would you?"

Maybelle froze. Edmund wanted to see her? Even after she had outright rejected him? Why?

Hawksford sidled up beside her, leaned in with his large body, and slid a gloved hand around her shoulder, swallowing her whole. "Furthermore, there is this rather amazing widow Caldwell is inviting. She rarely makes public appearances and I mean to make the best of it. While you—you clearly need to finish this unpleasant business with Rutherford. It is affecting the quality of my education. Which is why I was hoping you and I could . . ." He made a rolling gesture with his free gloved hand as if that explained everything.

Maybelle moved out of his grasp and took another large step aside. She crossed her arms over her chest and narrowed her gaze. "What are you suggesting, My Lord?"

He scratched at his chin, eyeing her. "That wasn't plain enough for you?"

She rolled her eyes. "*No.*"

"I see." He cleared his throat. "'Tis simple, really. Make my widow jealous, and I will make your Rutherford jealous. What say you?"

Maybelle dropped her hands to her sides. A rather devious, not to mention absolutely ridiculous, approach in dealing with the opposite sex. Then again, it's not like she'd been able to come up with a better way to approach Edmund after telling him to more or less sod off.

She'd been thinking about things these past few days. About how miserable she was. About the fun times they'd shared. About all the amazing sex they'd had. And she'd come to the conclusion that she could manage, at the very least, being his mistress. And if they happened to be ill matched?

Oh bother. Why think about it anymore? "What time?"

A slow smile spread across Hawksford's face. "I knew you'd see reason."

To her utter and complete frustration, Maybelle had spent most of her evening searching for Edmund amidst the overcrowded and noisy townhouse. Hawksford took liberties by grabbing for her waist and pulling her close, instructing her to stay close and in the front parlor or they'd never be seen.

What if Edmund wasn't coming? What if he changed his mind and didn't want to see her? What if—

Maybelle froze, jerking Hawksford to a complete halt.

Edmund stood not even twenty feet away, dressed in perfect, black evening attire, jacket and all. His right shoulder was to her and he was gazing out at the crowds around him. In one gloved hand, he held a glass of champagne, while his other gloved hand was tucked behind his broad back.

Her pulse livened at the reality that she was actually standing in his presence. And that he'd put his respectability on the line again to see her.

Seeing him standing there alone, as everyone else around them groped, chatted, drank, and laughed, gave her pause. And for a crazed moment, she wondered how he would react to her if she abandoned all plans with Hawksford and simply went up to him and offered simple pleasantries? Would there be a loss of dignity by doing that?

A woman dressed in black satin strode in from behind Edmund. The beautiful dark-haired woman had a perfect curvy physique, beautiful porcelain skin, and sizable breasts that would have made her grandmother quite jealous.

She sashayed her way around Edmund, the way a vulture did around the food it was about to indulge in, and paused before him. She offered Edmund a rather provocative and inviting smile as she reached out a gloved hand and openly touched his arm.

Maybelle felt her throat tightening. Had they arrived together?

Hawksford tightened his hold on Maybelle's waist and positioned them both toward Edmund's direction. As if only now seeing them.

Maybelle narrowed her gaze as Edmund leaned toward the beautiful woman to receive her words. He shook his dark head and said something, yet made no effort to remove the woman's hand, which continued to rest on his forearm. They must have arrived together. They were rather friendly.

Hawksford leaned down toward Maybelle. "There she is," he whispered into her right ear. "My Lady Chartwell."

Maybelle's heart nearly stopped altogether. She glanced up at Hawksford. "Did you say Lady Chartwell? You mean, the same Lady Chartwell who is giving my grandmother usage of the school's passage?"

He grinned. "Indeed. And did you also know that she hunts down men like the poor sheep that they are, takes whatever she desires of them, and then discards them completely, leaving them to drown in their unrequited lust? She is quite vicious. Though I mean to change that."

Maybelle's eyes widened as she snapped her attention back to Edmund and Lady Chartwell. Had Edmund somehow met her during his journey through her townhouse and into the school? Impossible. She herself had never had a chance to meet the woman. Certainly she'd met all of the woman's servants, but never the woman herself. So why was it that while she had never met this Lady Chartwell while going in and out of her townhouse, all of the men seemed to know her?

This did not bode well. At all. There was a rather wicked purpose behind why Lady Chartwell supported the School of Gallantry. For no respectable, titled woman ever would. Which is why it bothered Maybelle to no end that the woman was now trying to engage in theatrics with her Edmund.

Maybelle turned back to Hawksford and demanded, "Did they arrive together?"

The onyx buttons on Hawksford's perfectly cut black jacket gleamed as he adjusted his hold on her waist. He glanced down at her. "I would only worry if they *left* together. Then we both have a rather serious situation on our hands." He winked.

Maybelle waved an agitated hand toward Lady Chartwell, who was still talking to Edmund. "As your teacher, Hawksford, I advise you to do something. Immediately."

He glanced down at her, raising both brows. "And what exactly do you suggest I do?"

She smacked at his arm. "What we had planned!"

Hawksford smirked. "Of course."

Maybelle glanced over at Edmund, who had completely turned toward the dark-haired woman and seemed genuinely immersed in their conversation.

A flare of jealousy pounded her brain and all

reason went out the window. The woman hunted men like the sheep that they were? Really now. What could that possibly mean? Furthermore, why did it bother her so much? She was supposed to be making Edmund jealous. Not making herself jealous.

"Shall I begin?" Hawksford offered matter-of-factly.

Maybelle set her chin. "Yes. Do."

With that, they strolled toward the two. Hawksford with his arm still around her waist and Maybelle holding her arm around his trying to act like it was the most natural thing in the world. And though she tried hard to exude calm and confidence, she could already feel her camisole melting into her corset.

"It's rather hot in here, isn't it?" Hawksford commented when they were within earshot. "Do you mind assisting me out of this jacket, love?"

Cue. Maybelle eased out of Hawksford's arm and turned toward him. Keeping her voice natural and steady, she replied, "But of course. I rather prefer a man without his jacket."

Hawksford grinned down at her and leaned his solid frame toward her, clearly enjoying their game a bit too much. "Remember," he whispered, "if you and Rutherford ever do decide to go your separate ways, you will always have me and the school."

Perish the thought. Maybelle ignored the spark of amusement in his green eyes and instead worked to slowly remove his jacket one sleeve at a time, painfully aware that she was touching a man who wasn't

Edmund. She slipped the jacket from Hawksford's warm muscled shoulders and held it up for him.

Hawksford adjusted his vest and his cuffs, then grabbed the jacket and flung it off to the side, missing a couple who were on the floor frantically groping each other and making disgusting sounds.

Maybelle genuinely grinned, took his arm, and leaned into him. Hawksford finally turned them toward Edmund and together they closed the remaining distance between all of them.

Both Edmund and the dark-haired Lady Chartwell were already staring at them. Lady Chartwell appeared quite fascinated by their approach, a dark elegant brow perched high.

Edmund, on the other hand, didn't. His dark eyes met hers, his lean face set and his smooth-shaven jaw clenched.

Maybelle tried to keep the heat from rising to her face as she tightened her hold on Hawksford's arm. She only hoped to God Hawksford would keep walking so she wouldn't have to say anything as of yet. For she still hadn't thought of anything to say to the man that wouldn't make her sound like a babbling idiot.

Hawksford drew them both to a sudden halt right before the two.

Damn him. He would.

"Rutherford," Hawksford drawled, gesturing toward him. "Where the devil have you been? We've had quite a few lessons since we last saw you."

Clearly, Hawksford had no trouble fibbing through every single one of his teeth. For the men had been completely deprived of a teacher. And mostly due to Edmund. Maybelle struggled to remain calm as Edmund continued to stare her down.

To her relief, he eventually turned his dark gaze to Hawksford. Edmund surveyed him for a long moment, then coolly replied, "Unlike yours, my life does not evolve around the school."

Hawksford grabbed hold of Maybelle's waist and yanked her hard against the side of his large frame, causing her to almost gasp from the crushing hold. "Pity." Hawksford eyed the widow. "Maybelle was giving invaluable advice as to how to deliver multiple orgasms to one's lover. Seems I am quite good at it. Isn't that so, Maybelle?"

Maybelle choked. She tried desperately to pretend she was coughing but it was no use. For there was no bloody way she was going to answer that.

Edmund narrowed his gaze in response, while Lady Chartwell had a gleam in her sultry brown eyes as she scooted toward the direction of Hawksford.

"Is such a thing even possible, My Lord?" she asked in a low, seductive voice.

Hawksford leaned toward the woman, forcing Maybelle to lean right along with him. "Anything is possible when you submit yourself to the right man."

Maybelle kept herself from rolling her eyes.

The supper bell rang in the distance, calling the first set of guests into the dining hall that was just down the corridor.

Beautiful timing!

Maybelle yanked Hawksford back. "Take me to supper, My Lord." She trained her gaze on Hawksford, afraid to even acknowledge Edmund anymore. What a dim-witted failure she was.

Hawksford paused, his brows coming together as he eyed her, but otherwise didn't argue. "Do excuse us." He nodded in the direction of his widow. "It was a pleasure. As always."

Maybelle could have sworn the widow was breathing hard. Apparently, it didn't take much to excite the woman. And Edmund? God knows what Edmund was thinking the way he was glaring at them. She'd be lucky if he ever talked to her again. Good at delivering multiple orgasms indeed. Romeo could have done better on opium.

Hawksford turned them away and led them toward the dining hall. "You think I overdid it?" he whispered down at her.

"A bit."

Hawksford chuckled. "I would not trust that woman to Rutherford."

"If we don't see them in the dining room in ten minutes, we will hunt them down."

He eyed her. "You do realize that anything can happen in ten minutes?"

"For heaven's sake, Hawksford!" She glared at him.

"Well, it is true."

When they finally arrived in the small dining room, Maybelle glanced around, surprised. Considering the sort of gathering it was, she was truly impressed by the effort Caldwell had put into it. For it appeared a bit more respectable than the last gathering of his she'd attended.

White garlands decorated the mahogany-paneled room. The china, crystal, and silverware were so well polished they reflected the candles around them, giving a glittering shimmer to the long dining table.

After making their way around other couples, Hawksford found her a seat and pulled it back and out for her. She nodded her thanks.

After she was seated at the crowded table, she picked up her lace napkin and laid it carefully on the lap of her burgundy gown. She didn't know how long she'd last knowing she'd left Edmund alone with that . . . *she-lion.*

Maybelle glanced around the noisy table wondering if she should already be heading back. She paused, however, when her gaze unexpectedly met Edmund's dark eyes just across from where she was seated. Her eyes widened and her breath caught inside her throat.

Edmund pulled out a chair for himself. He stared her down from across the table even as he seated himself.

Despite all common sense, Maybelle offered him a genuine smile, thrilled that he had actually followed her to the table.

He shifted his jaw, as if considering what her smile meant, then gave a curt nod in her direction.

She eyed their surroundings. What was even more promising is that there was no sight of the widow.

One of the servants paused beside her, leaned in, and held out a silver dish for her to look at. She paused. Lovely. Seems there was no soup or appetizers to begin the meal, but rather roasted partridges in mint sauce. Then again, what was she to expect from a gathering she was actually able to attend?

"Half of one, please," she said over all the loud chatter. Hopefully the man could hear.

The servant hesitated as he searched for the best piece of meat, and then gave her the portion she'd requested.

Hawksford leaned toward her. "Not to be rude, but I intend to excuse myself. I am not all that fond of little birds bathed in unidentifiable sauces."

Maybelle eyed him and hoarsely whispered back, "Don't you dare leave me."

"I promise to return, love." Hawksford planted a soft, warm kiss on the base of her neck, startling her out of her wits, and rose, leaving her at the table alone.

And yes. Everyone witnessed it. Including Edmund, who stiffened in response.

The men and women at the table started removing their gloves, preparing to eat their meal. Maybelle glanced across from her. Edmund was boldly examining her. He lifted his hand slightly above the table and slowly and seductively used his teeth to pull on the fingers of his white gloves. Watching her the whole while.

Maybelle swallowed hard against the clenching dryness in her throat, realizing only at a gathering like this would he dare to remove his gloves so animalistically. What was worse, it made her want him more remembering how that mouth had kissed her, how those teeth had nibbled on her during their lovemaking.

By the smirk on his face, she had no doubt he was doing it on purpose. And she had no trouble showing him up.

Maybelle stripped her gloves off one by one, folded them neatly into one another, then slowly slid them down the length of her throat and straight into the front of her bosom. A place where no lady ever tucked her gloves.

Edmund's brows rose as he eyed her bosom. He shoved his gloves beside his plate, looking agitated.

She smiled, pleased with the result. Just as she was about to pluck up her knife and fork, the side of a shoe brushed the leg of her skirt below the table. Her eyes widened as she glanced up. Was he actually flirting with her beneath the table?

Edmund shifted in his seat, the gentle pressure of his shoe disappearing, and took to eating his partridge as if nothing had occurred.

The tinkering of silverware against china surrounded her, along with the multitude of humming voices. Every now and then her gaze met Edmund's across the table. And every time, she swore his heated gaze grew in intensity.

By the time dessert was served, nearly an hour later, she was wishing she could crawl across the table, grab him by the collar, and have her way with him. If only to rid herself of the wretched yearning she felt for him.

When supper was finally over—*oh, thank goodness for that*—Maybelle rose and quickly left the table, hoping to gain a sense of composure. The biggest dilemma the evening presented was trying to figure out how she was to approach Edmund without appearing to be cork brained.

Hawksford reappeared and caught her arm just as she was leaving the dining room. "How was supper? Good?"

"Well, I—" Maybelle paused and noted that Hawksford's bronzed hair was scattered and hanging sloppily down into his eyes. And his cravat, gloves, and collar were missing. What was worse— she sniffed, leaning toward him—she smelled cognac. Which she hoped explained the visible wetness on the front of his vest.

She lowered her chin. "*You did not.*"

He grinned, his face flushing for the first time since she'd known him. "I did."

Maybelle leaned toward him. "You'll be taking arsenic treatments for it, you realize."

"Hardly. A man of my experience always comes prepared." Hawksford reached out and plucked her gloves out of her bosom as if it were the most natural thing in the world. He handed them to her. "What about you?"

Maybelle grabbed her gloves from him and yanked them on, strangely annoyed that Hawksford had received more than she had. "I received a foot from under the table. Nothing more," she muttered as they headed out of the dining room and back to the bustling festivities.

"We shall have to remedy that. Immediately." Hawksford held out his arm and gestured toward the crowded rooms beyond. "Shall we instate a bit of public display?"

She grabbed hold of his arm and smiled. "Yes. Only be sure not to get carried away."

"Me? Never. Now. Remove your gloves."

Lesson Twenty

When you realize that your conquest
is not adhering to the straight path
you have set out for her to follow,
it may be time to admit
that perhaps the road you have paved
is rather crooked and in desperate need of repair.
—*The School of Gallantry*

Edmund watched Maybelle as she rose and left the dining table, her burgundy gown shifting seductively around her slim body and small waist. The back of her soft long neck and her exposed, creamy shoulders melted him with the memory of their night together. A night that would forever be scorched in his mind.

She paused in the doorway and was greeted by a very disheveled Hawksford, who quickly caught her arm. Edmund narrowed his gaze. That is why the bastard left the table. To shag. And no doubt he did it before a cheering crowd.

Hawksford leaned toward Maybelle, plucked her gloves from her bosom, and handed them to her. Edmund's stomach knotted at the obvious intimacy the two shared. Regardless, no two-timing bloody son of a bitch who'd just left her side to go stick his cock into some woman was going to then try to stick it into Maybelle.

What shocked him to no end was that Maybelle didn't seem to mind. At all. She actually took the bastard's arm and offered him a smile as they disappeared out into the corridor.

What happened to that whole not wanting to be a demimondaine bit? He refused to believe the two were an item. Hawksford had always agitated her. But then again, so had he. Damn it all.

Edmund stood, leaned in toward the table, grabbed up his glass of wine, and finished it. Seeing one of the servants walk by with a decanter of wine, he waved the servant over, had another glass poured, and drank that one as well.

Slamming his glass onto the table, he strode down the length of the table and made his way into the corridor and into the crowded rooms of the townhouse. He kept walking until he paused just off a makeshift dance floor where a lone violinist stood playing the strings of his instrument with only a pair of trousers and boots on.

Edmund searched for Maybelle and Hawksford. And sure enough, there they were.

Hand in hand. Dancing. And neither one of them was wearing gloves. Hawksford's skin was touching her skin. As if they did that sort of thing all the time.

Suddenly, Edmund couldn't breathe. And though he tried to slow the beating of his heart, he could not seem to gain control over it.

Maybelle's beautiful, flushed face appeared in and out of view as she whisked forward and back, her full burgundy gown swaying with each brisk movement. Hawksford watched her intently the whole time. In the sort of way a man watched a woman before he threw her onto his bed. And the ass that he was went as far as stealing kisses from her by bringing her bare hand up to his lips every time their dancing brought them near.

Although Edmund wanted to murder the bastard there and then, he knew that in some way this whole matter was his own doing. His greed and his lust for her had publicly compromised her to such an extent that it made her appealing to the likes of Hawksford.

Fisting both hands, Edmund forced himself to turn away, before he gave into his urge to outright storm the dance floor, throttle Hawksford senseless, and announce to all of London that Maybelle was still his. Even if she didn't want to be.

Christ. He should have never allowed Caldwell to convince him into coming. Brilliant manner of resolving unfinished business. Idiot.

Blowing out an exhausted breath, he decided it was best to head to the refreshment room and cool his thoughts. If he was going to survive the remainder of the night without murdering anyone, he had better go off and numb his senses. Or at least damn well try.

When Maybelle left the dance floor with Hawksford, after a total of seven exhausting dances—which would have had the *ton* in a fit for months if they had been around to see it—she glanced around the room. Why hadn't Edmund followed her? She hadn't seen him in the longest time.

"I must find him," Maybelle insisted, yanking Hawksford, who was leading her, to a complete halt. "No more games. I must bring an end to this suffering of mine." She hated admitting that she was in fact suffering, but there was simply no way around it.

Hawksford turned toward her and after glancing around pointed at her. "If you and he do not resolve this within the hour, I will have no choice but to get involved. You understand?"

Maybelle smiled and patted him on the shoulder. "I appreciate your enthusiasm. Thank you." She gathered her silk skirts and weaved her way through people.

"One hour!" Hawksford called after her.

"Yes, yes," she muttered to herself. One would think *he* had something to gain.

As she wandered through room after room, past naked bodies and moans galore, none of the faces around her were familiar. Face after face and there was still no sign of him. Then again, there was no sign of the widow either.

An hour had already passed. And if Hawksford was at all true to his word, he would no doubt get involved. God forbid.

Maybelle made her way around the house again and prayed Edmund hadn't left. Prayed she hadn't lost the opportunity to see him. And explain everything.

She blew out a breath, exhausted, and made her way into the refreshment room just beyond the gambling room. Drifting over toward one of the serving tables, she paused for a long moment and couldn't even bring herself to consider what it was she wanted to drink.

She sighed, wondering if she should simply investigate every bedroom upstairs a bit more thoroughly, then finally said to the server, "Champagne, please."

"Not gin?" a deep voice drawled from behind.

Maybelle froze, recognizing the voice. Edmund? She slowly turned, inwardly yearning to see him, yet dreading that she would have to explain her actions with regards to Hawksford.

Edmund towered close behind her, a nearly empty snifter of cognac in his right gloved hand. He observed her with unusually heavy and hazy dark eyes. A slow, sloppy grin spread across his handsome face. "So." He jauntily cocked his dark head to one side. "How are you?"

She took in a sharp breath. Dear God. Edmund

Worthington, the sixth Duke of Rutherford, was as drunk as a sailor heading out to sea.

Edmund crooked a brow at her, whirling the remnants of his cognac inside the glass snifter. "I never realized Hawksford took your fancy."

"He never took my fancy." Maybelle lowered her chin slightly, still in disbelief, but did not break his gaze. "And you are utterly foxed."

"A *brilliant* observation. And I must confess . . . I haven't been this foxed since—" He looked around himself as if looking for someone to tell him, then shrugged. "Hell." He lifted his glass to her, but didn't drink from it. "Cheers."

Had her act with Hawksford actually led him to such a state? Her heart pounded. Impossible.

"You are beautiful, by the way. Dressed all in—" He reached out his other hand and fingered the upper sleeve of her gown. He then ran his gloved hand down the length of her bare arm. "Burgundy, is it?" He glanced down into his snifter and murmured, "I rather like burgundy."

Sparks skid across Maybelle's skin where he had touched her. She glanced around. "Your Grace, you should sit."

"Nonsense." He made a face as if she were being absurd and stepped back. He lifted his glass to his lips, but paused and lowered it back again. "I hate partridges. Hate eating them. You know that?"

Maybelle laughed and looked toward those around them and noticed people were beginning to take interest in their conversation. Fortunately, they were among friends, so to speak. "Your Grace, clearly you are not in any condition to—"

"Pardon." He swiveled away and waved over one of the servants who had a decanter of cognac. The servant hurried over, paused, then partly filled his glass with more amber liquid. Edmund tilted the decanter against the man's will and filled his glass completely to the rim.

The servant yanked back the decanter before the cognac all poured out and just as quickly departed, shaking his head.

Edmund swiveled back and lifted the glass to her. "To the most beautiful woman in all of London." He paused. "In England." He paused again, reconsidering. "In Europe." He paused yet again. "No. In this vast world." He nodded, then tilted his head back and drank the entire contents.

Maybelle choked. As if he'd poured it down her own throat. He . . . he thought she was that beautiful? Surely, it was the drink having this discussion with her. Not him.

"Edmund," she breathed in concern, reaching out for him. "How much have you had to drink?"

"Not enough." Turning away, he waved back the same servant. The servant hurried over with the decanter again, eyeing her nervously, and refilled it.

Obviously, this routine of waving down the servant is what had led him to the state he was in.

Edmund lifted the filled snifter to his lips.

"I think you have had more than enough, Your Grace." Maybelle leaned toward him and tried snatching the glass away from his mouth, but he held on to it with brute force.

"I refuse to let you—" She wrenched the glass away from him, splashing cognac all over the front of her dress. She gurgled out a laugh, and tried to brush off the beads of liquid, but her satin dress had already absorbed it. Yet another gown . . . ruined. Perhaps she should have taken the damn hundred thousand pounds for all the dresses she'd destroyed while knowing him.

"Hell." Edmund stepped forward and leaned toward her, also trying to brush off the cognac with his large hands, although he seemed more intent on brushing whatever had splashed across the rounds of her breasts.

She smiled down at him, enjoying the tender care he was putting into his efforts even if they were completely misguided.

The servant came by and gestured frantically toward the snifter she was holding. "No more," the man mouthed.

Oh dear. When the servant was complaining, clearly the drinking had to be brought to a stop. Maybelle held the glass out for the servant just as Edmund stepped away. The servant grabbed for the glass and scampered off before he was caught stealing.

Edmund glanced around, as if realizing something was missing, but couldn't quite figure it out. He blew out a heavy breath, raked his hands through his dark hair, and then dropped them to his sides. "I saw you dancing with Hawksford. Without gloves."

Yes. And it was about time to confess all, even if he wouldn't remember any of it in the morning. "About that. Understand that it was all a silly, silly game. I didn't know how else I was supposed to approach you after the horrible things I said. I was rather hoping that perhaps you and I could talk and—"

"We dance first. Talk later."

Maybelle's heart skipped as Edmund scooped her into his arms and commenced twirling her about the refreshment room, scattering people from their path. He pressed her firmly against him, his body and his sandalwood scent tingling all of her overextended senses. He was leading her to a rather bad version of the waltz.

"Your Grace!" she insisted, turning her head and trying to focus on their surroundings, which seemed to be growing more crowded with observers. And needless to say, when people at a risqué gathering stared, there was trouble to be had.

His arm tightened around her as he danced her past a group of men who had paused in their drinking to watch them. Edmund inclined his dark head toward them. "Good evening, gentlemen. This lady here is mine. All mine."

Maybelle scrambled to keep up with him, her skirts fumbling around her legs. "Edmund, you'll regret this come morning!"

"I certainly hope so." He then brought them both

to a rushed stop, his muscled arms keeping her in place. His face softened as he slowly pulled away. Drawing his left hand from around her waist, he touched her chin. "You left," he whispered hoarsely. "And I never said it."

"Said what?" Her heart pounded wildly at being touched by him again. And with such tenderness. Obviously, he'd forgiven her.

Edmund paused for a moment, then blurted, "I love you. There."

Her eyes widened as she sucked in a harsh breath. Oh dear God. It wasn't possible. How could he? How could he have fallen in love with her? She blinked several times and stepped outside of his reach. No. This was too soon. Much too soon to be love. What was she supposed to do now? What was she supposed to say?

He stared her down, strangely looking stunned despite his drunken state. "You've nothing to say? At all?"

She swallowed hard and felt herself actually shaking. He had to be saying it only to get her to give in. Truly. How could a man like him ever love a woman of her birth?

"Is Rutherford bothering you, Madam?" Hawksford's deep, timbered voice drawled from beside her.

Startled, Maybelle turned and glanced up toward Hawksford. To her further shock, Hawksford's dark brows were set and his hazy green eyes locked on Edmund as if he intended to gut him. And she knew. Hawksford was about as drunk out of his trousers as Edmund was.

"Everything is lovely. Absolutely lovely. Thank you." She patted Hawksford on the shoulder and then pointed toward the doorway. "Go. Please."

Edmund stepped toward Hawksford. "You heard her. Off with you, boyo." Reaching out, Edmund ruffled Hawksford's hair, causing some of his bronze strands to stand up on end. "There's no shagging to be had here. Sorry."

Hawksford smacked Edmund's hand away and staggered toward him. "Don't bloody touch me and don't bloody call me boyo. You know nothing of me." He pointed at him. "I suggest you go back to school, Rutherford, and learn a bit more about women before trying to overindulge."

Edmund stepped toward Hawksford, a dark look now crossing his face. "I suggest you leave and tend to that poor girl you keep locked up in your rooms. Don't you even feed her? Or are you too occupied with your own needs to remember?"

Hawksford narrowed his gaze and the color of his shaven face visibly heightened. "Is that a challenge?" he seethed through his teeth.

Edmund leaned toward him, also narrowing his gaze, and pointed a rigid finger into his chest. "*Pistols.*"

Oh, no. This was about to get out of hand. And though she knew absolutely nothing about some starving girl being locked away, it did not bode well for a reasonable resolution.

Maybelle hurried in between the two and pushed each one away from the other. "Gentlemen, please. Hawksford, enough. What I really need you to do is—"

Hawksford yanked her out from between them and shoved her behind himself. "I will defend my sister's honor."

Maybelle stumbled back, stunned. His sister's honor? What in—

"I'll have you know," Hawksford said, spacing his words out evenly as he drew steadily closer to Edmund, "that my sister is dying. So while you damn well go about and publicly insult a dying girl, how about I return the favor? Last night"—Hawksford hit his own chest with a proud, aggressive thud— "I fucked Maybelle. Repeatedly. And she loved it. Said that I was far better equipped than you ever will be."

Maybelle's eyes widened and she didn't know if she should laugh hysterically or cry from the shame of it all.

"How about I equip you with a new face!" Edmund snapped up his right hand and smashed his fist into Hawksford's face, sending Hawksford stumbling back into the waiter who stood by with the decanter.

Maybelle flinched, covering her eyes with both hands as cognac and shards of glass exploded everywhere. Oh dear God!

"*Hit him again!*" some want-wit yelled out from across the room. "*Agaaaain!*"

Edmund's chest heaved as he held his fist steady and clenched in midair, waiting for Hawksford to come at him. Hawksford scrambled up to his booted feet, growled something out, and charged back at Edmund, grabbing him by the throat and delivering a solid blow into Edmund's side.

Edmund stumbled back into the crowd behind him, who then playfully tossed him back toward Hawksford.

"Cease this nonsense! Cease this at once!" Maybelle rushed toward Edmund and Hawksford as they continued to thrash blow after blow at each other's heads, chins, guts, and God knows what else. "Edmund! Hawksford! Enough!"

She edged toward them wondering if she should try to get in between them. Then again, seeing how inebriated the two were, she'd probably have one of her breasts torn off. Or both, for that matter.

Everyone in the refreshment room was cheering and shouting louder and louder until her ears drummed and her head felt like it was about to explode. Edmund and Hawksford seemed to draw strength from it, for they continued thwacking each other all the more.

"*Five pounds on Rutherford!*" someone yelled out from the other side of the room.

"*Ten on Hawksford!*" another countered.

Oh God, oh God. They were going to murder one another and no one even cared! She frantically looked around wondering what on earth she should do.

Brayton and Caldwell suddenly appeared, storming past her, their tall solid frames dressed in only shirts, boots, and trousers. Relief flooded her body as both yelled out to the crowd and waved for people to step back.

Brayton swooped in and grabbed hold of Edmund, locking Edmund's neck in a tight arm brace. Brayton dragged him back and away from Hawksford. Caldwell did the same to Hawksford, although Hawksford kept trying to slip down and out.

Edmund thrashed and struggled violently against Brayton, his chest pumping up and down.

Hawksford also struggled as bright red blood poured out of his nose in a torrent, dripping down his lips and chin, quickly soaking Caldwell's white shirtsleeve. Hawksford gagged as if struggling to breathe.

Maybelle's heart stopped. "Hawksford!" She scrambled toward him, blindly yanking off one of her gloves. "Caldwell, release him! He'll choke!"

Caldwell immediately did so, sending Hawksford stumbling toward her.

Maybelle grabbed hold of Hawksford's staggering body and tried to steady him. "You are a damn fribble, to be sure," she snapped, trying to place her glove against his nose. "Was that necessary?"

Hawksford yanked the glove out of her hand and tended to himself. "Forgive me," he muttered, still staggering. "I am quite not myself."

Who knew she would actually grow to like Hawksford despite his devious shortcomings? "You are quite forgiven. Now go home. Rest."

Maybelle turned back to Edmund, and sighed,

ready to take on the last challenge of the night. Brayton had already released Edmund. Only instead of Edmund staring Hawksford down with murderous intent, he was now staring her down with murderous intent.

"Edmund." She rushed toward him, knowing there was so much to explain. She should have never even tried to play games in order to push her way back into his life. "I am to blame here. Entirely. I was searching for an excuse to find my way back into your life after everything I had said. Edmund. I have decided I can relinquish some of my independence if it means we'll be together. I can settle upon being your mistress and that way—"

"No," Edmund coolly said, raising a hand. He sounded strangely sober. "I refuse to settle on anything less than marriage and seeing that that is not something you want, and that you have already taken another man into your bed, there is absolutely nothing left to discuss. Good-bye." He then turned and shoved his way through all the people who had gathered around.

Maybelle stared after Edmund in disbelief as shock overtook her faint body. She struggled not to altogether collapse. No. He couldn't leave her. Not now. Not like this. She choked at the thought of never seeing him again. Especially because she finally knew she wanted him. Wanted him more than anything she'd ever wanted in her life.

Clearly, it was time to take off the damn thimble and face the fact that she was in love with the Duke of Rutherford. Or she would live with the regret of never knowing if it was possible for their happiness to exist.

Maybelle clenched her fists at her sides and squeezed her eyes shut, preparing herself for the big fall. "All right, Rutherford!" she yelled at the top of her lungs over the incessant noise of the crowd. "I'll marry you if that is what you bloody want! But I refuse to live in a separate townhouse! And you damn well better wish to see me for more reasons than the procurement of an heir!"

Laughter rumbled out from the noisy crowd.

Maybelle cringed and waited with her eyes still closed, her fists still clenched. Still nothing. He was no doubt in about as much shock as she was. Dread pooled in her stomach, and slowly she opened her eyes wondering if she could face Edmund's reaction.

Only Edmund wasn't in the crowd anymore.

He was . . . gone.

Tightness clenched her throat and she fought the burning sting that overwhelmed her eyes. She searched all the unfamiliar faces. Didn't he hear? Or had he decided to finally walk away? Decided he had finally had enough of her indecision and uncertainty?

"I think he missed all that," Brayton offered, coming up beside her. He crossed his arms over his chest, blew out a breath, and peered down at her. "But then again, the man was so far in his cups, I doubt it would have mattered. Give him a day or two. Until his head comes out from between his knees."

Indeed. Well, as grandmother always liked to say, "Where there is a will to conquer a man, there is most certainly a way to conquer a man." The trouble was, her grandmother had never really elaborated much further on the matter. And so, she would have to elaborate on her own.

Lesson Twenty-One

Considering the amount of suffering
love bestows upon the minions,
it never ceases to astound me
why love is still permitted to exist.
                    —*The School of Gallantry*

Morning

Edmund knew not where he was. All he knew is that he was in a parlor that wasn't his sprawled on a chair that wasn't his either.

He blinked, bringing on a relentless stabbing pain to the left side of his skull. He hissed out a breath. That's when a horrid, gut-wrenching nausea threatened to turn his insides out. He tensed, his sore fingers digging into the leather armrests, and waited for it all to come out. Only nothing did.

"Oh look." His mother swept into the room still wearing her green robe. Her hair was bundled up beneath a white silk nightcap, indicating that it was in fact quite early. "The savage has emerged from his deep slumber."

"Mother?" he hoarsely whispered through parched lips. "What am I doing here?"

She rolled her eyes and stopped before him, setting her hands on her hips. "You were pounding on the door last night and nearly woke up all the neighbors. I had to take you in before Scotland Yard did."

There went the last bit of whatever respectability he thought he ever had. And what was worse, he had nothing to show for it. Nothing but a vise-wrenching headache.

His mother pointed toward the center of the room. The chairs, side tables, and the settee had all been pushed aside, showing the expanse of the barren wood floor beneath. "You ruined my Persian carpet last night. Utterly ruined it. Soaked it to the floor with a week's worth of supper, I'd say. Which is why I am demanding a new one. And it will cost you twice as much as the first."

Edmund winced, wishing he didn't have to listen to her nag so early in the morning and in his condition. "I will buy twenty if it'll so please you," he groaned. "All I ask in return is that you not speak. I am in desperate need of silence."

"Really, dear." She dropped her hand back to her side and paused. Leaning toward him, she cocked her head and reached out, fingering his chin.

"What happened to you? I never noticed these bruises on your face last night."

Edmund felt like a thousand needles were pushing at the skin she was touching. He winced and moved away from her hand. "Must you poke?"

She glared at him and straightened. "I am your mother and it is my right to poke. This is your fault, you realize. Thinking you could claim a woman in public, instead of simply knocking on her door and paying a respectable visit like a gentleman. I take it you were brawling in the girl's name?"

Edmund didn't feel like responding. Hell, he wished he could admit that he regretted brawling with Hawksford, but knew he'd be lying to himself. He wanted to damn well kill the son of a bitch for publicly slandering and claiming the one person he wanted most—Maybelle de Maitenon. Why was it everyone always claimed what was rightfully his?

His mother sighed and shook her head, causing her silk nightcap to quiver. "Wait here, dear." She turned and hurried out of the parlor, her green robe rustling along with her.

At long last. Silence.

Edmund shifted, his body feeling heavier with each passing moment. He needed to sleep. Needed to sleep and regain his goddamn sense. Not to mention whatever was left of his gut.

He slowly set his head back against the wing-backed chair and stared blankly up at the boxed ceiling. If only his head would stop pounding. And if only his mind would stop reliving the moments of last night over and over and over.

He'd made a dolt of himself. Confessing to Maybelle and all of London that he was in love with her. Only then to discover that she and Hawksford were well involved. If he could bloody stoop so low, he had no doubt many a good man had outright killed himself trying to—

Edmund froze and momentarily closed his eyes. Even with the effects of last night still lingering heavily, he realized something. Something he hadn't been able to face or understand in years. Edmund opened his eyes and knew it was time to accept what it was his father had actually done. Shortly before the man's suicide, his father had confessed to him that he was in love with Lady Anne. So in love that nothing mattered. Edmund had never really understood what it was like to be on the verge of emotional insanity. Until now.

"Herc we are," the duchess announced, coming back into the drawing room with a jar of ointment. "How are you? Better?"

"*Better?*" He tried to focus. "You've only been gone a few moments."

"You look terrible, dear. Absolutely terrible." She paused before him and twisted open the lid of the glass jar. With her finger, she scooped up a large glop of the yellowish green substance. "This will help with the swelling. Then I suggest you rest. You won't last another hour sitting about like this."

He wasn't worried about lasting through another

hour. It was lasting through the rest of his goddamn life he was more concerned about.

She leaned toward him with the ointment.

The stench of fish and rotting fruit overwhelmed his already queasy senses. He snapped up a hand and leaned forward in the chair, trying to get around her and the smell. "Whatever that is, you are not smearing it on me. I am leaving. I have something to tend to."

She blinked at him and straightened, her finger still covered in ointment and her other hand gripping the glass jar. "And what on earth can you possibly be tending to at an hour like this? You're not heading over to her house, are you?"

"No. That business is done." Edmund paused, knowing he had to move slow, and eased farther toward the edge of the chair. "I am off to the cemetery."

She scrambled back, looking startled and alarmed. "The cemetery? What for?"

"To visit father."

Her eyes widened and the glass jar dropped from her shaky hands, shattering into clumps at her feet. She scrambled back, away from the mess, and after a few moments whispered, "But you never visit his grave. You swore to me after what he did to us that you never would."

"I was a different man when I made that promise." Edmund rose and disregarded the dizziness he felt. "Visiting him will do me good."

"Do you good?" she demanded. "Are you still inebriated?"

"No. I am about as sober as I am ever going to get." With that, he headed toward the doorway of the parlor, wanting to simply bring an end to a matter he hadn't been able to face in over six years.

The morning fog had long lifted, and the afternoon sun slowly peered through the clouds when Edmund arrived at the cemetery just outside of London.

The air smelled refreshingly crisp and earthy, unlike the stifling air of the city. He slowly walked the quiet, treed grounds until he finally came to the family crypt.

"So here I am," he announced, pausing. He leaned into the side of the oversized cool stone that housed several generations of Rutherfords and closed his eyes, realizing now more than ever why he never came to visit his father. It was because he couldn't stand the pain of knowing that his father had tossed so much away.

"I suppose you know why I am here," he murmured, digging his fingers into the side wall of the stone crypt. "I have decided to accept your apology. The one you gave before you dashed away to the other side."

He swallowed hard and nodded, remembering his father's aging, pain-stricken, and tear-streaked face that begged both him and his mother for forgiveness. It was the last Edmund had ever seen of him alive.

Edmund squeezed his eyes shut, refusing to give in to his emotions, but one lone tear slipped down his cheek. The one tear he'd never let slip even with the death of his father. Perhaps if he'd been more lenient and understanding, the man would have set off on a different path. One that he could actually return from.

Edmund opened his eyes, swiped at the tear, and cleared his throat. "It has taken me some time, I know, but you might say I finally understand what loving a woman can do to a man's soul." He smirked. "Not very pleasant, is it? You simply chose a better strategy, you bastard."

Edmund pulled his hand away from the stone and glanced around, listening for a long moment to the morning silence around him. "I have no doubt that if I were to stay here long enough, you would answer me. Which is probably why I should leave. Because there is no more to be said. All is well with me. Or at least it will be. And that is all you need know."

He sighed, patted the side of the smooth stone, and then pushed himself away from the crypt. "Don't know if Mother will ever come around. Don't count on it. But hell, if I can come around, who knows."

Turning, Edmund walked away and felt as if a small weight had been lifted. Now he had to simply decipher a way to move on with his life knowing that he not only still loved Maybelle but that he had to live without her.

When Edmund climbed out of his brougham after his journey back from the cemetery he paused, surprised to find the gate and the front door of his townhouse wide open. A huge wooden cart filled with four small baskets of flowers had been set just outside the length of the black iron fence that bordered his townhouse. Two men, dressed in dirty, wool clothing and wool caps, gathered the remaining flowers from the cart, then made their way up his stairs and disappeared through the open door.

What the hell was going on?

Knowing he probably shouldn't move too fast lest his head explode, Edmund made his way up and eyed the now-empty cart. The wood plank bottom was sprinkled with colorful crushed remnants of flowers.

The two men reappeared, and paying him no heed, reached around and started pushing the cart out of the way.

Edmund eyed one of the bearded men and pointed at the empty cart. "What is this? I did not buy any of this. Take it away."

The bearded man shrugged. "Not allowed to answer questions. If you'll excuse us, we'll be needin' our cart back."

Edmund stepped back and eyed the open door of his house. Yes, why not announce to all of London that everything in his house was free? Where was the goddamn butler?

With whatever strength he had left in his sleep-deprived body, Edmund jogged up the stairs of his townhouse and entered the foyer. He slammed the door shut and bolted it. He stormed farther into the house and froze when he came to the entrance of his parlor. Or rather, what used to be his parlor.

Every bit of furniture, not to mention every bit of space on the floor, had been completely covered with roses, orchids, and daffodils. He swallowed and realized that they all had to be from Maybelle.

Although her words from last night were still a haze, he remembered her pleading to him about wanting to be with him. About wanting to be his mistress. After everything she'd put him through. But he refused to settle. Refused to settle for a woman who could easily turn from one man to the next.

"I tried to stop them, Your Grace," the butler frantically announced, coming up from behind. "But they threatened to leave everything, including the entire cart, at the gate."

There was no doubt this was Maybelle's doing. "Was there a note?"

"Nothing, Your Grace. Only these flowers."

Damn her. What? Did she expect him to call on her and say all was forgiven? Never. He had his bloody pride and there was no place for her in his life anymore.

Edmund stepped farther into the room, to assess

how many flowers there really were. The perfumed scent, however, overwhelmed his stomach. He froze as nausea rolled over him and forcefully pushed its way up his throat. Shit!

Edmund clamped a hand over his mouth, turned, and dashed out of the room and up the stairs. Damn her. Damn Maybelle de Maitenon for the rest of her days!

Lesson Twenty-Two

When love is on the line,
that is when we all learn to shine.
                    —*The School of Gallantry*

Early evening, 11 Berwick Street

When the clock chimed nine times and clicked back into place, Maybelle seated herself once again in her red velvet upholstered chair. She eyed her grandmother, Caldwell, Brayton, Banfield, and the very battered Hawksford as they all sat in silence. And they looked about as miserable as she felt. Thanks to her grandmother, everyone had no choice but to participate in her plan. As part of their schooling. Who knew that she herself would become a lesson.

There was still one empty chair and she had a sinking feeling it wasn't going to be filled. The half hour from the set time had long passed and the duchess still hadn't arrived.

The candles flickered in their glass lanterns, casting shadows across the velvet-lined walls, giving the room an eerie, deathlike feel. Reflecting her mood. If the duchess wasn't willing to help her, her plan to woo Edmund didn't look all that promising.

Hawksford shifted in his seat and winced from the effort. "I say we storm the woman's house and take her hostage until she agrees to any and all terms."

Maybelle sighed. "This is not a war, Hawksford. If she doesn't come, we will simply have to improvise."

Heavy footsteps now echoed from down the corridor. Maybelle glanced toward the open doorway, the candlelight barely reaching the fuzzy shadows within the corridor.

Harold loomed in the doorway and stepped aside. "The duchess is here."

Maybelle's heart jumped as a cloaked figure swept into the room. Oh, thank goodness! All was not lost after all.

Maybelle rose to her feet as the duchess pushed back the hood of her black cloak, revealing her flushed face and her tightly knotted salt-and-pepper hair.

The duchess nervously eyed everyone in the room, then quietly announced, "I apologize. I had trouble making my way through the tunnel. Whatever happened to the front door?"

The men chuckled but otherwise didn't say a word as they all stood to greet her.

Maybelle's grandmother rose to her feet with the

help of her cane and steadily made her way toward the duchess. "If men are willing to crawl through tunnels in the name of pleasing a woman, Your Grace, that is how I know they are deserving of enlightenment. Merci. Merci for coming and wanting to help my granddaughter."

The duchess nodded and turned her dark gaze to Maybelle. After a moment, she smiled and reached out a gloved hand from beneath her black cloak, revealing her bombazine gown beneath. "Come here, child," her soft voice broke with emotion and her eyes visibly glistened with tears. "Let me be the first to give you my blessings."

Maybelle stepped toward the duchess and told herself she wasn't going to blub right along with her. The duchess grabbed hold of her and Maybelle was instantly buried against black, stiff garbs and the comforting scent of lilacs.

"I have waited so long for this day," the duchess whispered against Maybelle's shoulder. "So long. Know that I would crawl upon my knees through countless tunnels if only to see my son happy."

Tears stung Maybelle's eyes. This woman was going to be her mother-in-law. She was going to have a family.

"Now, now, let us not get ahead of ourselves," Hawksford called out from behind them. "Rutherford hasn't said yes just yet."

Maybelle choked on a laugh and pulled herself away from the duchess's arms. "We have decided to bring in the French *ton* to help us, seeing the

British are all snobs. So it may be a bit involved, Your Grace."

The duchess rolled her eyes and waved her gloved hand about. "It can't be any more involved than the time Edmund popped his head out from between my legs. Let us have at it, I say."

Maybelle grinned, knowing they would get along just fine. It was now a matter of whether Edmund was ready to take on a wife and the fact that the School of Gallantry was here to stay.

Lesson Twenty-Three

My, my, my
how easy it is to catch a man's eye.
But catching his mind and catching his soul?
Therein lies the part that takes the toll.
                              —*The School of Gallantry*

Six days later, the onset of evening

Edmund tossed his newspaper onto his desk, tilted back his chair, and shook his head. Christ. More gossip to add to his name. His life resembled a damn horse market. And he, of course, despite being a duke, was nothing but a horse being sold off to the local butcher. The gossip and the complete back turning he could deal with. But knowing that everyone in London knew he loved Maybelle was simply not acceptable. At all.

"Edmund?" His mother paused in the entryway

of the study, dressed in a low-cut, rose-colored evening gown. "The carriage is here."

Edmund slowly brought the chair back to its four legs in disbelief. It was the first time since his father's death that he'd seen her in anything other than black. Even her black and silvery hair had been arranged beautifully into cascading ringlets held into place by gold and ruby hair combs.

He stood. "Mother. You look . . . beautiful."

She smiled shyly and placed her gloved hand to her corseted waist. "Thank you. With all the attention we've been getting, I thought I'd feed the fire." She quirked a dark brow, tilting her head. "You don't look all that bad yourself. Bruises aside, of course."

Edmund looked down at his freshly pressed attire and shrugged. "I will take that as a compliment." He eyed her. "Do I have to go? I don't even know who the host is and only have about enough enthusiasm to sit in a corner."

She waved a gloved hand. "Oh, come now. You don't expect us to give in to all the horrid gossip by altogether disappearing from public? They can all sod off. I've been waiting for this particular ball all Season long."

Edmund pulled in his chin. Never in all his thirty years had he heard his mother curse. It had to be one hell of a gathering. Edmund blew out a breath, turned, and picked up the newspaper he'd been reading. He held it up. "Did you read this?"

"No." A smile ruffled her mouth. "But clearly you did. What does it say?"

Edmund looked at the newspaper still clutched in his hand. He snapped the paper straight and read aloud:

The Duke of Rutherford strikes again. Quite literally. The School of Gallantry to blame. In the end, there are some things that simply cannot be taught to men.

Edmund shook his head and hit the newspaper with his good hand in agitation. "Damn these people. They don't even know whether I was enrolled or not. Who the hell would publish this goddamn nonsense?"

"The real question, dear, is who reads it?"

Edmund threw the newspaper aside. "Well said. Let us go and tell them all to bloody sod off, shall we?"

Maybelle tried not to shift from foot to foot as she impatiently eyed the large entryway from the distance she kept. It seemed all of France had come to her aid in the name of love. That is, her grandmother and all of her French aristocratic acquaintances. It's not like the *ton* was going to help. She only hoped this wasn't all for naught. "Where is he?" she muttered. "What if he doesn't come?"

"He will, chère," her grandmother assured her. "Do not allow your nervousness to get the better of you."

An older gentleman with too much tonic slathered in his hair strode by and grinned at them with too many crooked teeth to count. He nodded his pleasantries.

Maybelle ignored him and kept her eyes on the entrance.

Her grandmother nudged Maybelle. "That was a Frenchman, Maybelle. Never ignore the French. Especially with all the help that they are now giving you."

Maybelle sighed and was about to comment on it when an attractive older woman walked in arm in arm with Edmund.

She blinked at the realization that it was actually the duchess. She looked . . . amazing. At least ten years younger. And Edmund . . . oh, poor Edmund. His jaw and the left side of his cheek were still black and blue, with hints of yellowing. The man had endured so much for her. Which was why it was time to bring his suffering to an end.

She drew in a calming breath as their names were announced and they started heading their way. "He is here," Maybelle excitedly whispered, grabbing hold of her grandmother's arm and squeezing it. "At last."

"Yes, yes. Go." Her grandmother waved her off and eyed the doorway. "Before he sees you."

Maybelle kissed her grandmother's cheek. "I will see you at the end of the evening. Hopefully with a duke in tow."

Her grandmother grinned, waved her off, then

turned and walked toward the crowded ballroom, her ivory cane following each regal step.

Maybelle took in another deep breath, as if she were about to dive into the depths of unknown waters, and quickly stepped into a large group of people, removing herself from sight until it was time to make her appearance. It wasn't her reputation on the line anymore. It was love.

"Isn't this lovely?" the duchess cooed, dragging Edmund by the arm down the plush red carpet that lined the center of the enormous and luxurious high-ceilinged foyer after they'd been announced.

"Yes. Lovely." Edmund scanned the moldings that crowned the high ceilings, and noted the large portraits of overbred French bluebloods that lined the walls on both the left and the right. Ones that had no doubt fled France during the days of the guillotine. Ah, the French. They were always causing trouble.

He should know.

Just ahead, at the very end of the entrance, huge ferns and bountiful flowers were strategically placed alongside a sweeping staircase, giving it an exotic look of paradise. The long red-carpeted staircase wound up to both sides of the upper floor. A crowd of men and women made their way up to the balconies overlooking the ballroom.

A good place to be, actually. "We're going up-stairs," he quickly said, catching his mother's arm to keep her from leaving the red runner. "Away from the crowds."

She resisted his firm hold. "But I want to dance."

He paused and stared at her, not sure what to make of her new tastes. "You never dance."

The duchess released herself and set her chin to him. "I am not growing any younger, Edmund. And with each Season, I lose a year. Which is why I am going to dance."

Edmund glanced around, leaned toward her, and whispered, "You don't expect me to dance with you, do you? Because I really—"

She took hold of her fan and smacked his forearm soundly with it. "I, dear boy, will find another gentleman. One with less scandal attached to his sleeve."

Edmund bit back a laugh and stepped back. "Thank you."

The duchess eyed him sympathetically. "My dancing shan't last long, I assure you. In the meantime, do try and enjoy yourself."

"I will try," he muttered, turning and heading up the stairway behind a line of people.

Eventually, he found a small alcove off to the side. He sat in the far corner of a balcony near a row of ferns, where he knew he wasn't going to be disturbed.

He blew out a breath, crossed his arms over his chest, and watched as couples danced below, splashing the ballroom floor with vibrant and warm colors as they whirled to the music. He wondered how long he would have to sit and watch them before his eyes finally crossed over.

Someone suddenly came in from behind and sat next to him. Pale yellow skirts and a waft of cinnamon assembled next to him.

Edmund didn't bother to look at whoever had offered him company. Instead, he stared out before him.

A fan snapped open and began waving and waving, sending cool, quick drafts of air in his direction.

Though he tried to ignore the fact that there was someone next to him, the waving incessantly continued, and after a while, he grew irritated. Very irritated.

He shifted away. "Please, Madam. Do hoist all the air in your direction, not mine."

Her fan snapped shut and he hoped that he had offended her enough to send her back to wherever the hell she'd come from. Yet, to his surprise, she stayed.

He turned abruptly toward the woman and was about to say something more on the matter when he froze and clamped his mouth shut in disbelief.

Maybelle sat in the chair next to him, her smooth face faintly tinged with a hint of pink color. "Did you miss me?" she eagerly asked, leaning toward him. "For I certainly missed you."

He leaned back, trying to remind himself to breathe. Why did she sound like she meant it? Something wasn't right here. Even the granddaughter of a French courtesan wouldn't make public overtures unless she stood to benefit from it.

He slowly rose. He still had some dignity and planned on holding on to whatever was left. "If you'll excuse me, Madam. I'm looking to find a quiet corner for myself."

Before he could leave, Maybelle reached out a gloved hand and grabbed hold of his waistcoat. Hard. Her touch sent flaming heat through his flesh as the memory of her hands touching him naked unexpectedly hardened him.

He turned and glared down at her, annoyed with her ability to make his body respond so quickly. "What more could you possibly want?"

"Only you." She stood, bringing a scent of cinnamon toward him. One he never smelled upon her skin before but one he very much liked. She eyed him for a moment, paused, and very slowly slipped her two gloved fingers into the front of her bosom.

Edmund froze, and despite all common sense, couldn't keep his eyes from following her fingers. She seductively dipped her neckline just enough for him to see the deeper plunge between her perfect, powdered breasts.

The hardness he'd earlier felt in his groin throbbed again. She had far more power over him than he realized.

She smiled sweetly and slipped out a lace handkerchief, obstructing his view.

Edmund quickly looked away and wanted to

adjust the stiff collar that was beginning to stick to the growing heat of his neck.

"Did you receive the flowers?" She dragged the tip of her lace handkerchief across the bottom of her full lips, her blue eyes keenly watching him the whole while.

He glared at her. "I tossed every single one of them. They were a bit overwhelming."

"That was the point." She stepped closer toward him. "Forgive me. For everything. It was not my intention to hurt you."

Edmund pointed a rigid finger at her, wishing he could poke it deep into her heart and make her feel the pain and frustration he felt. "Setting aside all of your dirty business with Hawksford, did you forget that you never wanted to see me again?"

She drew herself closer, provocatively close, and looked up at him in a manner that begged for attention. "Forget everything that has ever passed from these lips," she whispered. "I simply did not understand my feelings for you. Now I do."

He stared down at her, his strength wavering. With such words, she never looked so damn alluring. Her thick golden curls framed her small oval face and her skin was slightly flushed.

More than anything, he wanted to believe that those lips he'd claimed for his had never touched Hawksford's. That none of her had touched Hawksford and that he could end his misery here and now.

"Edmund, please. Say something." She lifted herself up high on her slippered toes, and brought up her small hand, the one with the handkerchief, toward the side of his forehead. "Your poor face." She lightly brushed the bruises on his skin in the most provocative and tender way. As if she cared. Her gloved wrist smelled of powder and cinnamon as it teased his cheek with each soft touch.

He stood frozen and swallowed hard, wondering if it would be so bad to give in. Edmund snatched hold of her tiny wrist to push it away, but found himself unable to let go. The passion he felt for her dangerously raced through him, demanding he take her body.

A devious light lit up her blue eyes and a grin overtook her full lips. As if she knew the effect she had on him. She leaned toward him, not at all concerned about the fact that he continued to hold her wrist so tightly. "I love you, Edmund," she whispered. "And I know that whatever happens, we will manage. As will our children."

Edmund froze. Their children? He had expected everything to fall from her lips—excuses, explanations—but . . . this? He refused to believe it. No. If she truly loved him she would have said something to him that night when he confessed his love for her. And if she truly loved him, she would have tended to *him* before all of London. Not Hawksford's damn nose.

He narrowed his gaze, released her wrist by pushing it away, and growled out, "I am so pleased that you found my drunk proclamation amusing. Unlike you, however, I meant it." With that, he headed toward the main staircase, away from Maybelle.

"Edmund!" He could hear her skirts rustling after him. "Wait! Please! Edmund!"

He ignored her and kept marching on until his heavy feet pounded the runner of the stairs and led him back into the large foyer. He struggled not to replay her seductive glances, gestures, and words. In the end, they didn't mean anything. It was all a game. One she learned to play from her grandmother very well.

Edmund strode into the large ballroom. Finally surrounded by people, he propped himself against one of the walls just inside the entrance of the ballroom and momentarily closed his eyes. It was going to be a rather tedious night.

"Thought you could escape, Your Grace? You'll have to leave London to do that. And even then, I promise to follow."

His eyes popped open. Maybelle stood before him, her lovely face set in clear determination. A determination he simply did not seem to understand. What is it that she wanted? "I am not playing this goddamn game with you anymore," he sharply said, pushing away from the wall.

"I am not playing games." She leaned in, once again bringing with her the tantalizing scent of cinnamon. "Now. I vow to be patient, as clearly you are a bit overwhelmed by everything I am telling you. And I expected as much. But at least be rational. Dance with me."

He hesitated, still trying to make sense of everything. "I am not interested in dancing. At all."

"If you refuse to dance with me, Edmund, I'll be forced to draw attention." She leveled a serious gaze at him. "Don't think I won't. I can always think of something to entertain the masses. Although I will admit that the French are a bit more difficult to please."

Edmund glanced toward those around him and decided against his better judgment to give himself the pleasure of holding her. Just in case she really did feel what she said she was feeling. "One dance."

She held out her gloved hand for him to take as if she were the one leading them. "Splendid. The waltz is about to commence."

A waltz? Edmund blew out a breath, brought his hand beneath the warmth of her gloved hand, and guided her toward the dance floor. All he needed was to have her proclaiming her love and draping herself against him. The damn French were no doubt putting her up to this.

When they positioned themselves amidst the other couples, Edmund took her into his arms. She glanced up at him and grinned, her entire face beaming as if she was genuinely happy to be with him. Was it possible that . . . ? No.

"You have quite the grip," she commented, as they whisked across the waxed floor. "Do you mind loosening it? Just a bit?"

"Sorry," he confessed. Though he loosened his hold on her hand, he made it a point to draw her closer, trying to savor this splendid, bittersweet moment of having her soft, warm body against his.

A flush crept into her cheeks as they swept across the dance floor. "Edmund?"

"Hm?" He was trying to count his steps to further distract himself from noticing how beautiful she really was.

"Do you really love me?"

The question almost made him trip and he had to remind himself he was waltzing. She asked him the question like a child asked for a piece of cake—pleadingly.

He supposed there was no denying the obvious. Though he did not know why it mattered. "Yes," he muttered, his eyes now focusing on the small delicate feathers that were arranged in her hair. He had been so distracted, he hadn't noticed them earlier. He wondered what was softer. Her hair or the feathers.

"I apologize. For everything. Hawksford overstepped his bounds after what you said about his sister. You see, he and I earlier reached this godawful agreement. He wanted Lady Chartwell and I wanted you. But then you were horridly foxed and you said things you shouldn't have and he was horridly foxed and said things that were totally untrue so as to defend his sister's honor. And that, of course, is putting it mildly."

Edmund caught his breath and continued to stare down at her. That was Hawksford's sister? Of course he would be defending her honor. Did that mean . . . "So you and Hawksford never . . . that is . . . he never actually . . ." He couldn't even force himself to say it, he was so disgusted.

She heatedly looked up at him. "Perish the thought. Of course we never did. I love you, Edmund, and I am here tonight to announce it publicly so that you fully understand that I have no intention of ever hiding what I feel for you anymore."

Edmund jerked them to a complete stop as shock overtook his body. A dancing couple waltzed straight into them, jarring him and Maybelle and breaking their embrace.

"Hell, Rutherford," Caldwell cried, scrambling to resume his stiff position with his partner. "Learn how to dance!"

Edmund froze and looked around, noting not only Caldwell was dancing among them, but also Brayton, Hawksford, and Banfield. Even his mother.

What the devil was going on?

"Edmund?" Maybelle blinked up at him, and then glanced around, a baffled expression on her face. "Why aren't you dancing?"

Knowing all of London was watching, he did the only thing there was left to do. Claim her along with the rest of an explanation. He grabbed her gloved hand, led her off the dance floor, and did not pause until they had reached the far end of the wall.

Edmund felt his pulse thundering inside his ears, still in disbelief of everything that was happening.

He kissed her gloved hand and whispered down at her, "Meet me."

Her expression vividly perked as she lowered her voice in a conspiratory manner. "Where?"

He released her hand, cleared his throat, and thought of the best way they could meet without drawing too much attention. Which was going to be difficult regardless. "By the staircase."

The orchestra finished and a set of trumpets suddenly sounded, announcing a presentation was going to be given by the host. The bloody French loved attention, didn't they? People around them slowly made their way toward the far end of the ballroom to better hear the host, whose voice was barely carrying.

"Now is our chance," he whispered.

He then turned and walked away. He still couldn't believe any of it. How could he? But either way, he knew that if there was any chance that she did in fact feel the same way he did, he was going to damn well take it.

Lesson Twenty-Four

There is no such thing as a happy ending.
After all, if something comes to an end,
what sort of happiness can that bring?
Let us talk, instead, of happy beginnings.
— *The School of Gallantry*

When enough time had passed after Edmund had departed, Maybelle decided it was finally time to leave the ballroom. As casually as she could, she gathered her skirts and made her way through all the people who were heading in the opposite direction. Her heart still thundered in her ears with wild anticipation knowing that Edmund was waiting for her.

There was so much she wanted to say to him. An entire evening could not even begin to explain it all. Maybelle paused near the far right side of the long marble staircase and stood in the silence of the high-ceilinged corridor. Only Edmund was nowhere in sight. She glanced around. Where was he? He said—

"Pssst."

Maybelle frowned and turned to the sound at her left. Toward a thick arrangement of potted ferns set before a large, unfolded silk screen. "Edmund?" she ventured.

"*Yes.* Get in here. Before anyone sees you."

Her eyes widened as she quickly approached, refusing to believe that Edmund was actually hiding somewhere back there. "Edmund, you are not actually sitting in the ferns, are you?" She laughed at the thought and leaned every which way to find him. She had truly corrupted the man!

"I'm behind the screen," he snapped. "Now come here."

Maybelle made a face and straightened. "You are being utterly ridiculous."

"Do you know me to be utterly ridiculous?" he growled out, sounding as if he were losing patience. "Now come in before someone sees you speaking to the ferns and commits you to an asylum."

Maybelle wanted to join him. Desperately. But the reality was her gown was not going to all fit behind the small space of that screen. Not without knocking it over. And she'd already knocked over plenty of everything these past few weeks, thank you very much.

She placed her gloved hands on her hips. "Edmund, I cannot possibly fit in there with this dress. For heaven's sake, why not come out here? All of London already knows that you and I are well—"

Edmund's gloved hand reached out, grabbed her by the wrist, and yanked her straight through the ferns and behind the screen. Maybelle skidded across the marble floor as she stumbled to a halt just behind the silk screen. Not being able to keep her balance against the weight of her skirts, she grabbed hold of Edmund's muscled arm and together they fell back and hit the wall behind them.

Edmund's arms tightened around her as he held her in place. He chuckled and whispered down at her, "Why do you have to always make things more difficult than they actually are?"

"Oh, *I* make everything difficult?"

He grinned. "I did not mean for you to fall."

Maybelle shifted as best she could against him, enjoying their close quarters just beneath the staircase.

Their eyes met and Maybelle felt as if her heart was going to burst. Without breaking their heated gaze, Edmund turned her and gently repositioned her into the far corner of the wall, draping his hard body against hers. But instead of kissing her, he closed his eyes for a long moment and appeared to be struggling with something.

The tingling in the pit of her stomach refused to be quelled. This was it. She could feel it. And she was ready. More than ready for the adventure of taking him on as her husband for the rest of her life. Come what may. It was simply a matter of whether he was prepared to take her on for the rest of his.

* * *

Edmund tried to calm his whirling thoughts, readying himself for the consequences of admitting how he felt. Better to say it and regret it than never say it and regret it had never been said. Or something of that nature.

He opened his eyes and met that soft, blue gaze that seemed to plead with him to acknowledge how he felt.

"Maybelle," he murmured, lowering his head and nuzzling the top of her smooth forehead. "There is so much I want to say. I cannot believe that I thought the worst of you."

Her blue eyes searched his face. "All I want is for you to repeat what you did that one night. The night you told me you loved me. I was not given an opportunity to respond to it properly."

Seeing her looking up at him pleadingly, Edmund knew exactly what she wanted to hear. And he had no trouble saying it. "I love you."

Strangely, it felt different saying it this time. For one, he was sober. But the look on her face was no longer one of fear or confusion, as it had been that night, but that of softness and acceptance.

"And I love you, too, Edmund," she whispered, standing up on her slippered toes and kissing his chin. "I am so sorry it took me so long to say it."

She sighed and slowly closed her eyes. "There is so much I want to tell you. About me. About how I grew up. My father was the one who scared me away from ever wanting to marry. It sounds quite silly, I know, but it was real to me at the time. For even though my mother died giving birth to me, my father talked about her all the time. As if she still existed. As if she was going to walk back through the door."

She shook her head, a large tear slipping down the left side of her smooth cheek.

His strong, never-yielding Maybelle. Crying. It stabbed at his gut, not to mention his heart. He swallowed hard and gently brushed away the trail of wetness. "Please," he whispered. "Do not cry. I hate it."

She opened her eyes, blinked back her remaining tears, and forced herself to shakily smile up at him. "I want you to understand me in the same way you allowed me to understand you. Up until my father's death, Edmund, he made me wash and iron my mother's clothes. He bought her ribbons that matched her eyes and would set them upon her grave. Everything he ever did, everything he ever talked about, was for her. And I swore on the day when he was lying on his deathbed, clutching her lock of hair, that I would never hand over my heart to anyone in the way he had handed over his heart to my mother. But you made me realize, Edmund, that one extreme cannot incur another. And so here I finally am. Yours."

Hearing her words, her story, and knowing what she had suffered and lived through, overwhelmed him in a way he hadn't been overwhelmed since his father's death.

He leaned his hand against the wall and moved closer to her, wanting to feel her love. And wanting her to feel his.

Her slender arm wrapped around his waist. She sniffed and closed her eyes, tilting her head back. Ever so slowly, her full lips lifted upwards. Waiting.

Edmund let his hands slide to her slim waist and deliberately observed her in a moment he'd never forget for the rest of his days. The way her blond curls framed her face. The way her smooth skin glistened under two small trails of tears. The way her eyes were still closed, her blond, wet lashes shadowing her lower lids.

Yes. This woman, this incredible woman, was his duchess. Knowing she was expecting a kiss, he decided to surprise her with something else. Dipping his head toward the curve of her neck, he slid the tip of his tongue down the length of its softness. She let out a small sigh and leaned back against the wall, stretching her neck out for him.

He slid his tongue farther and farther down until he reached that alluring soft dip between her breasts, which she had been taunting him with all night. Pausing for a moment, he grabbed the front of her silk and lace bodice and pulled it down gently. He nudged her breasts out from her corset and brought them both into full view. The pressure of his cock began to build, demanding release.

Maybelle stiffened against him as her eyes fluttered open. "Edmund," she whispered intently, her hands suddenly coming between him and her exposed breasts. She glanced over his shoulder. "Here? Behind a screen in the ferns? What if—"

"Let them find us," he murmured, leaning toward her. "I am done pleasing everyone else."

He then brought her hands away from her breasts, and lowered his mouth to her left nipple. He gently sucked on it, savoring the soft, salty texture as his hand drifted toward her other breast. His fingers brushed her nipple lightly until it was taut.

A quiet sigh escaped her as her hands wandered across his body, as if searching for skin to touch.

"Remove your cravat," she whispered.

He pulled away from her for a moment, did away with his gloves, and hastily undid his cravat, pulling his collar away from his neck. He grinned down at her and leaned back toward her, draping himself against her. "Now what?"

A gleam overtook her blue eyes. She grabbed hold of his vest and ripped it as she watched him, spraying buttons everywhere. They tinkered to the floor. "You said to do that anytime I wanted to."

"So I did," he growled out, glancing down at the mess she'd made. "What else do you have planned for me?"

Her smooth gloved fingertips slid in beneath his shirt and, slowly, she dipped them toward his collarbone and toward the front of his chest. The sensation of her fluttering fingertips overwhelmed his body and Edmund knew there would be no controlling his appetite for her.

He grabbed two handfuls of her silk, yellow skirts and shoved them up past her thighs. He held them out of his way, his erection now bulging painfully against his trousers.

He ran his hands up her smooth stockings and searched for the one thing second to his love for her. Her core.

He slipped his fingers into her wet, warm folds. He shifted his jaw and closed his eyes, jealous of his own fingers. His thumb circled her nub as two of his fingers remained deep within her. He received a generous moan that made him want to thrust himself into her then and there.

"Yes," he hoarsely said, opening his eyes to watch her move against his hand. "Show me how much you enjoy this. How much you enjoy me."

She moved her hips against him. He quickened his wet thumb against her nub to heighten her pleasure and her breathing turned to pants.

Edmund withdrew his fingers and leaned away, momentarily bringing a gap between them. He hastily undid his trousers and yanked his undergarments out of the way until his shaft was finally free.

He heavily leaned into her body, wanting her very soul to become a part of him, grabbed hold of her thighs, then wrapped her legs around his waist. He propped her back up high against the wall, making sure she was just below the height of the silk screen that shielded them.

"I have been dying for you," he hoarsely confided in her ear, wanting her to know again.

"Not as much as I have been dying for you," she softly replied.

Edmund's fingers dug into her thighs. He adjusted her to the height he needed to enter her and thrust deep into her core.

He didn't know what he enjoyed most at that moment. Hearing her bite back a soft moan or feeling his shaft harden all the more as her tight wetness surrounded him.

He gritted his teeth and knew that his body was demanding he ride her hard. He slammed into her repeatedly, his cock aching with each thrust. He watched with half-closed eyes as her large breasts bobbed before him. Their frantic movement showed every time he thrust into her. He couldn't stop and simply drove her and himself toward the brink of bodily madness.

"Wrap your legs tighter around me," he quietly insisted, his hands gripping her buttocks. "I want all of you."

She obeyed, wrapping her legs so tightly around his waist, he slid in deep. Deep enough to feel the wall of her womb against the head of his cock. Not once did he stop thrusting into her wetness. Her core tightened as she panted more and more heavily.

She quietly choked in pleasured anguish and grabbed for him and the wall behind her to steady herself.

Edmund covered her mouth with his, and kept pounding in and out of her. He cupped her smooth bottom as tightly as he could, then pushed harder and harder against her, readying himself for his climax. He closed his eyes and groaned as his shaft pulsated and released every ounce of seed into her. The muscles in his body tightened, and every nerve, every sensation overtook his entire body until it exploded. He eventually relaxed and he was back in her arms and in the world.

He most certainly could get used to a life like this. Drained, he pulled out and gently let her slide down from around his waist. Slowly, he planted her slippered feet back onto the ground and her skirts cascaded down in a whoosh around her legs, brushing his own.

He smiled and when his heart had calmed to a normal beat, he tenderly adjusted the bodice of her gown, easing her breasts back into her corset.

She leaned back against the corner of the wall, tilted her head, and smiled at him as if she were far away and not with him at all.

"Where are you?" he murmured.

"I was thinking, is all."

"Oh?" Edmund carefully picked up his cravat and tried not to knock over the screen or rustle the ferns around them. "Of what?"

"Secretly, I have always wanted children."

"Did I ever tell you that I want a dozen children with eyes as blue as yours?" He grinned and tied his cravat. He then adjusted his trousers and secured them in the tight space behind the screen.

"You want a dozen?" She sounded rather concerned.

"Yes, but imagine all the fun we'll have making them." He waggled his brows and knotted his cravat into place. He leaned back into her body and tenderly observed her, making his eyes meet hers. Her, him, and the children.

A thunderous clapping echoed around them from the ballroom and their attention jerked back to their surroundings. He'd almost forgotten they were tucked beneath the staircase of a house that wasn't even theirs. They had to get out before people started stirring within the corridors.

"Come." He grabbed for both of her hands.

"No," she insisted, leaning back with her weight. "Not until I receive a proper proposal."

"I am not proposing behind a screen, woman. I have other plans." He tried pulling her toward the opening of the screen, but she leaned back in defiance, still hovering in the far corner.

"I want my proposal and I want it now."

"There is no time for this. And I don't want all of London thinking that—"

Loud voices rung out and numerous footsteps echoed all around them.

"Hell." He yanked her back and into the farthest corner. "Now we have to wait."

"Wait?" She stared at him. "What for?"

"Until no one is left in the corridor."

"Are you mad?" she hissed. "There are hundreds of people here. We cannot sit behind this screen that long. The festivities may very well last into the morning."

He glared at her. "If you hadn't argued, we wouldn't be in this dilemma. Now unless you wish to see all of these details written in every newspaper circulated in London, I suggest we stay here. Hell, even if we'd been married for twenty-five years, this would still make the papers."

Maybelle stifled a giggle and glanced around. "Do you suppose I should include this in a lesson as what *not* to do?"

"No. Let those bastards find out on their own." He grinned.

Maybelle paused, momentarily becoming quite serious, and eyed him. "Edmund. We haven't really discussed it, but you aren't going to force my grandmother to close the school, are you?"

Ah, yes. The school. The *ton* was going to hate him. Of course, he didn't care. "And deprive men of a good education? I think not. Though I am afraid they are going to have to find a new teacher. I have learned to despise sharing."

Maybelle smiled and cocked her head. "I promise to only stay long enough to help my grandmother. There have already been far too many interruptions in the school. Oh." She poked at him. "And you owe Hawksford an apology with regards to his sister."

Edmund brought her as close as their bodies would allow amidst the bustling of celebration. "Of course I owe him an apology. I didn't know. Or I most certainly would never have said what I did. I only hope that he will accept whatever it is I have to say."

She smiled. "He will."

Edmund grasped her chin in his hand and tenderly traced her flushed, soft cheek with the side of his thumb. There was no sense in waiting. Life was indeed too fragile and too unpredictable to wait.

He drew back his hand and cleared his voice in a theatrical manner. "Miss Maitenon, granddaughter of Madame de Maitenon, better known as the headmistress of the School of Gallantry, at least for the time being, will you give me the honor of becoming my wife, my duchess, my one true love?"

She sighed as if it were the best proposal ever given in the history of England's courtship. "Yes, Edmund. Yes." She reached up and traced a loving finger alongside his face. "Let us only hope we can escape this corner in time to announce our engagement."

Edmund chuckled as he gently pushed her back toward the corner of the wall. "Until then, duchess, let us enjoy our time together. Shall we?"

"Yes. Let's."

Epilogue

If you are in need of more lessons,
then I suggest you learn the art of patience
and wait for the next class to begin.
                    —*The School of Gallantry*

Six months later, Egypt

Through the thin, white veil that was held in place by her bonnet, Maybelle squinted up at the rough and faded façade of the pyramid looming several feet before her. Her loose, white muslin gown flapped about, cooling her sweat-ridden body. The sand spiraled at her booted feet, sending more tufts of grittiness toward her veiled face. She openly welcomed the pulsing dry heat of the sun and the sand as it hummed through every inch of her skin. The camels that she, Edmund, and their guide had arrived on grunted and shifted behind them.

Placing her hands on her growing belly, Maybelle thoughtfully rubbed it. A small smile lingered on her lips. She was finally here. At the place Belzoni wrote of. At the place of harsh beauty, wonder, and endless mystery. And it was far more than she could have ever expected. Far more.

"Amazing," Edmund announced from behind her, setting his hands upon her shoulders. "As you said it would be."

Maybelle nodded and slowly leaned back against Edmund's muscular frame. She tilted her head to the side, her oversized bonnet and veil following. As she wrinkled her nose up at the time-worn structure, an odd, wondrous realization settled upon her soul. It was a strange moment that openly mocked her in her own happiness. After all, without even knowing, she had almost given up her Edmund, her duke, her husband, the father of her child, for a pile of old rocks set upon endless hot sand.

And that was a very odd realization indeed.

Discover the Romances of
Hannah Howell

Available Wherever Books Are Sold!

Visit our website at **www.kensingtonbooks.com**